A STEALTHY SITUATION

FRANKLIN U2 #2

SAXON JAMES

INTRODUCTION

We're back with another season of Franklin U and it was so much fun to revisit San Luco!

In this book, Benny discovers that he has dyscalculia. I had a great sensitivity team who helped me make him the best character he could be.

If you're someone who likes to put a face to a character before you start reading, feel free to check out my Pinterest board here:

https://pin.it/74hcc65YV

And if you like music to set the mood, you can jump on and listen to A Stealthy Situation playlist here:

https://open.spotify.com/playlist/77IITxY1u2nAB1cQa HXBv2?si=1f889cd458bb4536

PROLOGUE

BEN

My head is spinning worse than one of those amusement park rides.

I stagger into my bedroom, literally bouncing off the door-frame, fingertips clipping the side of the door to slam it closed behind me.

The sounds of the frat party raging on dulls a fraction, which eases up some of the pounding in my head.

My chuckle turns into more of a giggle as I kick off my shoes and nearly hit the deck headfirst before catching myself. I've missed this. My frat brothers, the parties, the hot men who want to experiment in college.

It's all good.

Going home for break is amazing because I love my family and miss them while I'm gone, but when the new term is looming, I'm desperate to get away again. There really can be too much of a good thing.

It takes multiple attempts to struggle out of my shirt, and I give up getting undressed before I reach my jeans. It's not only my head but the room that's spinning now, and one moment, my bed looks like it's partway up the wall, and the next, I'm upside down.

What the hell was in that beer bong?

An annoying tapping starts against my eardrum that I try to shake away, but my foot slips on one of my shoes, and I go down hard.

"*Oww.*"

The yelp is more reflex, though, because nothing actually hurts. In fact, the floor is feeling extra comfy tonight. I flop onto my side on the hardwood, ignoring how much cum, piss, spit, and vomit has probably covered it over the years.

My eyes are growing heavy. That blissful, tipsy-turvy darkness that drags you under after too much alcohol tugs at me, and I relax, hoping for it to kick in faster.

But that stupid tapping won't leave me alone.

"Urg, stop it, brain." I slap my cheek a few times, trying to get it to quit.

It doesn't work.

Stupid, fucking—

"Benny."

I pause. Am I talking to myself? Did I just imagine my name?

More tapping. "Benny, open the fucking window."

Window?

I flop onto my back like a dead fish and tilt my head to look. The curtains are still parted, and there, on the other side of the glass, is me.

Upside-down me.

Only *that* me is wearing a hoodie pulled up over his wild hair and doesn't laugh when I laugh.

"You're supposed to be inside," I grumble at my reflection that's not reflectioning right.

My reflection gestures to the window. "Hurry up."

A barely human noise leaves me as I crawl in his direction. I pull myself up onto my knees at the window frame, unlock it, then push the window up and out of the way.

"Well, hellooo." I drag it out like a cartoon villain, realizing it's not my disobedient reflection at all.

"On a scale of one to five Jägerbombs, how tanked are you?"

I have to squint one eye and concentrate as I try to bring my thumb and forefinger a small distance apart. "I am this drunks."

"Phew. Here I was worried you'd overdone it." My perfect twin pushes me out of his way as he climbs into my bedroom.

And I don't mean perfect as in "wah wah he's so good, and everyone loves him, and I have a complex" perfect. I mean *identical* perfect.

So identical we switch places all the time and no one knows perfect. Our own family sometimes makes Em show them the scar on his hand just so they can be sure who is who.

All it takes is one of us to open our mouths though.

Emmett is sweet. Almost naïve.

I'm much more like our brother Asher eat-shit-and-die Dalton.

"You know I hate when you drink." He reaches under my bed to slide out the single mattress we have stashed there. "I always end up with a headache the next morning."

"Sacrifice I'm willing to make."

He strips off his hoodie and throws it at my face. "You need water."

"Too drunks."

He puts on a baby voice and pinches his thumb and forefinger together. "But I thought you were only this manys."

"You're killing my buzz. This room is for fun times only."

He laughs and pulls my arm over his shoulders to help me to my bed. I fall down face-first, and *ohhh*, this is much more comfortable than the floor. "Are all your frat brothers drunk?"

"Yuuup."

"Good. Stay here, and I'll be back in a second."

The music gets louder for a beat before he closes the door behind him. He could be gone for a second or five years, but next thing I know, a cold glass of water is bumping my cheek.

"Drink it."

"Yes, Captain Serious." I snicker as I take the glass and open my mouth greedily, only I misjudge the distance, and water gushes over my face.

"Fuck." I shoot upright, coughing up the drops I inhaled and shaking the rest from my frizzly hair. I'm suddenly a whole lot more sober than I want to be. "You did that on purpose."

"I let go of the cup about five minutes ago."

Urg. I drain what's left and use the glass to push aside the red Solo cups cluttering my nightstand. Apparently, someone other than me has been in my room tonight. Maybe the floor *was* the safer option.

"Did you lock the door?" I ask.

"Of course."

Slowly, my brain cells blink back online. "As much as I love our sleepovers, it's been a week since term started. You can't be missing me already."

Em doesn't meet my eyes as he pulls his pajamas out of the backpack he's brought with him. He forces a laugh, and it still weirds me out that I look that sweet when I laugh as well. I certainly don't ever fucking feel it. "I, umm, might have missed you so much that I started a fire on campus, got expelled, and am now your permanent roommate."

My vision goes wonky again.

"*Huh?*"

"It was a dare. A dumb dare. And apparently, I'm good at starting fires because next thing I know, the dorm is going up, and I panicked. Starting it was easy. Putting it out was not."

I'm not sure when my mouth fell open or when Emmett's body started to warp in and out, but I can only assume there was way, way more than beer in those beer bongs, and I'm hallucinating that my sweet, good brother got *expelled*. "Huuuuh?"

"Stop being dramatic."

"You ... fire?"

"Yes. Also expelled. Lucky me."

Holy shit, I might be sick, and it's not the alcohol this time. "They threw you out? What the fuck, dude? Need me to go down there and talk to them?"

He grins my way. "You can't even talk to me right now. What are you going to do? Throw up on the dean's shoes?"

"I'll make him take you back!"

"First, that's impossible. Second, you go to San Diego State, and then they'll realize there's two of us, and we'll be in even more trouble than I'm already in."

Please, *please*, let me be hallucinating.

I lurch to my feet, too worked up to sit still. "Why aren't you freaking out?"

Emmett climbs into the bed he's made himself on the spare mattress. "Dunno." I'm sure I spot a smile slipping onto his face, but I blink hard to clear my vision, and it's gone again.

"We have to do something," I slur, pacing. "If West finds out ... or Asher—"

"We're not telling them."

That calms just a smidge of my panic because our older brothers are going to be *pissed*. They're both huge hockey stars —West is retired and a head coach now—and all our lives, they've pushed us to follow in their footsteps. We were on that path too. The Dalton duo. Set to enter the draft and be some of the top picks. It was only a few months before it happened that Emmett and I decided we fucking hated the pressure we were under, the way the media treated our brothers, and how much we'd have to sacrifice just to play a sport we didn't love anymore.

We ran to the other side of the fucking country, from Vermont to California, to go to college where no one gives a shit who we're related to.

And what did we tell our furious big bros? We were getting our degrees to make a difference in the world.

Holy fuck, they're going to kill us.

I glare at Emmett standing right in front of me. "You're an asshole."

"I'm over here."

I sway on the spot, turning to find he is, in fact, still in bed … and I'm abusing my reflection.

"*Fuck.*"

"We'll talk about this some more tomorrow."

"Talk about your face tomorrow."

"That sounds like a funner topic."

I groan and stagger over to collapse again, hoping the third time's a charm. Alcohol really doesn't like staying upright.

But even as I try to switch off my brain, the worry is over-riding it.

We came to California with a plan. We were going to succeed.

Now, Emmett has nothing, and even though it wasn't my fault, I can't help but feel responsible.

I'm him. He's me.

If he's struggling, then so am I.

There has to be a way to get him back in. This can't be it.

My last memory before passing out is reaching over to pat him on the head.

I try to tell him everything will be okay, but the words don't make it past my lips.

1

HARRISON

Plants have always been my thing. One of my earliest memories was digging in the dirt, uncovering a small burst of green, and getting Dad to help me replant it. That thing grew like a motherfucker, and Dad didn't have it in him to tell me it was fire bush, and you can't spit in Florida without hitting one.

I was so proud.

The fire bush prompted a vegetable garden, then a fishpond, where I was more interested in the reeds and water lilies than the koi, but it was right around then, when I was excitedly showing my friends from school how tall the cattail had grown, that I got my first life lesson.

People don't give a shit about plants.

All my friends wanted to do was watch the fish swim.

I'm still annoyed about it.

I slow my jog by the Bean Necessities coffee cart on campus and order a green tea, then move off to the side to wait. From this exact spot on campus, if I tilt my head just right, I have a straight line of sight to the beach across the road. It's the smallest view of the water, but something about seeing the way the sun reflects off the waves gives me a boost to start my day.

Nature is incredible.

Making the move from Florida to here for college was a big call. It's something I debated about endlessly with my parents, but not once in all my years at Franklin U have I regretted it. I have great friends, the weather is always sweet, my professors are mostly awesome, and the greenhouse on campus is one of my favorite places in the world.

I'm always so happy to get back here after summer break, and while I still have time to enjoy it while I complete my master's, my goodbye to this place is getting closer, and I have no fucking clue what to do next.

Something with plants is my aim, but unless I want to work in a nursery, ecologist positions aren't exactly easy to walk into.

"Harrison," Austin, fellow redheaded king, calls, holding up my tea. Even with the steady orders at this time in the morning, he's fast. I've never asked, but I think he's learned I'm here at around the same time every day because I never have to wait long.

He was confused when I started asking him to call me Harrison and not Bowser. It was my nickname for so long—hello, red hair and loving video games—but now that I want to be taken seriously as an ecologist, I'm trying to break away from that. Get serious and whatever.

Sometimes I slip—like the friend I made in stats class, I accidentally introduced myself as Bowser—but I've gotten good at stepping into grown-up me.

My walk home is longer than it used to be. I miss living in Liberty Court, but now that I've graduated, it didn't make sense to keep on living with a bunch of undergrads, and my best friend and his boyfriend needed a roommate. Thank fuck they chose to stick around because looking for a room to rent is a land mine of bad experiences.

I swing by home for a quick shower, as quietly as I can since Felix and Marshall are either still sleeping or have left already and I don't know which, and then I leave again to check on my plants before class.

The greenhouse on campus takes up the rooftop of one of the science buildings and is a fucking godsend. Not only for my plants; it's an amazing hookup and date location too.

The number of chicks who've put out up there would horrify Professor Nottering if he ever found out. Which he won't. Because I'm a star pupil.

I jog up the stairs to the rooftop and take a moment to look out over campus. To recenter myself before the madness of the day starts. You can't help feeling like a king up here, above the streams of college kids passing below.

I shuck off my shirt and tuck it into the waistband of my shorts before I step inside.

The first thing that hits me is the familiar scent of dirt. The floral scent of the magnolias. A tinge of manure that's mostly smothered by the overpowering lemon of the cleaning chemicals. This greenhouse has been used by a bunch of Franklin U students over the years. There are aisles of projects, towering trees, a Zen Garden near the back, and a series of mini biodomes, which were one of the first things I was shown in science, and I'm still obsessed with them.

My section is in the furthest corner from the door, where Professor Nottering and I cleared out space for my regeneration efforts. The amount of flora that's dying out is concerning, and if I can prove that reintroduction is not only easy and cheap but necessary, the world will be in a better place than it is now.

Which brings me back to my first life lesson: how to get people to give a shit about plants.

To get people to fund animals, all you have to do is shove a cute koala in their faces. Plants?

Fucked if I know.

"Hello, Stacy," I coo, checking in on my flame lily. She's flowering perfectly and has really taken to the environment I created for her. "What do you need today, my sweet?"

I check her over and make sure the soil is hydrated enough before moving on to my next plant. They're all pretty, all useful, but none of them are enticing people to come and see them. There's a big difference between picking a girl up and promising her pretty flowers and getting serious investors to fund wildlife ecosystems.

"Jesus, Rich," I say when I reach my white roses. "Big weekend?" Some of his petals are dull, and there's a brown tinge to his leaves I don't like. I make myself some notes with possible scenarios and proven treatments. "Y'all are going to give me a heart attack. We don't need that today, thanks. All I ask is that you lot grow how you're supposed to and get greedy with those nutrients." I give the soil at Rich's base a soft pat. "You'll be okay, mate. We'll have you feeling better in no time."

Of course, they don't answer me back, but sometimes it's fun to pretend. Plants are living, growing, photosynthesizing beings, and they should be treated as much our friends as animals are.

I close Rich's mini greenhouse and move on to an experiment that I started for funsies. It's been done a thousand times before, but the results never fail to delight me.

Three plants, side by side, in their own mini greenhouses. I have everything in there controlled down to the temperature, the water volumes, the air quality ... and the ambience.

One plant has silence, and the other two are played a constant track of my voice.

The first is told it's doing good. I'm so proud. It's such a pretty little mother-in-law's tongue.

The second is told I hate everything about it.

From the display of one proud, green plant standing tall against the stunted brownish tuft, the results are indisputable.

If words can affect plants in such an obvious way, imagine what they do to other humans.

I sigh as I lock up, wishing people were more responsible with their lives. We're here for such a short time and somehow have such a big impact—yet so many people strive to have that impact be a shitty one.

Whether it's being an asshole, or littering, or living in excess.

So often, the human race is given a choice.

Too often, it chooses wrong.

2

BENNETT

I look down into my brother's face. He's lying on the mattress, making no effort to move, and I've got a class he normally takes for me this morning. There's nothing concerning coming through our twin bond, so I assume he hasn't died.

"Em?" I tap his side with my foot. "You up?"

All I get back is a long groan.

"Dude, you slept in."

"Didn't." He turns his face and squints up at me, his skin a concerning tinge of white. "Been up all night. Feel shit."

"You look shit. What's wrong?"

"Everything hurts."

I crouch down to feel his forehead, then snatch my hand away again. "I think you have a fever," I tell him, pulling the collar of my sleep shirt up to cover my mouth and nose. "What do you need? Water? Some painkillers?"

"Sleep."

"That's not going to get the fever down."

He buries his face in his pillow again. Emmett's been staying with me for two weeks now, and I've loved having him here. It's almost like old times, sharing a bedroom, being inseparable, talking late into the night. But the longer he's here with nothing changing, the more I'm starting to worry about him.

No one knows I'm a twin, so we have to be careful about who sees us, and I'm worried Emmett will forget he exists. We've both been through those moments before.

"I used the last of my painkillers the other night, so I'll have to run to the store for more."

"Just go to class."

Cute he thinks he can boss me around. "I'm not leaving you like this."

"I really, really just need to sleep it off. And you snore. And talk. A lot. Leave me alone and I'll be fine."

The problem is that if Em's out of it, I'm going to have to take my own class today—the horror! Thank fuck my professors haven't taken to the pop quizzes of my high school days, or I'd be seriously worried.

"You sure you'll be okay?"

"Yes," he grumbles, voice lost in his pillow. "Go away already."

Kinda rude to be kicked out of my own room and be made to attend my own class, but whatever. Emmett gets away with more than most people would.

I'm anxious over the time, so I skip a shower and change from my pajamas into the first clothes I find on my floor, then shove some sneakers on.

"Just saying," I tell my brother. "This is a real low for you. You could have been sick any day this week. Any. And you picked the day I have statistics. That's plain evil."

Where Em finds all that deep diving interesting, I can't

wrap my head around it. Numbers have always been the dullest, stupidest things to exist, and attending this class is going to be painful.

Considering I plan to be reporting on hockey in an attempt to make sure more players don't go through the same harassment my brothers and I did, statistics is a waste of time. Hockey stats have been ingrained in me since I was born, and sure, I don't know what a lot of them mean, but I know how they sound and how they're written, and I have spreadsheets I refer to that tell me if someone is doing well.

I don't need this class for anything other than fulfilling my GE requirements.

Em turns an angelic look on me. "Next time, I'll enroll you in advanced calculus and make you take every class."

Urg. Asshole. "You're really going to hold this over my head now I'm not taking any classes for you, aren't you?"

"Sure will."

It crosses my mind, again, to push him to talk to his school. Hell, I could go there as him and do it for him. But while we might use our identities against other people, we never use it against each other.

So now I have to deal with the knowledge that he's helping me, and I'm ... doing nothing in return. Some brother I am.

Still, even though I'm gambling with time until class starts, I duck into the bathroom, fill a washcloth with cold water, then head back to the bedroom again. Em doesn't hear me get back, so his eyes are still closed when I drop the cloth on his face. It hits him with a wet slap.

"The fuck?" He snatches it off and glares up at me. "Ohh, I *so* can't wait until you're drunk next."

"I'm really worried." I tug the cloth from his grip and this time lay it over his forehead, right above his still-glaring eyes. "Now, shut up and feel better."

I leave, swinging by the kitchen for a protein bar before heading out to my car. I could walk from here, but I'm nervous I'll be late and decide to take my chances with the student parking lot. It's right behind the Math department, and if the universe owes me one scrap of luck today, it'll give me a car space close to the building.

Apparently, the universe owes me jack shit, so by the time I get to class, almost everyone is inside the room, and I hurry to find a seat in the almost-full auditorium while I'm still finger combing the bed head from my hair.

I spot some spare chairs toward the back and hurry to slip into the row before I draw attention. Relief puffs from me on an exhale as I fall into a seat and pull my laptop from my bag. Once I'm not on the edge of panic, I cast my eyes over the rest of the class, and movement a few rows away catches my eye. A big dude with red hair, freckly, almost tan skin, and a backward hat stands and slings his bag over his shoulder.

Holy fucking damn, he's hot.

Maybe I should have sat next to him?

Not that it matters because he grins my way, then jogs up the stairs and slides into my row. Right next to me.

"Cutting it close," he says through his smile.

And ... I've lost my fucking tongue. Normally, I have no issues with guys. Sure, a lot of the time when I pick up, I've been drinking, but even without alcohol, I can flirt up a storm. Apparently, after a mad dash here, where I'm left sweaty and unsure if I put on deodorant, is all it takes for me to lose my game.

"Yes," I manage. "Just made it."

"Lucky. I still can't believe Brooks locks the bloody doors. There should be rules against that."

I double take. "Bloody?"

The big guy waves a hand. "British sitcoms. They're the tits, and I retain *way* too much of their slang."

"I don't think I've ever seen a British sitcom before."

"Dude, you're missing out. They're so witty and hilarious." He reaches over me and starts typing on my laptop. His arm keeps brushing the side of mine, and unlike me, *he* put on deodorant this morning. He smells amazing, but also kinda like dirt? Grass?

Fuck, he's close.

I'm about to introduce myself when he jabs a finger at my screen.

"There. Start with those. Binge them all, then we can talk."

His raw enthusiasm helps relax me. "What? We can't talk before then?"

"Sure, but not about *them*. This one, for example." He jabs a thick finger at my screen. "Not a sitcom, but I get full-on belly laughs whenever I watch it."

I eye him, trying to pick up whether he's flirting or just being friendly. "Maybe we could watch it together sometime."

"Really?" For some reason, that amuses him. "Okay. You're on."

"Fair warning, I will be shocked if it makes me laugh."

"Eh. I'm confident."

Professor Brooks walks in and locks the doors just like this guy said he would. That's fucking weird, but whatever. It's lucky Em has been taking this class for me because I struggle to be anywhere on time.

We fall quiet as Brooks talks, and while the guy beside me takes notes, I tilt my head closer to see if I can get any information from his screen about what the hell his name is. Sure, I could introduce myself, but it sort of feels like I've missed that chance.

He inputs a note in the margin of the document he's typing in, and bingo.

Harrison Dunn.

Ah. Dunn and Dalton. I ship it.

Harrison's paying a whole lot more attention to the class than I am, and so, reluctantly, I pull my attention away from him and back to the front. Considering I have no fucking clue what Brooks is talking about, I'm struggling to follow along, but I type everything I can keep up with, word for word, figuring I can ask Em about it all later.

Welcome to the downside of cheating: apparently, you don't learn anything.

Though, in my defense, no one understands numbers anyway. Who can math? That whole subject is a con.

After trying and failing to keep up, I cut another look to Harrison.

"What got you into sitcoms anyway?" I murmur.

"My mom."

"That's a weird hobby. I don't think I've heard of anyone our age watching ... *The Vicar of Dibley?* What?"

He snickers, and it's adorable. "Trust."

"Should we make a little wager out of it?"

"What do you mean?"

"Well, you say I'm going to laugh. I'm confident I won't. So, let's make it interesting."

Harrison thinks about it for a moment. "Okay, do you have class after this?"

"Nope, a free, then I'm full for the rest of the day."

"Here's what we'll do. Straight after class, we'll head to the dining hall and watch an episode. If you laugh, you owe me lunch. If you don't—"

An idea jumps into my head, fully formed. "You come to a party at my house this weekend."

"You're having a party?"

"We are now."

"I'm guessing you don't live alone?" he asks. "How will your roommates like that?"

"Considering I'm a DIK and my brothers throw random parties always, I don't think they'll care."

Harrison holds out his hand. "Deal."

I shake it, trying to ignore the sparks going off in my palm.

I guess the universe owed me one anyway.

3

HARRISON

There's something different about Benny today. He seems ... distracted. Normally he's super invested in class, and I have to ask him to break things down for me, but today, his brain is elsewhere. I only met him at the start of the semester, but he's been a savior in wrapping my head around this class. I originally took it in freshman year, and considering I need to take advanced stats soon, I decided to audit this one as a refresher, which is lucky because I hadn't realized how much I'd forgotten.

Benny's also never been interested in hanging out before. I've asked once if he wanted to grab lunch, but after it was clear he was only interested in small talk and statistics, I let him be. There was no hesitation today though. British sitcoms really can win anyone over.

"Okay." He drops his bag under the table, then grabs a chair that he flips around and straddles. "Do your best."

"Because I really love a free lunch, we're going to skip the sitcoms and go straight to a comedy panel that will have you dying."

"You're totally overhyping it."

"Benny-boy, let me introduce you to *Would I Lie to You?*"

He just stares at me. Benny is an interesting guy to look at. He has this young face, big lips, but eyes that give off the feeling they've seen too much. And those eyes couldn't hold more skepticism if they tried.

"You'll be eating your words," I promise him.

"There you go assuming I have a sense of humor again."

I like this version of Benny. Hell, he's cool otherwise, but this is the first time I've seen him so relaxed. Because I'm determined to win and only have half an hour to do it in, I go right for one of the funniest episodes I've seen lately and click on it to start.

The first couple of minutes, he keeps shooting me confused looks. Then when they get into the game, I catch him smiling a time or two. One of the stories a guest tells has me hunched over, trying to catch my breath, even though I've heard it all before, but when I peek up at Benny ... his eyes aren't even on the screen.

He's watching me—but at least he looks close to amusement this time.

"There's something wrong with you," I say when I catch my breath.

"They're funny, just not ..." He waves his hand over me. "You looked like you were about to suffocate."

"Because that's how normal people react to comedy."

"You are *not* a cute laugher, FYI. I recommend you never use this as a date suggestion."

I twist my cap forward, then backward again. "Noted."

The show wraps up, and a smug look crosses Benny's face. "I guess I win."

"Did you? I think enjoying myself makes me the real winner."

"A prize makes you a real winner. Enjoying yourself is a given when you hang out with me."

"Suddenly so confident."

"As the youngest of seven, I needed *something* to make me stand out from the others. Confidence is my thing."

"Aren't youngest siblings supposed to be all ... neglected and spoiled at the same time?"

"Eh, maybe if they have parents."

My eyebrows shoot up. "Shit, I'm—"

"Don't say sorry. It's cool. They died a long time ago, and I remember less of them than I'd like, but I have my siblings and their partners. Still lots of love going around the Dalton household."

"Yeah, fuck. Hard to know what to say about all that."

"Most people want to know how it happened—they hit a moose, never came home, that kind of thing." Benny is talking like he's completely disconnected from the situation.

"A moose? Fuck. We don't have those where I come from."

"Where do you live?"

I frown because I could have sworn we'd covered this. "Florida."

"Ah. So, if we lived there, maybe they would have been eaten by an alligator instead."

"Should we be joking about your dead parents?"

"Would you rather I cried about it?"

I laugh, tugging my hat off with one hand and dragging my hand through my hair with the other. "Do you want to cry about it?"

"Not really. Like I said, it was forever ago. I remember being sad for a long time, and then I just *wasn't*."

"Still. Wish you'd never had to go through that."

"Thanks. So do I."

The conversation has taken a fast turn, and I'm not sure how we get back to the joking side. Not that I don't like Benny actually sharing something for a change, but ... well, apparently, I'm not great when it comes to sympathy.

He looks me square in the eyes, lips tilting up on one side. "So. I take it *your* parents aren't dead?"

And there's something about the way he says it that has me laughing again. I can't tell if I'm amused or uncomfortable though.

"I don't think you get to tell people what's funny anymore," he says. "Apparently, you'll just lose it at anything."

"That show *is* funny. Wanna double or nothing our wager?" I suggest. There's still just enough time to sneak in another episode.

"Sorry, I would, but I really like winning. That, and I need to duck home to drop something off. Here." He hands over his unlocked phone. "Put your number in there, and I'll text you the party details."

I do as he says and hand the phone back. "Can't wait."

"Yeah." He holds my eyes again. "Me too."

UNKNOWN:

Where are you?

I STARE AT MY PHONE, wondering who the hell is after me. Just about everyone I know would assume I'm in class or studying.

· · ·

ME:

Class

UNKNOWN:

Yeah, but WHERE, dummy?

I CHOKE a laugh at the tone, suspicion sneaking in about who it could be.

ME:

That depends. If this is Benny, I'm in the science block. If it's a stalker who's going to kidnap me and demand a ransom: I'm way too poor for that, man. Give up now.

UNKNOWN:

Guess you'll find out soon enough.

"SOON ENOUGH" is exactly fifteen minutes later when I step out of class and find Benny leaning against the wall opposite my classroom. He has a takeout bag in one hand and is thumbing through his phone with the other.

"Tell me there's a cheeseburger in there for me, and I'll

come to all of your frat parties."

"You sure you wanna be making me promises like that?" He smugly pulls out a burger that he tosses to me. "We throw a *lot* of parties."

"You got me lunch."

"Yep."

"But I lost."

Benny shrugs his slim shoulders. He's not a small guy, more ... streamlined. Like he's built for running rather than taking on a football team. "You pointed out how much you really love a free lunch, and I just couldn't disappoint you like that. Besides, you *did* make me laugh. At you. That was valuable entertainment."

"I'm pretty sure you're not supposed to tell people you're laughing at them." We walk side by side, heading for the exit doors.

"Hey, don't blame me. I grew up with no parents, remember? How am I supposed to know those things?"

"And now I get the feeling you're fucking with me."

"Good. You're a fast learner."

I tear open the cheeseburger as we walk across the grounds. "Goddamn, I'm glad I made a wager today."

"Bet you're glad you switched seats too."

"Duh. I watched you walk right by me, and I was like, nope. I need to sit next to you."

For some reason, that surprises him. It's not like I've made a secret about needing that extra nudge for statistics, and he's always been happy to give it. Maybe Benny's one of those guys who likes when people need him. He clearly didn't see me this morning, and I wasn't letting him get away that easily.

"Well, I'm glad you did."

The sentence hangs between us for a second because it's an odd response. Like we don't always sit together.

We reach a bench seat, and I drop onto it to finish scarfing down my burger before making a dent in the fries Benny bought me.

"You want some money for these?"

"You keep that money for a future ransom. You might need it if you have that many anonymous people messaging you."

"In my defense, you literally just asked my location. Who does that?"

"A dude who wanted to surprise you with lunch." He tilts his head. "Next time, if you'd rather be kidnapped, just let me know though. I'm not going to kink shame."

"Not my kink, but good to know there'll be a next time." I stuff a fistful of fries into my mouth. "*Damn*, I love a free lunch."

"You have sauce all around your mouth," he points out.

Instead of putting down my food, I lean over and wipe my mouth on the shoulder of his T-shirt. "Gone?"

"You're an animal." He shoves me off, then checks the shirt like I've somehow stained the black material with ketchup. Judging by the way he's holding back a laugh, he's not too bothered about it. "I can't believe you just wiped your face on me."

"You pointed out I was a mess. I got self-conscious."

"Yeah." Benny drags the word out. "I doubt a guy like you has ever felt self-conscious in his life."

He's got me there. I might not be at the same level of snarky confidence that Benny is, but I'm ... settled in who I am.

Benny inviting me to his frat party reminds me that I haven't been out since I got back. Haven't slutted it up, haven't got drunk, just sat around the house playing video games with Marshall.

Dammit. Am I ... maturing?

I shudder the responsibility off me and put it down to moving away from Liberty Court. There was always a party or casual drinks going on over there.

"Shit," I say, catching sight of the time. "I've gotta run. Text me the party details, okay? Is it cool if I bring a friend or two with me?"

"What kind of friend?" he asks, head tilted to the side.

"Just my roommates."

"Yeah, they're cool, then."

What, was he expecting me to bring my bible group or something?

"I'll see you then."

Benny's smile stretches wide. "Can't wait."

4

BENNETT

"Thank you for forcing me to class today," I say, banging into the room.

Emmett is sitting by the window, tissues littering the ground around him as surprise pulls at his face. "You liked it?"

"I like the guy who hit on me."

He snort-laughs that quickly turns into a cough.

My good mood dips. "You okay, Emmy?"

"Fine. Just blocked up. Who hit on you?"

"A guy named Harrison. He's droolworthy. Hot as fuck."

Em shrugs. "Don't know anyone in our class called Harrison and definitely haven't seen anyone in our class who classifies as droolworthy." Emmett's eyes get unfocused. "Except maybe Professor Brooks."

Before I can groan out my disgust over Em having the hots for that train wreck, he continues.

"Tell me about this guy."

I dump my bag. "Not much to tell. He's hot, flirty, and we had a mini lunch date. I've invited him to a frat party this weekend." I don't want to give Em too many other details—like Harrison's red hair is a dead giveaway—because Em's always been great at sticking to our rule about not talking to people in class. I'm the one who struggled to keep my distance. And if he goes around looking out for Harrison in class, Harrison will definitely spot him and zone in.

Em perks up. "You're having a party?"

"We are now."

Whenever our house has a party, it's the one time we can get sloppy about being in the same place. With a full house and everyone too drunk to see straight, someone bumping into one of us in one room and then seeing the other in the next room is easy to pass off as alcohol. If they even remember it the next morning.

"Did you get out today?" I ask him.

Emmett shakes his head. "Felt too shitty."

"Well, once you're better, make sure you do. You can't just live in here all day, every day."

"Okay, West."

I grunt, hating when he acts like my being worried about him is the same as our eldest brother fathering us. "Fine. Live in here all day. Become a mole man for all I care."

"It's sweet when you don't care."

"You're so annoying. You're also killing my chances of hooking up. I can't bring guys back to my room and be all 'don't worry about the other me in the corner, he's not watching,' can I?"

"I dunno. Some people like that. Twins."

We both pull an identical face. While I share literally everything with Em, neither of us wants to share a hookup, and because we've had the offer many, many, *many* times is yet another reason we wanted our own lives out here.

Emmett snatches up his painkillers and tosses them to me. "I can't remember what it says, and my head hurts. If I took some at two, can I have more yet?"

I read the bottle and toss it back. "Every four to six hours. So, if you took it at two ... and it's five now ..."

"Another hour."

"Damn."

"Wanna get me some water?"

"Can do. I'm going to let some of the guys know about the party, and I'll be back, okay?"

He manages a pitying smile. "You don't need to babysit me. I'm sick, not dying."

I don't even like him joking about that. My morbid sense of humor over my parents' deaths only stretches so far, and when I try to imagine life without Em, I go cold all over.

We've always talked about what life will be like when we're older. We'll graduate, get our own careers, our own partners, and live within walking distance of each other. We'd be happy to live in the same house, but that's not for everyone, and we can't expect our partners to feel the same.

I might joke about Emmett cramping my love life, but if he needs me, I wouldn't want it any other way. Most people might find living in a tiny bedroom with someone else stifling, but it makes no difference to us. I figure we were smooshed together so much in the womb we came out mentally resigned to be that way our whole lives.

I reach the kitchen to grab Emmett's water and find two of my frat brothers at the kitchen island.

"Sandman." I greet the guy who pledged with me and has had the stupid nickname ever since. For the pledge party he threw, he thought he'd make it Hawaiian themed, only instead of filling the backyard with sand, he covered the house in it instead.

I swear I still find grains randomly around the house.

"Hey, Dalton. Just talking about weekend plans."

"What plans? We're having a party."

"We are?" He nods. "Cool."

"Theme?" Big Wally asks.

"Nah, just the usual."

"I'll hit up the guys at the stoner house. They always have good weed."

"Cool." It doesn't make a difference to me. Most of my siblings are into hockey, and the two who aren't, one is a math genius with a sensible streak, and the other is way too into her appearance to take anything recreationally. Drugs weren't something on our radar growing up when it was practice, school, practice, homework, conditioning, conditioning, conditioning. When Em and I first got to Cali, we thought it would be cool to try it, but being under the influence and hiding a secret as big as ours doesn't mix.

Even drinking, we have to be more careful than we would if we were at a party solo.

With any luck, I can use this party to pull Harrison, hook up early, then kick him out of my room before Em wants to go to bed.

"Let's make it a free ladies' night and ten a head for dudes," Big Wally says.

I grunt. "You guys are so straight. Ever think about little ol' me? Why don't we ever have a free night for queer dudes?"

"Because then you're the only one who would hook up," Sandman points out.

"You're a fucking idiot if you think I'm the only queer dude in this house." I take a sip of Em's water. "Statistically, there's no way that's possible."

"I'm not saying I *wouldn't* suck a dick," Sandman continues, "only that I'd have to be really drunk and desperate."

I pat him on the shoulder. "Real stand-up man, you are. Truly selfless."

He smiles like I've complimented him.

The thing is, I love my frat brothers; they're always here for a good time, and none of them have ever cared that I'm gay. Their number one question in life is "Is it fun?" and if the answer is yes, they're game. But I've never gotten particularly close to any of them. That's partially my fault for having my brother to confide in and not needing anyone else, and partially theirs. They say a *lot* of dumb shit.

"Okay, I want to make this party really good. I've got a guy coming, so let's get it up on socials. Have O'Toole fill the place with beer. Ooh—who was that sophomore DJ we had last time? The girl with the cat ears—you know the one."

"Yeah, she was great."

Sandman snickers.

I sigh. "You hooked up with her, didn't you?"

"Nope." He points at Big Wally. "He *tried*. She shot him down. I like her."

"Finally, a chick who has some sense. I don't know how you two get laid so much."

"They don't call me Big *Wally* for nothing."

"It's literally your name, and you're about ten feet," I deadpan.

"Yeah, but ... But ... Wally. It's innuendo. For my dick. Willy. You know."

I love hearing him splutter through the explanation. "I've literally never heard anyone else say that but you."

"I fucking hate you all."

"It's love like this that really makes me glad I moved in here."

Sandman chuckles. "I remember you all but begging to become a DIK."

"Begging to *suck* a dick, there's a difference."

"Pfft." Sandman flips me off.

I wouldn't say *begging*, but he's right that I wanted in. Wanted to be a part of something outside of my siblings. Outside of hockey. I've only had one of my frat brothers ask if I'm related to Asher Dalton, and after telling him no, he dropped it. A Google search could possibly pull up some random local articles on the Dalton duo, but unless someone is interested enough to go looking, I'm safe here.

It's one of the things I love about Franklin U. We're a Division One hockey school, but people are way more interested in football and lacrosse. Here, I'm just a random face in a sea of thousands.

"You know what we haven't done in about a year?" Sandman asks. "Jell-O wrestling. I miss that."

"You just miss seeing the chicks wrestle."

"Always so cynical. Sure, that part is cool, but it's just ... fun."

I can't disagree. Throwing each other around and having an excuse to play fight is a good time. Who knows, maybe I could get Harrison in on it? He'd probably kick my ass, considering he's bigger than me, but I wouldn't say no to feeling all that rubbing up against me.

There's a part of my brain that wishes I didn't bother with the whole frat party cover-up and had just asked to go to his house tonight to get it over with, but unlike some of my friends, I actually like the buildup. The anticipation makes good sex so much better, and if Harrison's confidence was anything to go by, I can trust the sex to be good. Maybe better than good. Though, when it comes to having my dick sucked, I'm not exactly picky on technique.

I drain Em's water and refill the glass, then raid the fridge for some fruit and the pantry for potato chips. I have no idea if he's eaten today, but if he hasn't left the room, there's a good chance that's a no.

I'm not much of a cook beyond pasta, so he'll have to deal with this until dinnertime.

"What time Saturday?" I check.

"Probably open up at nine," Big Wally suggests.

"Okay, laters." I nod their way before disappearing back to my room.

Em's face lights up when he spots what I'm carrying. I hold up the apple, and he barely catches it before it hits his face.

"Should have told me you didn't eat yet," I grumble.

"I wasn't hungry until I saw the food. Besides, I slept most of the day."

I dump the rest of the food on my bed and then grab my bag and pull out my desk chair. "Statistics sucks, by the way. I have no clue how you follow that class."

"And I have no clue how your whole dream revolves around writing for a living. Look at that, we are different."

I purse my lips, not wanting to bring up the future and next plans while he's sick. Technically, he already has a lot of course credits ... maybe he could enroll at Franklin? Just because we're twins, it wouldn't *mean* they'd automatically assume we've been cheating this whole time. Hell, they probably wouldn't be able to prove it if we continued. Unless they figured out the scar thing.

Considering no one other than our family ever has, I'm confident.

"So ..."

Emmett's grunt cuts me off. "No. No school talk. Sore head. Talk later."

Talk later. Sure. Those two words are his go-to these days.

5

HARRISON

Is risotto the greatest food ever? Or the greatest food ever?

First, they're cheap. Second, they're easy to cook. And third, they're versatile, so I can make them as fancy or plain as I like.

Felix stumbles inside from a long day at the veterinary clinic and collapses into the chair next to Marshall. His head drops onto my best friend's shoulder, and Marshall immediately wraps his arm around him.

I love how happy they are together. I'd been worried when they first showed interest because they're both friends of mine and total opposites, but I've never been so happy to have been proven wrong.

"Hard day?" I ask.

Fe peeks up at me. "Pup we couldn't do anything for. It sucks."

"Damn, I'm sorry."

"I'll desensitize to it. Eventually."

"And until then, you have us."

"Thank goodness." He sniffs. "Is that dinner?"

"Nearly done."

Marshall gives Fe another squeeze before releasing him. "Go shower and get changed."

Felix leaves us, and Marshall turns back to his books.

"Whatcha reading?"

"Literacy through the ages and how it helped shape civilization."

I pretend to snore, and Marshall flips me off.

"It's really fascinating."

"I bet."

He smirks my way. "And how *is* your flower shop?"

"Incredible, thanks for asking!" I've long since stopped biting whenever he calls my plants that. What are friends for if not to give each other shit? And Marshall and Felix are more than just friends to me. They're my family away from home.

He closes his book and looks over at me. "Figured out what your major project is yet?"

"Nope. I *know* it's about making plants fun, but I haven't figured out how to do that yet."

"Maybe it's because plants *aren't* fun?"

Marshall and I both love studying the world, but where his interests lie in people and how the world has changed, mine lies in making people not change *so* damn much. We've been given a fucking gift with this world, and we're ruining it.

Felix ... he's an animal person. I try not to hold it against him.

As a future ecologist, I understand the need for animals in the ecosystem, but it doesn't mean I have to like them. My bias mostly comes from resentment at the fact they get all the attention when the very thing that sustains all human life is forgotten about.

"I'm going to do it," I say. "You'll see."

"Hey, if anyone can, it's you."

"See? That's real support. You don't think it'll happen, but you encourage my delusions anyway. You get extras for dinner."

Marshall pats his jiggly stomach. "Like I need extras."

"Excuse me?" Felix walks in with his hands on his hips, and I choke back a laugh at how fierce the little dude can be.

Marshall throws his hands up. "I was *joking*."

"You better have been."

"I know you love my fat belly."

Felix rolls his eyes. "Duh. It gives the best cuddles."

Before Fe can perch himself on Marshall's lap, I interrupt them.

"Wanna grab plates and cups? It's ready."

He switches course for the kitchen instead, and I breathe a sigh of relief that I escaped that grope fest. I love that they're happy, I love that they're comfortable in their home, but I do *not* love the constant wandering hands reminding me that it's been a while for me.

All through college, I've been a hookup guy. I tried a relationship once with a chick I really liked, but things just fizzled out. It's not that I don't want to find someone, and it's not that I'm actively looking either, but at the moment, school has to come first.

Scratching an itch is second, and finding someone to settle down with can wait. I figure I'll either end up with some corporate type, saving the world one rainforest at a time, or some hippy chick who chains herself to trees.

All I know is that we're bound to have shared interests because I can't *not* talk about what I'm passionate about, and what I'm passionate about is usually boring to most people.

It's why my one and only college relationship fizzled out, and it's why, whenever I see someone a couple of times and think there could be something there, it never comes to anything.

If we have nothing to talk about, what's the point? I don't want a partner just so I can do the marriage and kids thing. I want someone I'm friends with. Who makes life better.

I know I'll find her one day, but the two women in my course haven't spared me a second glance, and in a school this big, it's hard to cross paths with someone who shares my interests.

Until then, I'll keep focusing on my goals and try to keep my roommates from humping each other around me as often as I can.

"So, family," I say once we're all seated and eating. "Guess what we're doing this weekend?"

"Studying?" Marshall immediately answers.

"Hard no. Frat party. The three of us. And do not exchange that look that I know you're about to exchange because you've both been behaving like an old married couple since we got back."

"I've never been that into parties," Marshall reminds me.

"No, but Fe's always been a party animal."

"That was because I was looking for people to sleep with. The only person I'm sleeping with is right next to me in bed, and I don't have to get out there shaking my ass for it to happen."

"I dunno, I'd like a bit of ass shaking," Marshall teases.

Felix narrows his eyes at me. "A frat party? Really? When was the last time you went to one of those things?"

He's right. Now that I'm doing my master's, I feel like the old guy trying to hang out with the kids when I go to an under-grad party. It's mostly why I've stayed away. Benny is a junior, so there's really only two years between us, but between him being an undergrad *and* one of those frat bros, we couldn't be more different.

"I lost a bet," I tell them. "To a junior in my statistics class."

"Isn't that the one you audit?" Marshall asks. "I didn't realize you were friends with anyone there."

"The guy's a math whiz, and I get help from him sometimes. I needed the refresher, but there are still things I don't fully understand, and Professor Brooks just flies through the material. Some days, I wonder if he realizes he's talking to a full classroom at all or if he's just that nervous he's trying to get the words out as quickly as possible."

"He's young for a teacher, so he probably *is* nervous," Felix says. "It's cool you have a friend. Outside of us."

"Fuck off, I have plenty of friends outside of you two."

Well, I did last year. Most of those friends have moved away or gone back home after graduation. Those who stuck around, I don't see as much because I'm busy with school, and they're busy with life.

As though proving my point, my phone lights up with a message from Benny.

> Saturday at nine. Don't bring anything. When the pledges at the door hit you up for money, just let them know Ben Dalton says you're on the list. They'll know what that means.

"Why the frat party?" Marshall asks.

"He's a DIK, and they're having one."

Felix laughs. "A math genius DIK, who would have thought?"

"No offense," Marshall continues, "but why the hell would a DIK care about you going to his party? Why was that the prize for the bet?"

I blink at Marshall because I hadn't thought of that. "Umm ... good question. To hang out, I guess."

"Have you hung out before?"

"Well, other than today, no."

Felix and Marshall exchange a look.

"What was that?"

Felix is struggling to hold back his smile. "Can we be absolutely sure that he's not into you?"

"Into me? Like ... gay?"

"Or any other flavor of queer, but yeah."

I don't immediately deny it because I don't want to assume anything about anyone, but as I think back over today, I'm not getting the vibe. "I don't think so."

"Why?"

"Well, if he wanted that, he'd be ... flirty, right?"

"Probably."

"Then, nah. It didn't feel like he was trying to pull me. Frat boys just always want their parties to be big."

"True."

"Besides, it's not like I'm not open to it, but I'm straight. I've never had the urge to go there with a guy, and Fe, you're one hell of a cute guy." I hold my hands out to the side. "Still nothing."

"Aw, well, I guess frat boy is shit out of luck."

"If he even wants that, which I don't think he does."

Thankfully, they let it drop, and Marshall takes over the conversation, filling us in on the drama at Shenanigans. The college bar is a great place to hang out, but when you hire a bunch of college students, they bring the drama, and Marshall always ends up with the best stories from work. Ever since his colleague Brax hooked up with a lacrosse player at work and Marshall almost walked in on them, I've been invested. And now, with the lacrosse player's illegitimate baby brother working there too, I'm just waiting for the next scandal.

Since I cooked, they clean up after dinner, and I finally grab my phone to text Benny back.

ME:

> Sounds mint. We'll be there. Can I tell the pledges my friends are on your list too? We're all kinda poor college kids.

I ADD A BEGGING EMOJI. Felix and Marshall both get regular work, but between vet school and Marshall doing his masters, it cuts into what hours they can take. I'm living off scholarships and a stipend my parents send me, plus the occasional hours I pick up mowing people's lawns and tending to their gardens.

BENNY:

> Sure. But please take a photo of their expressions when you do.

ME:

> I get the feeling this is a joke I'm not in on.

BENNY:

> Stupid frat boy stuff.

. . .

ME:

Isn't ALL frat boy stuff stupid?

BENNY:

Well, now I'm super offended. SO offended.
You'll have to make it up to me.

ME:

I'd offer you dinner, but my roommates just ate
it all. And you call me an animal.

BENNY:

Well, did they wipe their faces on you when
they were done? No? Then you still win. Also,
good point. You owe me a meal.

ME:

Fair, but I'm poor, remember? So, it'll either be
something I cook or the school dining hall.
Your call.

BENNY:

Well, most of the home-cooked meals I've had
over the years have been burned, so I'm
interested in seeing what you can do.

ME:

Deal, I love cooking.

BENNY:

What a coincidence: I love eating.

ME:

Match made in heaven.

I READ over my words for a second before I think through
what Marshall and Felix said. This doesn't feel flirty to me.
We're just talking, and he's an easy guy to talk to, but I guess
there's more than one way that could be taken.

ME:

Having friends you click with is the bomb.

I'M HAPPY WITH THAT. It doesn't sound too "sorry about the last message, I'm definitely straight" type of correction, but it lets him know he's in the friendship category. That's the main thing.

BENNY:

So, what are you going to cook for me?

I LET OUT the bated breath I'd caught when his reply dots had started on the screen. See? Zero weirdness. Thank fuck for that.

ME:

Risotto is my favorite, but I can do casseroles, fried chicken, anything with seafood …

BENNY:

Considering I live off pasta all of those sound fantastic. Surprise me. Make my mouth water, big guy.

I SNORT a laugh because that's maybe the flirtiest thing he's said all day, and I wonder if *he* knows it can be taken more ways than one. I might have questioned shit if he'd sent a message like that before we'd established the friends thing. Instead, I just get to be buzzed that I've made a new friend.

Even if he is a DIK.

6

BENNETT

I cruise through the party, marveling again at how easily we're able to pull something like this together. The house is full, and we only opened the doors ten minutes ago, but I can pick out my brothers by the random hoots and hollers coming from various rooms. It's gotten clammy inside with all the body heat filling the space, so I've taken off my shirt and tucked it in my shorts— it has nothing to do with wanting Harrison to see my abs the second he steps into the house.

"Dude, Devon is about to start a fire in the kitchen," Holmes says, almost knocking me over. "He dumped a whole bag of potato chips, M&Ms, and toffee into a dish and covered it in whipped cream. No fucking clue why he's putting it in the oven, but he's drunk off his tits already."

Motherfucker. Given I decided to stop at two drinks, I'm probably the most sober one here, which means it's on me to put a stop to the house burning down. That would be a fast way to end the party before Harrison even got here.

So reluctantly, I leave where I'm hovering by the entrance and follow Holmes toward the kitchen. The music is thudding so hard the walls shake, and we have to push our way through sweaty bodies to find the commotion. Lots of drunk men cheering and egging on the dumbassery.

I approach the huddle of bodies, not loving the smell starting to build in here.

"Hey, what are we cooking?"

"Munchie cure," Devon grunts.

"You sure? Because it smells like burning plastic."

They all snicker like they have a joke I'm not in on. Knowing they're drunk and stoned, I wouldn't be surprised if that's the case.

I crane my neck to look into the oven, and even through the grubby front glass, I can tell it's getting dark in there. I hate to say it, but I think Holmes was right.

"Question: is it the charcoal or the smokey flavor that gets rid of the munchies?"

I'm met by five blank faces.

With a sigh that's as dramatic as me hanging out by the door for Harrison, I hook my foot into the oven handle and kick it open.

A cloud of smoke billows into the kitchen, followed by the sound of coughing. Someone hurries to close the door to the hallway before the alarm can go off.

I tug my shirt from where it's tucked into my shorts and press it to my face while my brothers argue amongst themselves over whose fault it was. I've dealt with more than enough kitchen mishaps that this one barely fazes me. I just flick the knob off, grab a towel, and pull the charred mess out.

Then, because I really want to make sure they clear out of

the kitchen before they do more damage, I drop the dish in the sink and turn the cold water on high.

Sizzling fills the air, steam roaring up around us, making the room smell nastier than before. A few people cheer, so I indulge them in a bow and am about to tell them all to get their asses out when I glance over and spot Harrison.

He's in the doorway, red Solo cup in hand, gorgeous broad smile sitting clean on his face.

"You know, when you said you grew up on burned food, I didn't realize you were the one cooking," he says as he approaches.

"I wasn't. And I wasn't this time either." I hold up the soggy dish. "Want some potato, choc smash?"

"Some what?"

"Had to give the stupid-ass idea a name as dumb as the things that they put in it. I love my brothers, but damn do they switch off at parties."

"And you're the mature, responsible one, right?"

I laugh because I don't think I've ever been called that in my life. "I grew up in a house with six siblings making shit up as we went along. There's nothing mature about me. I just know how to thrive in chaos."

"That's a good quality to have."

"Sometimes. Other times, when everything is calm and normal, life feels way too boring."

"Boring?"

"Yeah." I dump the dish back in the sink and throw the towel over it. "Makes me restless. Down. I hate it."

Technically, with the secrecy Em and I are going for, it would have made more sense to get an apartment together. We would have had our own space, wouldn't have had to hide, and it would have been so much simpler than locking my bedroom door every time I leave my room.

But Em wanted to experience the San Diego State campus, and the thought of having an apartment to myself? Off campus where there were no people around?

How fucking depressing.

In some ways, the DIK house reminds me of my childhood. It's loud. Busy.

When things get quiet, that's when I start thinking, and I don't like where my brain goes.

Harrison shrugs, taking a long sip of his beer. "I love the stillness."

"You are one weird dude."

"I just think that if you don't stop once in a while, really pay attention, appreciate what's around, that things move too quickly. Sometimes you miss it."

"Miss what?"

"The good in the world."

I stare at him for a beat, then hold my arms out toward the drunken laughter, stumbling couples, and beer bong chugging around us. "Are you telling me this isn't all good?"

"This is fun, but I wouldn't call it good."

"Chaos is my everything. A night like tonight, it'll give me a buzz for the rest of the week."

Harrison still looks skeptical.

"Come on, I'll show you." I grab his hand and pull him through the house after me, up the stairs, and through the halls until we reach the attic entrance. I pull down the string and climb up first, his heavy footsteps on the rungs letting me know he's following.

"This seems like the opposite of what you wanted to show me," he says, stepping into the bare roof cavity. The music is muffled up here, and yeah, it's quieter ... for now.

I cross to the large window and slide it all the way across.

Music and the sounds of the party going on below filter up to us again, and I cross my arms over the ledge.

From here, I can see the entire backyard and everything happening in it.

"This is my kingdom."

Harrison watches for a second. "People have always disappointed me."

"What? Why?" Considering how over-the-top friendly he is, I would have thought he was one of those hypersocial extroverts.

"Dunno, really. I think it's more of a me problem. I just get so invested in things, excited over them, and it's like no one else cares."

"Like what?"

He drags his bottom lip through his teeth. "Eh, it's not important."

"Of course it is."

He glances my way, brown eyes meeting mine for a second. "I'm kind of a plant guy. Really into the environment and think nature is one of the coolest things ever, but as you can imagine, most people find that weird. It's always 'are you a dog or a cat person' but never 'are you a Venus flytrap or house fern person,' you know?"

I don't know. I have literally no clue what he means. A *plant* person? Is he one of those nutters who sits out in the forest to study fungus? Does he wear a tinfoil hat while he does it?

Harrison takes one look at my face and cracks up. "See? There. You're mentally calling me a weirdo, but your face is screaming it at me anyway."

"Not weird ... umm, different?"

"Uh-huh. Right."

"Well ... are you going to answer the question?"

He looks at me like he isn't following.

I roll my eyes. "Flytrap or fern?"

His smile swiftly fills his face. "Out of those two, definitely the Venus, but overall, monkey face orchid. They make me laugh. Every. Damn. Time."

"Yeah, but we already established that doesn't take much." I pull out my phone to look up whatever the fuck that orchid is. When it hits my screen, my lips twitch. "Okay, that thing is pretty funky-looking."

"See? *See?* And there's just so much cool shit like that out there. Not even cute like that, but really bloody mind-blowing. We wouldn't have half the medicines and cures we do now if it wasn't for plants, and they literally balance the entire ecosystem. Need food? Shelter? Water? Plants!"

There's something about seeing this hulky, handsome guy totally nerd out that makes me weak. I have never, ever thought a plant was cool or interesting in my life. The best use I ever got out of them was when Em and I would use branches and sticks to sword fight as kids.

So, I might not share his passion or his interest, but I can grudgingly admit he kind of makes me want to.

"I take it you're studying something plant-ish?"

He frowns for a split second. "Sorry, I thought I already said. Yeah, I want to be an ecologist. Still a lot to do to get there, but it's happening. What about you? Something with hockey, right?"

Did I tell him that? I wouldn't put it past me because once I get started on that sport, I'm like Harrison—can never shut up about it—but it's not in a good way.

"That's the aim. Get my journalism degree and become a sports reporter for hockey. A decent one, not one of those assholes who are always after a sound bite."

"That's a cool goal."

"Thanks."

"I don't know a whole lot about sports, but would hockey be hard to get into? It's pretty popular, right?"

Pretty popular? He's cute. "Something like that. But I'm confident." Nothing like cashing in on the bit of nepotism that goes along with my last name.

Harrison points at something below us. "Are those two in the bushes over there fucking?"

"Probably. It happens at least a few times a party."

"Can't say I've ever wanted to have public sex like that."

"It's fun." I grin his way, and he plays with his baseball cap in a way that makes him look adorable.

"Of course a DIK knows all about that."

"Hey, I'd rather they do it down there than in my bed. I've lost count of the number of times I've had to stand in the hall and wait for people to be done in my room."

"Jesus," he mutters, sounding scandalized.

"Eh, I come from a big family, remember? I'm used to boundaries not being a thing."

"Surely common decency helps you realize you don't fuck in someone else's bed."

"Nah. You know what it's like. When you're with some-one." I sweep a look over him. "That tension building and building ... then you give in, and it makes you so high there's no stopping it. You don't give a shit where you are, you just need to get off."

Harrison turns his head slightly toward me, and the idea to kiss him briefly flickers through my brain. Sure, it's not the most romantic place to do this, but I'm not after flowers and songs—I just want to suck his cock.

Something makes me hold back though.

Something in his expression.

We're so close our shoulders are almost touching, so I can see every detail on his face. The freckles over his nose, the long, strawberry blond eyelashes, his strong jaw, the muscle in his cheek ... and the doubt in his eyes.

I groan and drop my face onto my folded arms. "You're straight, aren't you?"

He chuckles. "Yeah. Sorry."

"But ... but ... class. And the dinner date you promised me."

"I just wanted to sit next to you." He holds up his hands like he's been busted. "And I'm still all for that dinner date, uh, platonically."

"Fuck, did I misread things." I'm expecting him to do the awkward duck out, but Harrison stays put.

He's still grinning. "You were really into me, huh?"

"Duh. You're hot."

"What did you think would happen up here?"

"Not gonna lie, blow jobs would have been my first pick."

Seeing that huge frame on his knees for me, cap swung backward, soft eyelashes fanned out over his cheeks ...

"Damn it." My stupid cock is getting stupid hard.

"What was the first thing you noticed about me? Go."

I cut him a look. "What?"

"Well, there had to be something. Let's call it research."

"You wanna know what I was attracted to?"

"Sure, doesn't everyone?"

I turn to face him, elbow still propped on the window, while I try to figure out if he's for real or is just baiting me to earn a punch to the face. "Seriously?"

"It's as good of a conversation as any."

I know what the real answer is: his friendly confidence. Sure, I'd noticed how hot he is first, but that would have been easy enough to ignore if he hadn't acted like we were already best of friends. Still, I want to test this supposed coolness.

"Those blow job lips. Sorry to tell you this, but they were made for sucking dick."

His mouth hangs open for a second. "Like you can talk. Your lips are like little pillows, dude."

That shocks some of the disappointment from me. "Pillows? That was a gay thing to say."

"Which is how you know it's true. If I even noticed them, then yes. They're big."

"What else did you notice?"

"That someone likes to be complimented."

That almost makes me laugh. "Wanna give me more?"

"It would actually be easy to give you a lot, but I'm not going to risk them going to your head."

"Too late." Just knowing there's a lot makes me feel good. "Thanks for not freaking out and being a dick. It's happened before."

"Shit. I'm sorry. It's not something you should be thanking anyone for though, like, fuck. Wires get crossed all the time. I *did* ask you out on a date, after all."

"True." I debate whether to push my luck. "Just let me know where and when."

"This week sometime." Harrison's gaze catches on something. "No way. Is that Jell-O wrestling?"

"Sure is. Wanna go watch the hot chicks go at it?"

"Nah, I want a turn. You in?"

Rubbing our bare, slippery skin all over each other? Kill me now.

"Did you miss the part where I have *six* siblings? I'm a wrestling pro, big guy."

"Guess we're about to find out."

7

HARRISON

Turns out Marshall and Felix were right. Benny wanted my dick. It's not the first time I've been hit on by a guy, and it won't be the last, so him thinking I'd freak out about it makes me sad. We established he wanted to hook up. We established that's off the table. Now, we move on.

That's what you do with misunderstandings.

I'm still down to hang out and cook him dinner and force him into watching more shows with me—those are all things I wanted to do before our conversation, so nothing has changed.

It's a tight squeeze through the house, and I have no idea where Felix and Marshall are, but Benny and I stop to grab a drink as we make our way outside. The party is stupidly fun, a real vibe, but it's hitting me that this isn't the kind of thing I'd want to do on a regular basis anymore.

We have to fight our way to the front of the crowd that's

formed around the wrestling. And by "we," I mean Benny pushes his brothers out of the way while I duck in behind him.

The two women wrestling have their shirts off and are covered in Jell-O while the guys around us are acting like it's the greatest thing they've ever seen. It's not surprising to see Chase and his best friend, Tatertot, at the front, leading the cheer squad.

Welcome to college, lads.

I duck my mouth down near Benny's ear. "Should we have another wager?"

"You mean the last one didn't scar your ego?"

"My ego is big enough to take a beating. What do you say?"

"I'm always game. What are you thinking?"

That part is harder. Bets are fun; thinking of a prize is not. "Fifty bucks?"

"Money? Pfft."

"Fine, fine ... Ah ... okay. If I win, you come to work with me next weekend."

"Work?"

I nod. "I have some lawns to mow. Sweaty work. Takes me all day. It'd be way better if I had someone else I could palm it off to."

"Fine. Agreed. No risk since you won't win anyway."

"Okay, smart-ass. What are you getting?"

A teasing glint hits his eye, and he pumps his eyebrows at me.

"No." It's a real struggle not to laugh, but I don't want him to think he's cute. "No BJs."

"Oh, damn," he says, not trying to sound believably disappointed. "In that case, cleanup tomorrow. You can come help."

"That sounds easy enough."

He gives me a pitying look that tells me I don't know what I'm getting into. "Deal?"

"Deal."

I strip off my shirt and we both ditch our shorts. Then, I pause to finish draining my cup, before I step over the side of the little kiddie pool and into the calf-deep Jell-O.

"Ready?" a black-haired frat boy calls, smacking Benny's ass.

"Fuck yes."

"And you?" He leaves a stinging slap on my butt cheek too.

"Sure am."

"Okay, let's go! Make the DIKs proud, bro," he calls before waving his hand between us and jumping out of the pool.

Benny lunges for me, and I'm not expecting the impact. His compact, muscular body collides with mine in a way that forces the air from my lungs.

Okay, he wasn't lying about all that wrestling experience. I push Benny off me, but he comes for me again just as fast. We tussle for a moment, me trying to keep my footing on the slick surface, but then he hooks his foot behind my ankle and tugs. My feet slip out from under me, and I hit the pool base hard. He's like a feral little gremlin when he climbs on top of me and tries to get me in a headlock, body panting hard, thighs straddling my torso, skin soft and slick against mine.

Gah, wake up already!

I try to grab a hold of him, but the Jell-O makes it almost impossible. He's slippery and fast, and I have *way* underestimated him.

Now that I know he isn't holding back, neither will I. Using the Jell-O to my advantage, I slip to the side, throwing him off me, before taking him onto the ground. We fight and slip and shove and wrestle, trying to get the other out of the kiddie pool.

Benny's laugh rings out in my ears, oxygen struggling to fill my lungs.

"Give up," I grunt.

"No goddamn way."

"You are such a little shit."

He cackles and finally gets me into that headlock, but because I'm so much taller, it puts him in a vulnerable position. I get my arms around him, hooking one up between his legs and the other behind his back. Then, I pick him up and—

Pop him over the side.

"What the fuck?" He releases my head and looks down at the grass he's standing on. His chest is working overtime, abs sticking out with each inhale and ... huh. He's very, very obviously half-hard, and his briefs aren't doing much to hide it.

"Woo!" One of his frat brothers slaps me on the back. "Who's versing the winner?"

"Nope." I hold up my hands and climb out too. "That's me done. Finished."

"He'll only fight people smaller than him."

"Exactly." Whatever I have to say to get out of another round. Not that it wasn't fun, because it absolutely was, but I'm here to spend the night with Benny. And also, the guy is savage. I'm pretty sure I'll have bruises tomorrow.

He glances up at me, curls plastered to the side of his face and neck with sticky Jell-O, and laughs. "Your whole face is bright red."

I point at my hair. "The smallest amount of blood flow will do that. Good genes." Being a redhead hasn't exactly been easy —especially since it's red-red—but I've learned to love it about myself. It's a talking point. Makes me different. It also helps me sort the trash out of my life pretty fast.

"I love getting a guy's blood pumping."

I gesture toward where his dick is still trying to escape his briefs. "I can tell."

He reaches down, kinda cupping himself to cover up. "I made no secret I'm attracted to you, and you wanted to roll around all lubed up and half-naked. Surely you know a little chub isn't something you have control over."

"True." Still weird to think that I made another guy hard. "You got towels inside for us to clean up?"

"If I say no, will you stay naked for the night?"

Ballsy guy. "If you say no, I'll have to leave."

"Damn ..." His gaze flicks away and then back to me. "So, like, you still want to hang out?"

"I said I did, and I meant it. My two roommates are boyfriends. I don't give a shit, really."

His smile is hesitant. "In that case, we better get you cleaned up."

We pick up our clothes, and Benny leads us back inside. We get to what I'm assuming is his room, and he cracks open the door to peer around before letting me inside. Cute of him to try and protect me from a potential orgy.

He opens an old set of drawers and tosses me a towel. "You can shower down the hall, but I'd recommend against it."

"Yeah, I'll just towel off and get dressed."

His eyes immediately drop to my damn briefs and away again. "I don't think my underwear will fit you, dude."

"I'll figure it out." And to figure it out, I turn my back on him and drop trou. He's moving behind me, I assume getting changed as well, so I focus on drying myself down as best I can before tugging my clothes back on. The cotton of my shirt catches against my sticky skin, and I'm definitely going to need a shower once I'm home.

I glance over, expecting to find him dressed too, but he's still in his briefs, back to me, hand firmly covering his eyes.

"You're not getting changed?"

"Dude, I just saw your ass. You're going to have to give me a minute."

I choke, not sure if I'm going to laugh or ... "Fuck. Sorry."

Getting changed in front of other guys isn't something I've stopped and thought about before.

"Goddamn, you have so many freckles." His voice is husky.

"Are you hard?"

He snickers, head dropping forward. "Please get the fuck out of my room."

I hurry for the door, still a bit thrown over my ass getting him horny. It's not an uncomfortable feeling, just ... different. "I'm gonna get us drinks. Meet in the kitchen?"

"I'll be there."

He doesn't meet my eye as I slip out of the room, but I do peek back at him.

My gaze skims down his tan, muscular back and lands right on his ass.

I've never noticed before, but hot damn, Benny has some cake on him. If that ass was on a chick, I'd probably pop wood too.

Right. Drinks.

Leaving now.

I've just finished pouring out our drinks in the kitchen when Benny walks in. That was fucking fast. He's fully dressed, and even his hair is out and dry. He's clutching a red Solo cup in one hand and is wearing an unnervingly happy smile.

"Bowser!" He throws his arms around me. "Fancy seeing you here."

I chuckle and pat his back before he pulls away. "Real coincidence."

"Love these parties," he says, a slight slur to his words.

Wow. Not only is he a fast dresser, but he's a fast drinker too. I nod to his cup. "What was in that drink?"

"Something delicious." He grabs the beer I've poured for him and takes a gulp. "Gah. That tastes like shit in comparison."

"Cheap beer tastes like shit? No ..." I spot Marshall and

Felix passing by the door. "Ohhh. Wait here a sec. I'm gonna grab my friends for you to meet."

I dart out into the hall to chase them down, hoping to grab them before they disappear again. Felix's bright auburn curls should be easy enough to spot, and Marshall isn't exactly small. I catch sight of them as they turn a corner, heading down the hall toward where Benny's bedroom is. Thankfully, I manage to reach them before they've taken a few steps because I don't want to know what they're doing sneaking off toward the bedrooms.

"Where have you guys been all night?"

"Enjoying the party." Felix looks me over. "Where have *you* been?"

"Narrowly avoided a house fire, got the view from the roof, and then Jell-O wrestled. Oh. And found out my new friend wanted to fuck me."

Marshall and Felix high-five. "Called it."

"Shut up. Anyway, he's a cool guy, and we're friends, so I want to introduce you. He's—"

Approaching us from down the hall. His hair is back up, that same curl stuck to his neck as earlier, and he's in different clothes again.

I tug his tank top. "You changed."

"Well, I wasn't going to give everyone a show all night."

It's definitely a relief to be introducing a fully dressed Benny to my friends. I plant a hand on his shoulder and turn him to them. "Guys, this is Benny. Benny, Felix and Marshall."

"'Sup." He eyes them both. "I take it you're the boyfriend roommates."

"And you're the—"

I shoot Felix a look to be careful of his next words.

"New friend."

The sly eyes Benny sends my way makes it clear he knows

something else was going to come from Felix's mouth. "That's me. The new friend with the hots for the straight dude. Tale as old as time, am I right?"

Marshall and Felix laugh as I look between them all.

"What?"

"It's a joke that's not really a joke that all queer guys have to have at least one tragic straight friend crush. Actually, that's probably true for all queer people, but hey!" Benny gestures to me like a magician revealing his secret. "You're mine!"

"Crush?"

"Okay, that's overexaggerating, but you know what I mean."

I throw an arm around his neck. "If I could be gay for anyone, I'd want it to be you."

"And now you're just making things worse."

Felix plants his hands on his hips. "Hey, I thought you said it would be for me."

"Wait." Benny shakes me off him. "You just go around telling all the boys that?"

"Can't help it that I'm in high demand."

"Am I the only one in this hallway who hasn't wanted to sleep with you?" Marshall asks, and Benny and Felix answer "yes" in unison.

Gotta say, it feels good to be wanted.

"I think we need another drink," Marshall tells Fe, and just as they're about to walk off, Felix tugs me down to reach my ear.

"It's my duty to inform you that your new friend is a total ten, and all your straightness is going to waste."

I roll my eyes as they leave, and Benny leans against the wall, folding his arms over his chest.

"What did he say?" His cocky tone makes me pretty sure he heard.

I fake a confused look. "Dunno. Something about barely a four. Run away. Stage-five clinger—"

Benny thumps my arm. "He said I'm a ten. I'm glad you know that you're missing out on all this."

"I have so much regret," I say, leaning against the wall beside him.

"I can live with that." His puffy lips curl into a grin. "For the rest of your life, you'll always think back on the DIK you never had."

"The memory will keep me company on my deathbed."

"Hot. Think by that point you'll be too old to even get it up over me?"

I glance down at my pants. "Apparently, I'm already suffering from that issue."

"Hey, maybe you're not straight, just impotent."

I slap my hand down over his mouth. "Don't put that into the universe."

His pretty bluey-hazel eyes shine teasingly up at me.

I only remove my hand when I trust he's done talking about it. "What time tomorrow?"

Benny tilts his head. "Huh?"

"For cleanup. What time do you want me here?"

"I know I got some good hits on you, but none of them were to the head. You won, remember?"

"Oh, I remember. Kicking your ass won't be forgotten in a while."

He gives me a flat look.

"But I'm going to help you anyway."

"Well, now you've said it, I'm going to hold you to it." He grips my shoulder and leans in close. So close. Close enough that for one second, I actually think he might kiss me. He doesn't, but I also didn't pull back from him either. "You are going to regret every minute of your life tomorrow. And you'll only have yourself to blame."

8

BENNY

I have a niggling headache, thanks to Emmett's drinking last night, but it's nothing some painkillers don't squash. Since I'm planning to be at the house all day—my party, which means I'm in charge of supervising cleanup—Em's gone out. Knowing he's not locked away in my bedroom helps lessen some of my anxiety around him and what he's doing and means I get to funnel all that anxiety toward Harrison instead.

Good times.

I shouldn't. I'm being a dumbass. The dude is straight and off the table, which isn't an issue, except when I mentioned a crush last night, I might not have been far off. Stupid things. Crushes are pointless and meaningless. A bit of attraction and the excitement of someone new is all well and good until the newness wears off and you realize you don't actually like anything about them.

That's where I am with Harrison.

He's the shiny new toy, and I'm the bratty toddler who doesn't want anyone else to play with him.

He said that he was coming around today, but we never talked a time, and after downing a few more drinks once it was established hooking up was off the table, I wouldn't be surprised if he's forgotten all about it.

Bad ideas are always great when you're having fun. Following through is a whole other story.

So now I'm doing that annoying thing where I'm bouncing from room to room and definitely not straining my ears for any sign of someone at the front door.

"You call that floor clean, Harper?" I call from where I'm perched on the kitchen counter, smashing my way through a bag of Takis and ignoring the way my mouth is burning.

He flips me off with one hand and keeps scrubbing with the other.

Having pledges means I don't have to do any of the actual cleaning myself. We've all been there on the bottom rungs of the frat, and one day, these guys will be the ones sitting on the counter, watching. We all know I'll end up getting my hands dirty eventually though. That's brotherhood. Give them shit for an hour, then everyone gets into it and gets the job done. Sure, the house smells of sweaty gym gear most of the time, but none of us like living in a dump.

I flick a Taki onto the floor in front of Harper. "Missed a spot."

"Fuck you, Dalton." He picks up the bright blue tube, jumps to his feet, then crushes it in my hair before I can stop him.

"Hey, uncool."

He slaps a hand on the bag and crushes half of them for good measure. "Keep them in the bag, you dick."

Oh, the images of upturning the crushed chips all over the floor are sweet, but even I'm not that much of a jerk.

Harper gets back to work right as there's a familiar, warm chuckle behind me.

"What the hell is in your hair?"

I turn toward Harrison's voice, gut doing this fun, bubbly thing, and smile. "You really don't know how to quit while you're ahead, do you?"

"What do you mean?"

"You're here. To clean. A frat house post-party."

He shrugs, drawing my attention to his freckly, unevenly tanned shoulders. "If you think this could be any worse than cutting lawns, you're mistaken."

Poor man. With a smirk, I drop from the counter, cross to one of the stools, and lift the butt cushion. It unearths the sight and smell of puke.

Harrison takes a swift step back. "Right. Well, that's fucking disgusting."

"Too late to back out now."

He drops his phone and keys onto the counter, then rounds it and starts pulling cleaning stuff out from under the sink. "You're surprisingly well stocked."

"This isn't our first party."

"True." He fills up a bucket with sponges and chemicals. "Where are we starting?"

"*We?* Oh no, friend. You're on your own here."

Harrison laughs and steps forward. He plucks the chip bag from me and sets it aside, then combs his fingers through my hair, clearing the crushed chip out. That happy bubbling explodes, and I growl at it to shut the hell up.

"There is no way," Harrison says, in an overly happy voice, "that you're getting out of this. You're going to grab a trash bag and come to the front living room I passed that hadn't been touched yet, and we're going to scrub the hell out of that thing."

"But ... but ... then who will supervise?"

"Anyone but you," Harper snarks, flicking water at my leg.

"Ahhh ..." Harrison points at Big Wally, who's just risen and walks in wearing an open robe, Kings football socks, and a pair of tighty-whities. "That guy."

Big Wally pauses by us. "Who, me?"

"Yup." Harrison passes him *my* chips. "Good luck."

Then, he takes my hand in one of his large ones and tugs me from the room. The only thing that stops me from being pissed he gave my food away is the curse from Big Wally as he swallows a chip whole, then scrambles for a glass of water.

"'K. That was fun."

"This won't be though."

We step into the living room, and I seriously regret throwing this party just to get laid. Especially since no dick sucking was had. It could have happened, too, if I'd wanted to ditch my new friend and pick up any number of the guys who'd been there last night that I know would have been down. That's another point for the stupid column when it comes to crushes. All your good sense goes out the window.

Who the hell passes on an orgasm just to hang out with someone *platonically*?

"Trash," he says. "Off you go."

"What'd you call me?"

"I'll call you a lot worse if we're stuck doing this all bloody day."

So, I might not have planned to help for a while yet, but here we are, so I might as well just get on with it. Besides, I get to do it hanging out with Harrison, so that makes it less bad, even if the urge to give myself a minor injury just to get out of it has only decreased by a smidge.

"You guys know how to throw a party," Harrison says, wiping spilled drink off the wall. "It was a lot of fun, but I think I've officially hit the age of hangovers making me question if it's worth it."

"Wait. You're here *and* you're hungover?"

"I thought my jog and tea would help, but I ended up puking behind some bushes off campus."

"Wow. Someone is going to get a nice, early morning surprise."

"I didn't *leave* it there." Of course not. Harrison is Mr. Responsible. "I snuck the people's hose and used it to wash the mess away."

"I don't know of a single person who would have done that."

"Maybe you need new friends. Besides, their geraniums needed watering, so ... two birds."

I laugh. "Geraniums. You're such a nerd."

"You say that like it's a bad thing, frat boy."

"Tell me something cool about plants."

"Ohhh, okay!" He thinks for a second. "Did you know there are more microorganisms in one teaspoon of soil than there are people on Earth?"

I think my brain short-circuits. "Wait ... that's like ..." I try to picture a teaspoon and make my fingers in the rough size of the spoon I had breakfast with this morning. "No way."

"Seriously."

"I don't fucking believe you."

Harrison tips his head to the side. "Want to make a bet of that?"

I'm not stupid enough to fall for it. "Nope. I'll accept your word."

"Smart boy." He keeps scrubbing. "Tell me something cool about hockey."

I get that one-second tension that always hits when someone

mentions the H-word to me. Then I remember that Harrison isn't a sports guy, and while I might tease him about being a nerd, I way prefer that and his plant facts over him catching on to who I am.

"Umm ..." I try to remember all the things I actually liked about the sport before everything went to shit. Before the pressure and politics outweighed the fun of skating. I can't tell him that Em and I were a force to be reckoned with. That once we hit the ice together, we were so tuned in to each other that it almost didn't seem fair to the other team. *That's* the part I miss. The part I used to thrive on. I might have had a reputation for not following the coach's directions, but none of that was intentional. I'd even argue it was on him. Calling out left and right when I'm skating at those speeds is ridiculous.

Too bad the flip side of being that good and being a legacy meant that whenever we fucked up, people got nasty. Catty. Cranky coaches and people online saying we wouldn't make it through a game without each other was common after a loss. It hurt every time. Then there was the ever-present threat of us being drafted to different teams on opposite sides of the country. Em's fear of never being able to live up to the Dalton name that our brothers set for us, when he was easily the better out of us two.

Fuck hockey. Fuck those assholes who thought writing about goddamn kids in high school was the place to be a condescending asshole.

Always thought the Daltons were overrated players, anyway.

Westly never even won a Stanley Cup.

Asher Dalton is trying to live up to big brother's skates and embarrassing him in the process. His entitled attitude is everything wrong with the NHL.

Bennett Dalton is going the exact way of big brother Asher— and I don't mean that as a compliment.

Emmett was the golden child of the Dalton duo, but even that didn't save him from scrutiny. So, Harrison asking for something "cool" when it comes to hockey? I can't separate anymore.

So, instead, I go for the douchey answer. "The coolest thing about hockey is the ice."

Harrison laughs, because of course he does—the guy laughs at anything. "You're a twit."

"Guilty."

"But maybe so am I because you were right: this sucks."

Like he's just given me permission, I dump the trash bag and fall back onto the couch. Harrison joins me.

"How the actual fuck do you guys have parties every week?"

"Well, it's not, like, *every* week. We have to make time to study and shit too."

"Still, if I had to deal with this much cleanup, I'd never have a party, ever."

"Prez will be up around lunchtime. If it's not done before he wakes up, then everyone will be dragged from their rooms to pitch in."

Harrison looks confused. "It doesn't piss you off that he's getting a lie-in while you deal with all of this?"

"Nah. We all have our place. Prez and Laurie—our treasurer—would have been up late after the party checking off the takings and notarizing everything. They also run all the meetings and shit that we have to show up to. Most people don't realize that fraternities answer to a national org. They're like little businesses. We have a cook who makes a shitload of meals and all that needs to be coordinated. Then there's rooming, rush, philanthropic events. Just, like … a lot. Prez handles all that. He has members who are also in charge of different things, and next year, I wanna be a Big. I've been spending a lot of time with the pledges to prepare for it, and sure, it seems shitty that they're the ones on cleaning duty, but it's because they're so green. They don't know about all the different responsibilities yet. Their only duty is to do what they're told, and the rest of us in the house, we've been there. We know not to take advantage, and for the few shitheads who step out of line and take things too far, the risk manager and Prez step in."

"Huh." Harrison rubs his jaw. "Like your own little social community. Or ecosystem."

I have no clue what he's talking about. "Sure."

"It's a lot more complex than it looks on the surface."

"Exactly. But the one thing we all have is brothership. We bond hard. We go through shit together. We know that any guy in this house will have our backs. DIK for life."

"I still have no idea how a national organization allowed the name DIK."

"Technically, it's Delta Iota Kappa."

"They knew what they were doing."

Those geniuses sure did. "Eh. Our school is literally FU. It's on all the sweatshirts. It's a crime that I don't have a FUKing DIK hoodie by now."

"But you're not a King."

"I'm not above sucking off the entire football team to make it happen."

"Talk about jaw cramps."

I swipe my tongue over my bottom lip, trying to tell myself not to tease him but not able to stop myself. "No jaw cramps for me. I've had a *lot* of practice."

He leans forward, and I'm unsure if he knows he's done it. "When you say a lot ..."

"I'm gay. I'm living away from home, and turns out college is where queer guys get to be free, at least in places like this. There're gays after their first time, some living uncloseted, others who want to experiment freely as much as possible, and

..." I nudge him. "A hell of a lot of straight dudes who want a taste. Present company excluded, of course."

Harrison frowns. "But ... if they're straight. Why would they want to sleep with a dude?"

"That's the age-old question, right? Some people try to blow it off and say they're all secretly bi, but ..." It's hard to put the next part into words without sounding like I don't care. "Some just really want to know how sex with a dude differs from sex with a chick. Others are open-minded and curious if they'd like it, some dudes think it's kinky, and the fuckwits of the experimentation world just get off on using gay men. I hate the saying that homophobes are all closeted because it's like people are excusing them. Giving them a reason. No, some people are just dicks. And those people like to fuck a man to show how much more powerful they are than them. It doesn't mean they're queer. I don't want those people as part of my community. It just means they're assholes." And now that I've gone off on that tangent, I shoot Harrison a quick smile. "I learned how to avoid those toxic types. In my experience, the straight guys I've slept with have been genuinely curious, and I was okay about helping them figure that side of themselves out."

"I've never considered people would do it for that reason. Like ... just wanting to know. Being curious. I've—"

He cuts off, and damn do I want to beg him to continue. But while I might still low-key flirt with him, it's just for fun, and I'm not going to cross any of his boundaries. That door is firmly closed in my mind. So, whatever he cut off is probably not something I want to hear anyway.

"We should keep cleaning," I say, trying to move the conversation away.

He agrees so quickly it makes me think he wants to do the same.

9

HARRISON

The whole day I spend with Benny messes with my head. We clean and have lunch and then end up camped out on his bed, watching more of my shows that he claims he hates but smiles at anyway. But even as I laugh my way through *The Inbetweeners*, my mind keeps slipping back to our conversation. To all the reasons why a straight dude might have sex with another man.

Honestly, I can't say I'm not curious. Have been since high school. It's more in an anthropological way though, and that's not enough of a reason to have sex with someone.

See, I notice when guys are hot, the same way I notice that girls are hot. The first time Fe hit on me, long before he met Marshall, I'd been confused. He's pretty, really pretty, but he didn't make my dick hard or make me want to sleep with him. Still, I thought twice about giving it a go.

What would have happened if I had? Would I have been able to get it up? Would I have enjoyed it?

Obviously, I'm glad it never happened because he found Marshall, and I have no regrets or anything about not taking my chance, but Benny has me wondering. Thinking a lot of thinks. What would have happened if I'd taken *him* up on the blow job?

I chance a quick look his way, finding him amused again. He's not pretty like Felix, but he's definitely good-looking. Even when his face is resting, and he looks ... haughty? Is that the word for it? Benny is brimming with confidence, and he knows how to use his looks to his advantage. I shift closer on his bed, making out like I'm trying to see the screen better, but really, I just want to see if I'll react to the closeness. If it will do anything for me.

My dick doesn't shift, but I can't deny there's ... something. Something prickly all along my arm resting beside his. Something jittery in my stillness.

What would I do if he kissed me?

Well, I obviously wouldn't want to embarrass him and stop, so I'd kiss him back, but ... would someone totally and completely straight do that?

I try to compare my interactions with men versus women over the years. I'm probably scrapping a seven in the looks department, but because of my size and that I find talking to people easy, I draw attention. I'm not exactly sure what it is, but I get hit on a lot. Mostly women, some I sleep with and some I'm not feeling, but every guy who's hit on me, my response is always, "Sorry, I'm straight."

The automatic no. It shuts down every possibility, and now I can't figure out if it's just become my default response or if I'm really not interested.

The women I find attractive get a chance. We talk, hang out, then get into things later.

It's not like I'm popping wood at first sight. Would it be the same with a man?

Is the fact I'm even considering what it would be like with a man an indicator that I should try it?

I glance back at Benny's lips, imagining leaning over and catching them with mine. Biting down into that plush bottom lip. Slipping my tongue past his teeth.

The jitteriness cranks up a notch. I don't hate the idea. Still not sure if my dick's on board, though, since the fucking thing is taking a nap, apparently.

Fuck, I hate that I'm having these thoughts. I hate even more that I'm having them with Benny.

When I told him that nothing would happen, he backed right off. His cheeky flirting is cute, but I can tell there's no substance behind it, and ... I sort of like it. He's fun. Makes me laugh, though that's not much of an accomplishment.

Does all of that translate to attraction? I don't even know at this point. I do know that I need to get home and give myself some time to work out what's on my mind. Benny said he's more than happy to experiment with people, but I like being friends with him. I don't want to mess that up by asking him to blow me and having nothing happen.

When the episode wraps up, I let him know it's my turn to cook dinner and I have to go. It's not until I get out of the house that I realize the expectant look he gave me was him hoping I'd invite him to come. I *did* say I'd cook for him, but we're going to have to take a rain check on that one. I'll apologize when I see him next.

Right now, I need to figure out if these thoughts are something that's coming from me or our conversation.

I SHUDDER as lips find my neck again, skin lit with ripples of pleasure with every swipe of tongue or hint of teeth. I'm panting, needy, cock steely hard and weeping at the hand wrapped around it. My hips buck, loving the friction, and the groan I let out doesn't come close to conveying how this feels.

Teasing, bluey-hazel eyes blink up at me. So cocky, so deep, watching me pant my way toward my orgasm. I'm achingly close, waiting for it to hit, for me to tip over that ledge.

I bite into a soft lip, and it drives me wild. Makes my balls tighten.

"Fuck," I moan.

A soft chuckle. A chuckle that makes my gut sing.

More lips at my throat. Tighter grip on my cock. Body warm and writhing on top of me.

"Close ... so close ..." I gasp.

"Me too." The voice is familiar.

"Gonna come ..."

Benny gazes down at me, eyes confidently locked on mine, puffy lips parted, hand jerking me toward the edge.

My orgasm hits hard, cum filling my fist as my eyes fly open.

I'm gasping into the dark, struggling to catch my breath and work out what just happened, and as my brain cells come down from that mind-spinning high, one thing becomes clear.

I just came in my pants.

I strip my sheet off with one hand and look down at where my other is tucked into my pajama shorts. There's a wet stain on the front that's yet more evidence of me being twenty-three and having a wet fucking dream.

Goddamn it.

I'm frozen for a moment, scared to withdraw my hand and also still trying to get my breathing back in control. I can't even remember the last time I had a sex dream, and I have never, ever had one about another man.

Did I come because of him? Or was I just too far gone by the time I'd seen his face to stop? Whatever the reason, seeing his face didn't turn me off. Didn't make my orgasm any less intense. In fact, I don't think I've ever gotten off so hard with my hand before.

I manage a long, steadying breath before I sit up, pull my spunk-covered hand out, and strip out of my shorts. I use them to clean up the mess and then pull some new ones on before heading out to the kitchen to wash my hands and grab some damn water.

Turns out having a wet dream over your new friend makes you thirsty.

The light is on, keying me into the fact that someone is still up, and when I enter the eat-in kitchen, I'm not surprised to find Marshall at the table, hunched over his books. He pulls all-nighters more than I can count.

"Hey," he mutters, not even looking up.

I slink toward the sink to wash my hands. "What are you doing?"

"Reading up on the archeological evidence of Atlantis."

I snort. "A myth?"

"It's fascinating."

"Know what else is fascinating?" I ask, filling up a glass of water.

"What?"

"Having a wet dream over Benny."

Marshall pauses, and it takes him a second to look up. "Over ... Benny?"

"Yup."

"Right. Huh." He scratches his pen against his temple. "How does that ... work?"

"Beats me." I take a long sip of water and lean back against the counter.

"So ... are you queer now?"

"I don't bloody know. Awake me has never gotten hard over a dude, and it's not like he was in the whole dream, just right at the end ..."

Marshall nods. "I have lots of experience with wet dreams."

"You do?"

He laughs, eyes bright behind his glasses. "I was a virgin until I met Felix and not interested in anyone. Yeah, I had a vague dream person who felt familiar, and we had a lot of fun together."

"But you didn't know the person?"

"In my dream, I did, but they weren't anyone from real life. Just speaking from an ace perspective, someone doesn't have to get your dick hard for you to be attracted to them."

"Yeah, but I'm not ace."

"You also didn't think you were anything but straight, and yet you had a wet dream over a guy."

He's got me there, kinda. "Getting horny isn't an issue for me. I guess ... how do I know it was him that did it? Earlier today, we talked about how he's hooked up with straight dudes before—"

"Don't let him pressure you," Marshall says, suddenly sounding protective.

"No, it was nothing like that. Swear it. We were just talking, and I asked why a straight dude would hook up with a guy."

"They wouldn't."

"Yeah, but from his explanation, I kinda think they could."

Marshall's lips flatten. "Guy-on-guy sex is gay. Or bi. Or pan, or ... look, it's anything *but* straight. The guys who claim to be straight are closeted or something."

"He said some are, sure. But he also was adamant that he'd slept with some open-minded guys who wanted to know what it was like and ultimately decided that nope, they're still straight."

Marshall narrows his eyes. "Are you sure he wasn't pressuring you? Like, did he tell you all that after saying, 'Hey, Bowser, I can totally suck your dick, and here's why' type of thing?"

"Jesus, dude." I drop into the chair opposite Marshall. "Look, I've always wondered. I didn't tell Benny any of this, and he wasn't pushing. He just wasn't. The thing is, I've never considered that there was a safe way to try out my vague curiosity and see if it did anything for me."

"What are you saying? You want to sleep with him?"

I face-plant onto the table. "I can't work out where my thoughts are at. I'm open to it, sure, but I don't know if it's because our conversation got me thinking or because I specifically want to sleep with him."

"Have you had any, uh, moments to make you think you might want to have sex with him?"

"There's definitely something there. I was testing myself out today. But what if I bring it up and he's open to trying and then ... nothing?"

"Then it's your right to say no."

I look up again, propping my head on my hand. "That's not the part I'm worried about. I don't want to mess him around. If we try and I'm not into it, I don't want him to feel bad or whatever. I also don't want to get him all into it and then leave him high and dry. That's mean, innit?"

"You can't get him off just so he doesn't get blue balls."

"That's not what I'm saying ..." But what am I saying? I can't blame Marshall for not following when I can't even work out what the hell this is supposed to be about.

"I know why you're confused," he says. "I also get that for allo people, sex is like this big deal or whatever, but is it possible to just ... not put so much pressure on it? Maybe the dream was just a dream, or maybe your curiosity goes away, or *maybe* you wait. See what happens. Then find yourself in a position that you *know* you want to try it out and it all happens organically." Marshall screws up his face. "I can't think of anything worse than an arranged hookup to see if a guy can get you off. The pressure alone would stop me from performing."

He might be right about that. Marshall gave me some good points, but I'm someone who's all for living in the moment. For feeling and experiencing. Waiting for some hypothetical future event isn't something I usually do.

I'm having these thoughts now, and I want to act on them. The scientist in me is especially curious.

But I also understand better than others how circumstances and environment play a large part in something thriving or failing.

I don't know what to do.

10

BENNY

ME:

> Dude, we're watching a show, and they just
> called the other person a "wanker." Made me
> think of you.

HARRISON:

Naw, you're so obsessed. It's kinda cute really.

ME:

> Calm down, big guy, it just sounded so dumb
> and British, who else was I supposed to
> think of?

HARRISON:

"Big guy"? And now you're hitting on me. My
ego is inflating at such a rapid pace, I might
need to develop a degradation kink to bring it
down a little.

ME:

> And now you're talking kinks. Remind me of who is hitting on who? You know I'm skilled at insulting people.

I lock my phone and set it aside, sure that if he messages back, I'll be glued to my phone all night. The second I see his name on my screen, I'm a fucking mess of excitement over seeing what he's texted. I need it constantly. Maybe he's right that I'm a little obsessed?

Fucking crushes.

It's gotten so bad that I actually considered going to my statistics class tomorrow just to hang out with him, but thankfully, I haven't reached that level of desperation yet.

"Hey, Em?"

My brother glances over from where he's swinging on my desk chair.

"Remember how we have that 'no talking to people in class' rule?"

He gives me a funny look. "Yeah, why?"

"I'm just worried that tomorrow, Harrison will try to sit with you, and that could get awkward."

Emmett shakes his head and turns back to the screen. "I've got it covered. Don't worry about it."

"You sure?"

"Yeah, I'll sneak in right before doors lock and wear my hoodie up."

"Won't it be too hot for that?"

"Nah, the room has AC. We're good."

While I completely trust him to handle it, I also know how quickly Harrison pounced on me that day we met, so I wouldn't put it past him to be watching out for me either. Would he do that? Sure, we're friends, but I'm assuming he has other people he knows in that class.

Emmett suddenly reaches forward to pause the movie we're watching. "What's wrong?"

"Nothing."

"Are you seriously trying to play the nothing card with me? *Me?*"

He's right. We know each other way too well for that. Back to front, inside and out. We've never kept a secret from each other because it's not who we are. "Fine. I'm just worried. Harrison's turning out to be a really good friend, and I don't want to put you in the position of having to act like me one-on-one."

"There's, like, three hundred students in the class, Benny. We'll be okay. If some strange guy sits next to me and starts talking like I know him, I'll play sick and leave."

I suppose that could work. "Are you sure you still want to do this though? I'm not exactly giving you anything back at the moment. Maybe you should—"

He cuts me off. "Don't bring up San Diego State again. It's fine. I *want* to do this for you. If you don't pass this course, there goes your chance at being a sports journalist, and your reasons for wanting that are good. I'm going to help you however I can. Plus, you *are* giving me something. You're letting me stay here and haven't spilled the beans to Asher and West."

Emmett knows I'll take his secrets to the grave; help him carry them there and bury them if I have to. It's pissing me off that he's keeping our older brothers in the dark though. "When are you going to tell them?"

"When I have a plan for what's next. You know what West is like. If I go to him and say I've been kicked out of school, his dad voice will come out, and then he'll start freaking out about not being able to fix it. Then Jas will lay down the guilt trip and make me move back and enroll at CU. I'm not doing that."

Just the thought of Em on the other side of the country makes my chest get all tight. "FU is still an option."

"You've said." He drops his voice to a grumble. "About a million times."

"Don't get snarky with me."

"You're starting to sound like West."

"Fuck off, I'd never be that uptight."

He gives me a look. A look *I'm* known for giving. "Then why are you starting now?"

"Because I love you, you ... wanker." See? Even fighting with Em, I'm thinking about Harrison. "This is stressful as fuck. In high school, it wasn't so bad because people expected to see both of us around, and we were trading from the get-go. Wanting to separate once we got here, and now living together, it's a lot. Plus, the whole Harrison thing ..." I let out a huff of air, realizing Em is right. "Fuck. I *do* sound like West. When the fuck did that happen?"

He laughs and throws a pen at me. "Exactly. So shut up."

I love West, but there's no way I can live with his state of worry all the time. He didn't always use to be like that, apparently, but after our parents died and he had to retire from the NHL to play dad to us kids, it changed him.

It changed Asher, too, but in different ways. West felt too much. Asher shut that shit down.

It's a skill of his I've tried to follow because the less you feel, the less people can hurt you. Walking around all vulnerable all the time is a good way to be trodden on. Em's my weakness though. He's so open to everything that I'm constantly worried about him.

"Fine." I kick back on his mattress and tuck my hands behind my head. "Nothing changes. If you see him, you play sick and leave, then we'll go from there. The last thing he's going to assume is that I have a twin running around."

"Exactly. Gotta say it, though, you're kinda cute about this one."

"Shut up. He's straight."

"Yeah, that sucks. Do you really think being friends is smart?"

"I don't see why not." I try to shrug, but it's awkward. "He's a fun guy to hang out with, and once my stupid dick catches up and knows he doesn't equal playtime, it'll be easier. Just gotta wait until then."

"Is it bad I'm kind of hoping he *does* sit next to me just so I can check him out?"

That doesn't surprise me at all. It'd be killing him that he doesn't know who this guy is. He's already tried to bully me into online stalking him, but I can't remember what the fuck Harrison's last name is. Something that starts with *D*. I could ask him, but also, there's a small part of me that doesn't want Em to know. If he sees Harrison and agrees with me that he's hot as fuck and validates the horny feelings I'm having, it'll be so much harder to tamp down this interest.

Maybe one day, they'll meet. Far, far away from here.

But the more likely option is that our friendship will fizzle out, and I'll never have to face the awkward conversation of why I'd never mentioned my twin to him.

"No talking to people rule, remember?"

"Who said anything about talking? I said I want to check him out."

"Check him out all you like," I answer. "It won't change his sexuality."

"Hmm ... maybe we should go out soon. It's been forever since I've hooked up, and I'm starting to get antsy. There was a really cute guy at the party you had, but I obviously passed. Hardest decision I ever made."

While we have no issues with playing fast and loose with

our grades, we won't hook up with someone as the other person. It's way too fucking weird and gives me the ick to think about men thinking they've slept with me and haven't. Neither of us likes the idea, and it blurs all kinds of consent lines anyway.

So yeah, with Em having been here for almost a month, I bet he's getting the urge.

It might help calm down this want for Harrison too.

"We'll do something soon. That bar in Encinitas?" We've been out together a couple of times and found a gay bar we both like where no college students hang out.

"Sounds good to me. Now, can we get back to this movie, or do you want to giggle over your not-boyfriend some more?"

I fling the pen back at him and completely miss his head. "Fuck you. Put it on."

But the second it starts playing, my attention goes right back to my phone. To the burning knowledge that I probably have a message waiting. Can I ignore it until the next scene break? And then the next? Nerves amp up in my gut, and I figure enough is enough. It's just a goddamn text.

HARRISON:

I guess not having parents means you didn't
learn it's not okay to call people names.

ME:

Hey, fuck you. Only I get to joke about my
dead parents.

HARRISON:

Shit, sorry! I'm so, so sorry. That was
insensitive as hell, I wasn't thinking.

ME:

You are too fucking easy. **kissy emoji**

HARRISON:

I officially hate you.

ME:

Yay! Does that mean I get out of manual labor this weekend?

HARRISON:

Nope, it just means I hate you so much, I'm going to get extreme satisfaction over watching you do it all solo.

I KNOW I shouldn't reply with what I'm already typing out, but he makes it too easy.

ME:

Oh, yeah? You enjoy watching hot, sweaty men "do it solo"?

HARRISON:

skull emoji Your ability to turn everything dirty is a real skill.

ME:

Thank you.

HARRISON:

Was it a compliment?

ME:

Depends. Are we still on for this weekend?

HARRISON:

Sure are.

ME:

> Then it was definitely a compliment. Geez,
> Harry, stop hitting on me.

HARRISON:

You'd love that, wouldn't you?

THE LINE IS flirty enough to give me pause, but then he follows it up with a winky face. A *winky face.* The international sign of "oh, yeah, I'm definitely flirting." My jaw is somewhere around my balls when I finally type back.

ME:

> As fun as this conversation is, I'm really not
> looking forward to this weekend.

HARRISON:

Relaaaax. I'll even give you half my earnings.

ME:

> No fucking way, man. You need that money.
> I'm freeloading off my rich big bros.

HARRISON:

Fine. What if I promise to make it fun?

ME:

> I'd say you're a big, fat liar.

HARRISON:

Oh, yeah? Wanna bet on it?

ME:

That's an easy one to make. Mowing lawns is the devil's work.

HARRISON:

Maybe.

THERE'S no reply for a second.

HARRISON:

But what if I promise to do it shirtless?

FUCK ME. Suddenly sounds like a whole lot more fun.

Emmett's laugh breaks through the images of Harrison with his shirt off, and he starts singing, "Benny is fucked ... Benny-boy is fuuuucked."

Brothers are the fucking worst.

11

HARRISON

If nothing else comes from my friendship with Benny, at least I'll walk away a grade A texter. My message game is strong, and somehow, we're up until 2:00 a.m. trading stupid response after stupid response, and I have to pry myself away from the damn phone.

I have no idea if he drinks coffee or not, but I swing by Bean Necessities on the way to class anyway and go for a hot chocolate. They're usually a safe choice, right? Fucked if I know, though I'd take a wager that he's not a green tea guy.

I'm at class early and take a seat where I have a prime view of the room. Students trickle in, and a couple of them I know send me waves or smiles, but most of them are complete strangers to me.

Just when I think Benny won't make it, he steps inside.

I picture him running late again, and the image of him all frazzled makes me soft.

He looks around for a second, hoodie pulled up over his head, and when his gaze lands on me, he upnods and heads my way.

It wasn't the stupid, cocky smile I was expecting, but hey, it's still early.

Before he can say anything, I plop the cup down on his desk. "Morning sugar."

"We're getting each other drinks now?" He drops his bag and slides into his seat. "What is it?"

"Hot chocolate."

"Huh. Nice." He takes an experimental sip, and it mustn't be hot because he goes back for more. "Cheers, Bowser."

"It's the least I can do for—"

Professor Brooks slams the door and locks it, cutting off our conversation. "Silence. Calm down, please, we have a lot to get through today."

Don't we ever? I roll my eyes Benny's way, but he's already paying attention, sitting straight, gaze locked on the young professor like he's worried about missing something. Other than the few times I need him to break something down for me, we don't talk like last time, which is a bit disappointing, but I get it. It's a hard class to begin with, let alone if you miss something important, and by the way Professor Brooks talks, you'd assume *everything* in this class is important.

"Some days, I swear he *wants* to put us to sleep," I mutter, getting an immediate laugh from Benny. The sound lights me up. "It's not the math and science that's the hard part. It's resisting his hypnosis." I glance over at him, but he's not looking. It ... *bristles* me a little bit. Usually, I catch him looking all the time, so this should be an improvement. Should be but isn't.

I want to see his eyes. I like his eyes.

He's smiling softly toward the front of the room. "This is his first semester teaching, right? He's still green. Give him time."

"What'd you do last night?" I ask him, even though I know he watched a movie at one point.

Benny's back to typing intently though. "Sorry, what?"

Okay, okay. I get it. This isn't the place. Benny is trying to focus, and it's not fair of me to distract him.

But damn is he distracting me.

I can't stop watching the way he's typing. He's got these long, nimble fingers, but he keeps hitting the wrong keys and is punching them hard, almost hunched over the keyboard he's concentrating so intently. He's got a prominent vein running along the back of his hand, a thin wrist, and then the rest is hidden by the hoodie he's wearing. The weather has cooled off a bit, but not *that* much.

His dirty-blond hair is flicked over to the side, giving me a good view of his neck, strong jaw, five-o'clock shadow, and those fucking lips. The lips I imagined sinking my teeth into the other night.

That same unexplainable feeling builds in my gut, and for the first time ever, it starts to form into something recognizable. Something that feels a lot like want.

What kind of want, I have no idea, but it's the type that makes my fingers want to meet his jaw, the type that makes me want to tell him to look at me, the type that very strongly responds to the way his mouth is moving along with the words he's typing.

I pull my gaze away and try to tune back in to the class.

Even with all that want, there's still nothing going on between my legs. It doesn't have me convinced that I'm not so desperate to give things a try that I'm tricking myself into feeling what isn't there. Surely if I was into the guy, my dick would know.

Maybe it's slow on the uptake?

Because my gut seems to think I'd like kissing Benny. Even considering that makes me a delicious kind of light-headed.

"You have a free period next, right?" I ask. "Want to do something?"

"Sorry," he whispers, sending my hope crashing through my ass. "Can't. I've got a class to study for."

Other than last week, he always has studying to do, and if we hadn't been up all night texting, I'd worry he's cooled on me already. Clearly, he's trying to protect himself or maybe even trying to prove to me that he respects my straightness or whatever, so I suppose I have to play along. The longer we're friends, the easier it'll be for him to realize I don't run scared from a little flirting. Fuck. Some of the shit we both said last night should have proved that by now.

Five minutes before the end of class, Benny sighs and slumps back in his chair.

"Do you ever get the feeling you're too dumb for school?" he asks.

I chuckle. "You're a junior. You've made it through fifteen years of schooling already. You have less than two to go. I'd say you're good."

He doesn't look happy about that response, and it hits me a second too late that he's serious. *Serious.* He's taking college-level statistics, understanding it all, and he thinks he's dumb?

"Benny, look at me."

He's reluctant, but he does. There's none of the usual warmth. None of the teasing. None of the feeling that he's seeing too much of me. "Yeah?"

Shit, what was I going to say? "You're not dumb. I can't believe we're even having this talk when you're one of the most confident people I know."

"I am?" He looks at me like I'm confused, and I give it right back. Benny is never lacking in anything.

"It's one of the things I like most about you. I mean, fuck, I'm auditing this class. I might have passed the first time, but it was by the skin of my teeth, and this time, I want to really wrap my head around it. Understand it. You're way better at that than me, so if you're dumb, I'm dumb, and I don't think of myself as dumb at all."

He processes that for a moment. "Thanks, Bowser."

I smile, glad we could at least clear that up. I'm hoping he'll hang out for a minute after class anyway, but as soon as Brooks wraps everything up, Benny stuffs his laptop into his bag, cuffs me on the shoulder goodbye, and then is out of there like his ass is on fire, hood pulled up firmly over his head again.

I have no idea what that was about.

Instead of heading to one of the study carrels like I'd hoped, I head to the science buildings and take the stairs to the top.

There's a class happening in the greenhouse that I bypass as I head down the back to check on my babies. Rich looks like he has a case of rust, but thankfully, I've caught it early and cleared the two leaves it had started to grow on away. I'm heavily monitoring him after his baking soda spray bath, so he should be okay, but if the rust keeps coming back or spreads deeper, it will be bye-bye, Rich. I haven't had the heart to tell him that.

All of my other babies are growing perfectly, and I can't help feeling a little guilty that I've exposed Rich to something.

Would Benny like him? Or Stacy. Or any of them. He was interested in the microorganism fact, and I have a lot of other plantoids I could share with him. I pull out my phone and send him a photo of Stacy.

ME:

Did you know the fire lily is poisonous enough
to kill a human, but has been used for ages in
treating everything from acne to cancer?

BENNY:

Did you know … you're a nerd?

ME:

Sure did.

BENNY:

If it's so poisonous, who the fuck was like,
"Yeah, I reckon this will fix all the problems I
have?"

ME:

That's how people had to do it before Google.

BENNY:

Cool fact, grandpa. Makes me not miss
having one.

I GRIN and send him back a slew of middle finger emojis, relieved that at least through text he acts like he always does. Then I close up my plants, sneak past the class in session, and head out onto the rooftop. Before I leave, I get a random idea.

I cross over to the spot I like to use to look out over campus, turn my back on the view, and then take a selfie.

ME:

You have your attic window; I have my rooftop.

BENNY:

You also have a sunburned nose and look
hideous. Don't send me selfies ever again.

A SMILE TUGS my lips because I'm ninety percent sure he's joking. Except about my nose because when I look at the picture again, it is a bit pink. The rest of me, though, looks exactly like I always do. Backward cap, hair sticking out the front. Ehh, I look more freckly than usual because of the light, but if Benny thinks freckles are ugly, he never would have been interested in me in the first place.

BENNY:

Because I'm not allowed to jerk off to them, so
it isn't cool, bro.

I WANT to write back that I never actually made that rule, but I stop myself. This is where the shaky ground is. The thought of him jerking off to me is one I kind of like, but saying that, opening up the possibility that maybe I want to test my straightness out ... I need to tread carefully. So instead, I do what he does when the flirting gets too much and he wants to smart-ass his way out of it.

I send him a kissy face emoji.

Then I tuck my phone in my pocket and try not to think about the weekend.

12

BENNY

I snarl as the stupid goddamn stupid fucking lawn fucking mower splutters to a stop again. And all the swift kick I aim at the grass catchy ma-thing does is send pain radiating up my foot.

"This is bullshit."

"You're too impatient."

I level Harrison with a glare that only makes him smile wider.

"You're cute when you're angry."

"Call me cute again, asshole."

Harrison laughs. "And you're adorable when you're stabby. I know this is hard to believe," he says, ducking down and tipping the mower on its side, "but if you go *over* large rocks, this beast isn't going to like it."

I gesture to the lawn—if you can even call it that. "If I stop to remove all the rocks, we'll be here all day."

"And I assume that's why this guy hired me instead of doing

it himself." Harrison scrapes something out from below and then stands it upright again. "Try now."

One pull of the cord has it roaring to life. "This sucks."

"Yep," he says before squeezing water from his drink bottle into his open mouth. "But it's honest work. Open."

Fuck, he's weird. I open my mouth, and he fills it with water. God, it tastes good, considering today is hot as balls. We've both done away with our shirts, and I'm still sweating like an ice cube in lava. I'm a Vermont boy. I'm not used to all this heat.

Harrison tosses the drink bottle back toward our stuff and then grabs some more rocks. The shirtless look with the thick, black gloves is doing it for me, and apparently, I'm at the point where I'll find anything he does hot. It's becoming a real problem. Even going out with Em the other night didn't fix it.

"Please tell me we're nearly done," I shout over the motor as I push the stupid machine around. Gotta say, this is better than shifting all that rock Harrison is moving, but it's still a pain in the ass. I'm no stranger to hard work; hockey is brutal training, especially at camps where we're at it every day, but this is a different kind of torture. If I wasn't so set on fulfilling my side of the bet, I would have tapped out by now.

"One more house after this."

Fuck me. How the hell was he supposed to get all of this done himself? It feels like we've been at this all day, and he probably would have been working well into the night at this rate. As much as I bitch and moan and will never admit this out loud, I'm glad I'm here. Apparently, I have some kind of nice person hiding under all my snark.

"I've just decided I'm cashing in on that dinner tonight," I warn him, shoving the mower over yet another whatever on the ground. Thankfully, it keeps chugging along, and even though

I'm trying to mow this stupid grass straight, I'm not doing a very good job.

"Ah, after work, you're putting me to ... more work?" Harrison asks.

"It's your fault for giving me an appetite."

"You're lucky I like cooking."

That gets me stupidly excited, which I should have learned my lesson about by now. I'd been looking forward to today all week, thinking it'd be slow and easy and Harrison and I would be able to hang out for the day, but between the hard work and the loud lawn mower, the flirty conversations I'd been envisioning are few and far between. By the time we climb into the car after each job, neither of us can be bothered to talk much.

At least by having dinner together, we might get some of the fun I'd been hoping for.

It's four by the time we finish up this lawn and head to our last one of the day. When we pull up, I nearly sob with relief.

It's a tiny grass strip in front of a garden bed.

"People *pay* you for this?"

He gets out of the car and heads for the back of his truck, where I meet him. "Not this one. I didn't have the heart. She's an old bird whose husband died last year, and the garden was his baby—he was very proud of his bougainvillea. She was terrified she wouldn't be able to handle it on her own and was willing to pay anything, even though she doesn't have much, so I do it for her."

I eye the nice cottage. "Pretty house for a poor lady."

"Shut up, Benny. All people have stories. You can't tell just by looking. Even if she is lying and doesn't want to pay, who cares? If we all stop doing nice things for people just in case they don't deserve it, then the ones who do will end up missing out as well."

Ooof. Straight to the heart. "Way to say I'm a shitty person without saying I'm a shitty person."

"You're not a shitty person." He looks genuinely confused. "Jesus, first dumb, now this. You play confident, but I'm getting the feeling it's a lie."

Dumb? When did I say I was dumb? It's exactly the type of thing I'd say as a joke, though, but apparently, he took it to heart. "My confidence is fine. I took you shooting me down in my stride, didn't I?"

He suddenly looks away, and for the first time, I'm getting uncomfortable vibes from him. It throws me because that was the least flirty thing I've said all day.

"It's not like ... I didn't shoot *you* down though, did I?"

Okay, now *I'm* confused. "That's exactly what happened." I eye the way he's fidgeting with the shit in his truck. "Why are you being weird?"

"Eh. Nothing. Come on, let's get this done so I can feed you."

I'm not going to argue with that, but if he thinks I can just let that go, he's wrong. I flirt with him because he's given me all the signs he's cool with it. It's empty flirting, just like what he gives me right back.

At least, that's the impression I was getting, but maybe it's changed?

Maybe the flirting is *too* much for him?

The last thing I want is to make Harrison feel weird around me, but now I'm having to go through and rewire all my natural responses to him. We built our friendship up one way; now, I have to unstack those building blocks and start over, I guess.

Jesus. This is why no good comes from friending straight dudes. And from crushes.

I mow the strip of grass while he plays with his plants, and I can't stop glancing over his way.

Dammit, why does he have to be so hot? Like, on the *inside* too. He's whistling as he tends to the plants, and I'm even finding that attractive. There's something wrong with me. Something seriously, seriously wrong to be standing here sore and sweaty and cranky and still be swooning over the guy who put us in this situation.

I finish mowing and switch the machine off, then fake sob as I hit my head against the metal handle.

"What's wrong with you? I thought you'd be happy we're done."

"I just really, really hate you. That's all. That's the story."

I ignore his laugh as I wheel the mower back to his truck and load it in again, then open the passenger door and throw myself into the seat to wait for him. The cab is stifling, there's no breeze, and I hate everything about sitting here waiting, except for the view of Harrison doing what he loves best.

Fuck, maybe I should turn myself into a tree? I wonder if he'd take a blow job from one of those flytrap thingies.

Once he's done, he wipes his dirty hands off on his gym shorts, sending his back muscles rippling. I'm too busy watching them flex under his skin to notice the little old woman approach.

They exchange a few words, and she squeezes his arm in what looks like gratitude. Harrison must say something about me because they both turn at the same time, and she gives me this adorable little finger wave.

Dammit. *Of course* she's a cute old lady.

I really am a dick.

I muster up a smile and wave back before she walks inside, and Harrison packs his shit away in the truck.

He climbs in beside me, wiping his face off with his shirt before pulling his cap back down. There's dirt smeared on his cheek, his neck, his shoulder ... and when I look down, I'm not much better.

I'm still sore.

I'm still sweaty.

But then I think of that cute little wave, and I grudgingly—so fucking grudgingly—have to admit that I'm sort of maybe just a tiny bit glad that I came today.

"So, your old lady looked sweet," I admit.

"Told you."

"Still bet she's got a basement full of dead puppies or something."

Then Harrison does something that stops all my thoughts in their tracks. He pats my thigh.

My bare thigh. His big hand. Making warm, sweaty contact.

"Your outlook on the world will never cease to amaze me."

I don't know what to say to that and don't trust myself with words anyway, so I stay silent on the whole drive to his house.

"Want me to drop you home to shower first?" he asks as we drive through the college district.

"It's out of the way. I could borrow something of yours."

"We could try." His eyes leave the road for a second to study my waist. "Marshall and Felix definitely won't have anything to fit you, but I've got some elastic gym shorts we can try."

"Sounds good."

So instead of taking the turnoff to DIK and having to explain to him why he can't wait in my room, we head for his place instead.

I'm expecting the house to have gardens and greenery everywhere, but it's a tiny cottage like we've just come from, with red stones covering the strip between the road and the house.

"I would never have picked this place to be yours," I say as we pull up out the front.

"Why's that?"

"Where are all your plants?"

He winks. "You'll see. Besides, this was the best the three of us could afford, so we love her anyway."

Of course he does. Harrison is just a happy guy, with whatever life throws at him. Maybe our friendship was never meant to be about shared orgasms, and instead, it's all about me finding some fucking perspective in life.

A well-rounded Dalton? That Dalton being *me*?

Nah, sounds false.

He'll make me a good person when I'm dead.

13

HARRISON

Benny's eyes have been on me all day.

I know because mine have been on him just as much.

Shirtless, tan, all those muscles glistening. His thick blond hair strangled by a hair tie even as a chunk flicks forward past his ear over and over.

Hell, if I tuned out his constant stream of profanities, I almost had a peaceful day. I really, really like spending time with him.

I also really, really like the look of him. And the smell, apparently, because every time we got close or were both in the cab, all I could smell was his deodorant mixed with his sweat, and something about that combo really got my dick moving. It was both a relief and made me nervous as fuck because if the sleeping tiger is getting on board, I really have nothing holding me back.

From making a move.

On Benny.

And possibly fucking our very new, very welcome friendship up.

"Come on," I say when we jump out of my truck. "We'll put dinner on and then shower."

"Why can't we shower first?"

"If we do, we won't be eating until late. I've got a chicken and some vegetables there with our names on it."

The promise of good food must spur him on because he follows me into the cool house without complaint.

"Marshall? Fe?"

There's no answer, so they must be out. That's another reason Fe is good for Marshall; before they got together, Marshall hardly did anything. He's still not the most social guy, but at least now he doesn't dread parties and meeting people for drinks.

I can't stop myself from throwing a wink over my shoulder at Benny. "Looks like dinner is all ours."

"House too." He opens his mouth, and I wait for something over-the-top flirty to come out, but then ... nothing. He changes his mind, swipes his tongue over his lip, and nods toward the kitchen instead. "Let's do this."

That was weird. But then again, it's been a long day, and he's probably getting hangry.

We wash our hands at the sink, standing side by side, that same scent from earlier filling my nose. Dammit. Maybe we should have showered first.

I move away from him and head toward the fridge.

"Can you grab me the measuring spoons?" I ask without looking at him. "We'll need the tablespoon and the quarter-size one."

The chicken is probably too big for us both to eat, but Felix and Marshall will be happy with any leftovers we leave them. I grab all the seasonings from the cupboard and then text Marshall to find out when he'll be home.

It's ridiculous how much I'm mentally crossing my fingers that the answer is late. Very, very late. Tomorrow morning, late.

He texts straight back.

MARSHALL:

Tenish. Why?

ME:

No reason. Just have Benny here for dinner. Thought I might … test your theory out.

MARSHALL:

Just text me when you're done.

WELL, that's one problem solved.

"Here." Benny dumps a whole handful of measuring spoons in front of me.

I glance from them to him and back again. "I only needed two."

He shrugs and moves to the fridge. "I'll cut the vegetables. You handle the chicken."

That sounds fair. "You sure you can be trusted with a knife? I swear you wanted to kill me a couple of times today."

His grin is evil. "You'll have to trust me and see."

"That's how people die in horror movies."

He carries the potatoes over and dumps them on the counter. "Nah, just these guys." He lifts the first one. "Don't kill me. I just want to provide for my family." And a second. "Family? What family? No one even likes you, Bill." Benny grabs a knife from the drawer and lets out an evil cackle. "You're at my mercy now."

He hacks into the vegetables, and I watch the side of his face, wondering how, *how* this is the man I'm fancying.

"Those voices are really doing it for me," I tease, hating that I think it's kinda cute.

"I'm tired and hungry, and I'll fake punish our meal if I want to."

"Oohhh, degradation kink *and* a punishment kink. Learning new things about you every day."

"You could learn—" His mouth slams shut.

I ignore the chicken and turn to him. "What?"

"Nothing."

"Nah, you were about to say something."

Benny moves on to punishing the carrots instead. "Just something dumb. Figured it was probably inappropriate."

"Can't I decide that?"

He sets the knife down and turns to look at me, and just like every other time, those eyes do me in. "You already did."

"What do you mean?"

"Today, when I said you turned me down and you started getting all weird about it. I crossed a line, so I'm sorry, and I'm just trying to be a good friend and remember what those lines are."

Wait. He thinks I got weird over what he said? Considering I never actually clarified anything, how dare he misunderstand me? I want to beat myself with the paprika shaker.

The tension wasn't from him.

The tension was from me wanting to tell him the shit going through my head. Sure, I turned him down, but I'm actually not so sure I meant it. I'm also not sure I didn't. The confusion is real.

But as he stands there, not even a foot away, the words that make no sense to me just ... drift away. Does any of it actually matter? Words are useless. Feelings are everything. And I'm having a hell of a lot of them now.

The urge to rub the dirt from his cheek with my thumb.

The curiosity of how his body would feel against mine.

The intense want to know what he tastes like.

My hands itch to touch, to feel his hair and grab his hip, and finally settle that burning in my gut.

His lips part, and fuck, they're pink. Kinda pouty, actually, which isn't something I'd think about a guy as cynical and cocky as him. Benny's face is a mix of contradictions. Soft cheeks, hard jaw, slender nose, intense, suspicious eyes. He's vulnerable and shrewd. Sweet and dangerous.

The nerves in my gut give a kick, and I move without thinking.

My mouth slams down over his.

I hold my breath.

Feel his soft lips under mine.

Wait for discomfort or indifference to hit, but instead, it's like all the blood rushes from my feet to my head.

I pull back with a gasp. "Holy fuck."

Benny's eyes are wide. "Umm ... what ... what was—"

I'm a fizzy ball of expectation as I bring our mouths together again. Still with no words but one.

More.

I need more. Need to know. Need to feel. And *god* am I feeling. The distance between us disappears, and his closeness brings my cock alive. My hand slides into the back of his messy hair to cradle his head, and just as my lips part, Benny pulls back.

"Wait, wait, wait, wait, wait." He's struggling to catch his breath as he stares at me. "You're kissing me."

"Yeah."

"Why?"

"I ..." Huh. Apparently, words are important in this situation. "I wanted to."

He makes a noise in his throat. "You wanted to?"

"Yeah."

"But *why*?"

Fuck. Don't ask me that. It requires answers I just don't have.

"You're curious?" he asks.

It's as close to an excuse as I have. "Yeah."

"Curious about ... kissing a man?"

I lean in so my teeth scrape his jaw, loving the salty taste of his skin. "And many, many other things."

"Ah. Fuck."

I know exactly what he's swearing over because his dick hardens against my leg. It's that moment, more than anything, that reminds me what this is.

I'm not just kissing Benny.

I'm kissing a man.

And I don't want to stop.

His arms squeeze between us so he can cup my face. "We can do this ... but I don't want it to be the kind of thing where you tell everyone I came on to you. Or where you never speak to me again. If this happens, it happens. It's just sex. We stay friends and maybe even joke about it like we do with everything else. I'm not saying you have to tell anyone, just don't be a dick. This is you making the first move."

"I am." I turn my head to nip at his thumb. "And it's too late not to tell anyone. I already told Marshall about the sex dream I had about you."

Benny's face lights up. "And why didn't I get to hear about that?"

"I thought maybe we could experience it instead."

He suddenly lets go of me and steps away. For one second, I'm lost for what I said to turn him off, but he just starts throwing open cupboards.

"What are you doing?"

"Normally I would have jumped on you by now, but I'm fucking starving. So, we're getting a goddamn pot, putting dinner on exactly as it is, and *then* I'm going to jump on you."

I laugh and flick open the corner cupboard. Benny all but dives inside for a pot, and while he fills it with water—cursing over how long it's taking—I dump the unseasoned chicken onto a tray and shove it in the oven right as he throws the vegetables in the pot.

Then we meet halfway, bodies colliding, mouths crashing together like our lives depend on it. His lips part this time, and I groan as I drink in how he tastes, how he kisses, how his tongue meets mine over and over again. The kiss is deep, full of need, and possibly one of the hottest kisses I've ever had.

His hands slide over my shoulders, and he pushes down, almost making my knees buckle as I drop to them. At first, I think he's about to ask me to suck his dick—something I need a second to think over—but then he says, "Sit."

"Sit?" I drop back onto my ass, trying to work out where he's going with this.

He doesn't leave me waiting for long. Benny steps either side of my thighs and then lowers himself onto my lap.

I tremble, wrapping my arms around his shirtless torso, skin still warmed from the sun. He smells like salt and sunshine and *him*, and it has my dick hard as fucking steel.

"You okay?" he asks, voice dipped deep and gravelly.

"Instead of asking me that, get your mouth back on mine."

He smiles, and the glimpse of it that I get before he's kissing me again lights me up inside. The kissing is as erotic as any porn

I've jerked off over, and while I wasn't sure if I was interested in more than this, I know I am now.

I think I'll die if this ends without seeing his dick.

But to do that, I have to stop kissing him. To touch it, I have to untangle my fingers from his hair. I don't want to do either of those things.

There's too much about Benny that I want. Too much I want to savor and experience and taste.

He's heavy in my lap, and I love the solid weight of him too. Love that when my hands drop to his back, muscle ripples under my palms. When I reach his hips, they settle there, and with a boost of confidence, I pull him down to sit on me properly.

"Shit," he rasps, rolling his hips. It's delicious torture as his hardness ruts against mine.

The way he works his steely cock against me has my head going fuzzy, and I can't help but sink my teeth into his lip. Just for a second. Just to ground myself.

My chest is working overtime as Benny tugs his lip away and pulls back to look down at me. Those shrewd eyes will be my undoing because I can't look away from them as he drags his thumb over my lips, then presses it inside.

"Suck."

I close my mouth around him and increase the pressure, stroking the pad of his thumb with my tongue. Benny's eyes are hooded as he watches, and a thrill passes through me at making him feel this good.

When he pulls it out, I try my luck.

"You were picturing that was your cock, weren't you?"

"Sure was."

"Is that what you want? Me to blow you? Swallow your cum?"

He grunts, frown creasing his forehead. "I want whatever you're comfortable with."

On impulse, I press my hand to his groin. I can feel every ridge of his dick through his loose shorts, feel exactly how hard he is against my palm. Strangely, it makes me feel powerful, especially when he rubs himself against my hand.

"Touch me. Please."

My balls ache at the rasp in his voice. At seeing Benny forget to be cocky or snarky. Maybe later, I'll have hesitations, but for now, I reach into his shorts and pull out his heated length. The hunger for him burns hotter as I stroke him, wanting more, wanting to see him come.

Benny slams his mouth down over mine again, pouring all the lust into the sloppy kiss. The air is crackling around us, desire pooling in my balls, and the heat from the oven is only making us sweatier. His body is slick against mine, and every inhale is full of his scent, making me delirious with pleasure.

I let go of him for a second to pull myself out too, and I give my dick a desperate tug.

"I knew you'd have a pretty cock."

I shift him forward until our dicks are pressed together, smooth tips side by side, and then I wrap my hand around us both.

Benny's head drops back, and I steady my free hand between his shoulder blades as I lean forward and kiss his Adam's apple. Nip it. Then suck it into my mouth. I kiss my way along his neck, loving the taste and the high of him consuming me.

"Jerk us off," he begs, thrusting into my fist.

I drag my mouth away from him to look down, and as I do, he lands a spit on our cockheads.

I gather it up, and the slickness helps my hand glide easier, makes him fuck my fist faster. His balls tap against mine with every movement as I creep closer to the edge.

It feels so good. So desperate. I'm so damn horny I need to get off. Now. But I don't want this to end.

I'm glad I waited for this to happen when it was supposed to. Here, in this moment, there's no overthinking. I'm ready to feel him with zero hesitation.

"I'm close," he warns, breathing labored. His hands are gripping my shoulders hard, hips moving overtime as I stroke us. The weight of us both in my hand really does something to me.

"Do it," I tell him. "I want to see."

It's only a few seconds until Benny's fingers dig into my shoulders as he lets loose. The ropes of creamy cum that shoot from him are so fucking hot I can't take it anymore. My balls tighten, zaps hitting the base of my spine before I let go too.

My head drops back against the cupboard door behind me as I breathe my way through to completion.

There's nothing but the low hum of the oven, the gently bubbling water, and our ragged breaths left to fill the kitchen, and as my senses come back online, everything sounds too loud.

Benny snaps his shorts back up over his dick, and he shoots a quick look at me from under his hair.

Even though I'm still coming down from my high, I know what that look is. And given what he said about afterward, I can only guess he's been with too many guys who've ended up regretting it.

I lean forward and press a soft kiss to his lips. "That was ... everything."

His lips tug with a smile. "Everything is overselling it."

"No. Really." I shake my head, dazed. "I'm still recovering."

"From a hand job? Easy man to please."

It's not entirely from the hand job, though I can't tell him that. All my curiosity is answered, and because it was with Benny just makes it so much better. Can you be attracted to someone's personality before you're attracted to their body? Marshall would argue yes since he's demi, but I know I'm not ace. I'm sexually active. I hook up. I have no issues there. But unlike those hookups where I've been attracted to their bodies and then walked away, this was the opposite. I wasn't attracted to Benny at all at first, and then the more I got to know him, the more curious I became.

Fuck it, there'll be time to sort those thoughts out later.

"Shower?" I ask because we both desperately need it by now.

Benny trails his eyes over the cum on our torsos. "I dunno. I think I like you like that."

My hand *whacks* his ass, and he climbs off me.

Then, he helps pull me to my feet, which is a good thing since my legs don't want to work properly.

"Are we okay?" he asks.

"More than. We just had incredible sex, now we're going to shower, and then we're going to sit down to a bland-as-fuck dinner since someone got too horny."

"You say that like you didn't kiss me out of nowhere after I've been dying for it for two weeks."

I shrug. "You said you're all about the tension."

"And was I right, or was I right?"

Oh, yeah. He was right.

Now I'm going to do what I said we'd do. Shower and dinner. Back to two friends hanging out.

Figuring out the rest will come.

14

BENNY

Am I in a fucking dream? Considering my dick is sleeping for maybe the first time ever around Harrison, I'm going to go with a no, which means that really just happened. We hooked up and showered, and now we're sitting down to dinner like he didn't just blow my brains out.

"It's not too bad," he says, digging into the chicken. "Would have been better if I'd been able to season the skin, really get it good and golden."

I'm eating so fast I've barely tasted a thing, so none of it matters to me. "It's delicious."

"Well, you *would* think that, since you can only cook pasta."

"Luckily, I found a man who can cook."

Harrison's knife clatters to the plate, and there it is. The first little chink in his coolness.

"Dude, I'm kidding. I don't want to date you."

"And why not? You said I'm hot."

Okay, *that* makes me laugh. "So are a million other people on this campus. I don't want to date them. Besides, what happened to being straight?"

"Well, we just washed the evidence of my non-straightness down the drain, so I doubt that still stands."

Huh. That response is unexpected. "What are you saying? You're suddenly not straight?"

"I just gave us both a hand job, and you're actually asking that question?"

"I told you. Shared orgasms don't mean anything."

"Actually, I think those guys who've told you that are lying, but okay."

Probably, but it's not our place to say. It's not up to us to tell someone they're wrong about their sexuality or they're not the right kind of gay, straight, bi person. Everyone's situations are different. "That's a bold statement, considering you've never met any of them."

"Fine." Harrison pins me with a look that makes my chest feel all weird. "From purely my own experience, I've had those thoughts a few times. How a guy would feel and sound and react. I'm highly attracted to women, so it's not something I've spent much time thinking about, but sometimes the thought pops in, and it always bothered me I didn't know."

"And now you do."

He reaches over and covers my hand with his. "Thanks. I really mean that. I'm glad it was you and that we're still able to stay friends. I don't know what this all means for me, but I'm glad we got to do that. Really, really"—a smile slips onto his face —"glad."

I can't help but smile back. "Yeah. I'm really fucking glad as well."

EVERY DAY, I expect Harrison to freak out, but every day, I wake up to a new message from him. Dumb shit, and funny shit, and GIFs I wish I didn't understand but now do because of all the movie nights he forces on me.

I hate to jump the gun, but I really do think we can move on from this with our friendship unscathed. Who'd have thought it?

And sure, the crush is still hanging around like a bad smell, but it'll pass with the next breeze. I've been keeping my eyes peeled around campus and during drinks at Shenanigans to find the next guy who's going to catch my eye. My options are still open; I'm not limiting myself to Harrison, and I'm definitely not going to turn into a pining little puppy over the guy.

So what that we catch up multiple times a week? That's what friends do.

I kick at the sand, sending it in an arch over the beach. It's near deserted here, and even though the DIK house is a few minutes' walk from Shenanigans and the beach there, Emmett and I have gone further out. Somewhere no one from FU will run into us.

"Are you going to tell me where you got that hickey from yet?" Em asks.

It's faded almost from sight now, but I'd loved having it. Showing it off. Watching Harrison's face every time his eyes caught on it.

I don't answer him, and Emmy laughs. "To be clear, I'm not actually asking. We both know it was your"—he lifts his hands for air quotes—"friend, Harrison."

"And that's exactly why you'll never meet him. We're friends. Nothing else."

"Friends who fuck."

"It was *one* time."

"But you did do it." The asshole smirks at me like he's won.

Whatever. It's not like he didn't know I hooked up with Harrison without me needing to tell him. Being subtle isn't something I'm good at, and showing off that hickey after getting back from his house was a dead giveaway.

My shithead brother just wanted me to say it out loud.

"Anyway, I've been there and done that. It was fun. Every bit as good as I knew it would be, and now we can move on and be actual friends."

"Mmm, uh-huh, yeah, okay."

"I know it's been a while for you, but that's what you do when you hook up with someone, unless you want to start getting into booty call or boyfriend territory. I don't want him to be either of those things."

"If he asked you to hook up again, it would be a no, obviously."

"Obviously."

"You *definitely* wouldn't go there."

"Nope."

"Even if he begged. You're better than that."

I narrow a glare at my stupid brother and his stupid dumb face.

He taps his temple. "We might not have the twin reading minds thingy, but I don't need it to tell me when you're full of shit."

I grumble and flop back onto the sand. "Nobody likes you."

"Actually, that's you. I'm the delightful one." He kicks off his shoes and moves down toward the water. It's almost sunset, and there's a crisp breeze that reminds me of back home, but the sand is still hot, and I'll bet the water is the same.

"Hypothetically," Em yells back to me. "If Harrison was standing here naked right now, how do you say no to that? If he's as hot as you say, and you have as little self-control as I know you do—"

"I might have no self-control, but I think even I'd draw the line at having sex with him in front of you."

"If I wasn't here, obviously. You're really telling me you wouldn't go for it?"

I press my lips together to stop the automatic lie that wants to slip out. If hooking up was on the table, it would be a real struggle to say no, but considering this crush is lingering, it wouldn't be the smartest thing to do.

But Em doesn't know how to shut up. "And what about the straight thing? Where is he at with that?"

"Dunno."

"You haven't talked about it?"

I sigh toward the sky. "Briefly. He said he can't be straight since he enjoyed it so much. That's as far as we've gotten."

"If he enjoyed it so much and he's not straight, then remind me why it isn't happening again? Frequently? You like this guy."

"Fuck off, I do not."

"You're such a baby."

"Why? Because I don't want to date my friend?"

"Because you can't even have a simple conversation with him."

I hate being a twin. He's got me there. Harrison and I are continuing our friendship as though nothing happened. *Exactly* like nothing happened. Sure, we'll get flirty and whatever, but that's nothing new for us. Whenever it gets too close to our shared orgasm moment though, the both of us nope out of the conversation fast. We're champions at redirecting.

The good thing is that Harrison has his roommates if he needs to talk through any confusing, angsty, coming-out stuff. That side of things was never an issue for me since Asher, West, Hazel, and Em are all queer, so I wouldn't be any help to him anyway. He gets all that self-discovery to himself; I've done my part, and I don't think I want to talk to him about it all anyway because I don't know where my head is at.

If he was here, naked, asking to hook up? Let's be real, it'd happen. I'm just not sure that it'd be a good thing for it to happen, which isn't something I usually have to think about. I really like Harrison; he's a great friend, and in a choice between hanging out with him versus hanging out with anyone else—Em not included—I'd pick him. Hands down.

But is it a *feelings* thing, or is it just that I'm emotionally stunted and suck at making friends, so now I'm clinging to the first real one I have?

Because I don't want to face any of these thoughts, I turn things around on Em. "So, told West and Asher yet?"

"You know I haven't."

"Made a plan?"

"Stop bugging me."

"Just saying, life is getting away from us. It's been a month since you were given the boot, and you still don't know what you want to do. You can't live off of a mattress in my room for the rest of the school year. What will you do then? Forge your diploma? Move to Mexico?"

Em's shoulders have gotten all tense in his silhouette made by the sunset. "Are you forgetting I'm the older brother?"

"There's no proof of that."

"Of course there is. I was born first. That's indisputable proof."

"Yeah, but we're identical. How many times do you want to bet our parents mixed us up, couldn't tell who was who, and just eeny meeny miny mo-ed it?"

"That's not a thing parents do."

"Why not? What the fuck does a name mean to a squishy flesh ball anyway?"

"Your lack of emotion scares me sometimes."

The excess emotions I'm feeling over Harrison is what scares me.

It's not until after we've taken a quick swim, climbed back in the car, wrapped up in towels, and driven all the way home that I realize Em didn't answer my question.

He's getting too good at distracting me lately, and I'm beginning to think it's on purpose.

But if he hasn't made a plan, and he doesn't want to talk to me about things, what the hell do I do?

I'm so fixated on my worry about Em through my shower that I even forget to jerk off over Harrison.

Who the hell am I turning into?

15

HARRISON

The second my eyes pop open, I grab my phone and check the screen, immediately grinning at Benny's name there.

It was around 2:00 a.m. before I texted him good night with a kissy face, but I couldn't keep my eyes open long enough to see his reply.

As soon as it's open, I snort back a laugh.

The middle finger emoji. Benny translation: multiple hearts.

My arms flop out to either side, and I stare at the ceiling with the dumbest smile on my face. All week on campus, instead of walking around with my head in the leaves, I've been paying attention to people. More specifically, men.

And I'm still no closer to working out my sexuality.

There are plenty of good-looking men. Pretty men. Sporty men. I notice them, and there's vague attraction, but I don't have the urge to go up to them and hit on them. Surprisingly though, I don't have it with a lot of women either.

I can't help but notice a pattern. If I'm approached by a woman who's attractive, I'll usually end up sleeping with her. If *I* do the approaching, they're usually someone I'm at least friendly with, who I like as a person, rather than just a pair of tits.

Is that what's happening here? I'm attracted to Benny because of who he is, not because he has a dick?

At the end of the day, it just doesn't bother me that much.

It'd be nice to put a label on things to help explain who I am to others, but for me? I'm into Benny. My brain and my body are both in agreement with that, so now the most pressing thing is figuring out what to do about it.

He's only ever mentioned wanting to hook up, and I'd be down for some repeats if that's on the table, but I don't even know if I have that. It's like our hand jobs never happened, and I love having the time to think things through, but I'm starting to feel a bit gross about it all.

Like I used him.

It's not what happened, but pretending like this great mental rearrangement didn't change my life is childish, and I hate that we can't talk about it.

Marshall's my best friend, but he doesn't see sex the same way I do. Felix ... he *has* been used by other people, but he put himself in those situations, so trying to talk to him about something like this is delicate.

I put a pin in it all and get ready for class.

I'm not as excited for statistics as I have been the last few times. Sure, I always like spending time with Benny, but he's a different guy in class. He concentrates really hard, makes notes all over paper, and types so intently I'm scared to say anything and have him lose his train of thought. He also usually has to run off right after, so while it's great just to be near him—okay and checking him out—I don't get that dose of fluttery nerves I usually get when we spend time together.

It's the same today. Benny concentrating. Me trying to pay attention. Him running right off afterward.

It's starting to get weird.

As I'm walking across campus, I have to send him a message to reassure myself it's his usual class standoffishness and that he's not actually going cold on me.

ME:

What are you doing?

BENNY:

Just at the house, should be studying, but really don't want to.

JESUS, he flew back to his place fast.

ME:

Well, I won't be a bad influence right now, but can I kidnap you tonight?

BENNY:

I don't think you're supposed to ask when you kidnap someone. It's way hotter to be caught by surprise.

ME:

He likes fear. Noted.

BENNY:

Where are you going to take me after you've
erotically kidnapped me?

ME:

I guess you'll have to wait and see.

AN IDEA IS ALREADY FORMING THOUGH. I'm going to take someone who's quickly becoming my favorite person to my favorite spot on campus. We'll wait until it's dark. No one else will be around. We'll take in the view and walk through the greenhouse, and I'll talk plants to him and let him snark about them to me, and, fuck. Maybe I'll kiss him again. Whether I do or I don't, I can't shake how obsessive I'm getting about not knowing whether he wants that again.

After classes, I get through as much work as I can, and then I cook us up some food. Sure, most people would view a packed dinner and a scenic location as a date, but can it really be a date when one person isn't aware it is?

Do I even want to date him?

He said no to wanting a boyfriend, but what about a hookup buddy? A fling?

The one and only person I was interested in dating since starting college began this way too. Kind of. We slept together a few times, hung out a lot, and then I took her on a date and asked her to be my girlfriend. It crashed and burned not long after.

I definitely didn't have the kind of nerves I do now. Whether that was because we were already sleeping together or because this is all Benny, I don't know.

It's almost dark by the time I leave.

Benny's been messaging me progressively more the later it

gets, and I haven't responded to any of them. I wouldn't be surprised if he's in bed by the time I show up, but he said he wanted to be surprised. Maybe I should climb in through his bedroom window and kidnap him that way? I laugh to myself as I picture his gorgeous face jumping with shock at a random guy climbing into his room.

But if the window's locked, my surprise will be gone, and I'll look like an idiot instead.

Front door, it is.

Sunset is well and truly over by the time I arrive, and while I would have loved to catch that with him, I also know campus is still reasonably full at that time, and I want to make sure there's no one in the greenhouse when we arrive.

I jog up to the front door and knock, holding my breath, crossing my fingers that Benny's been waiting and that he's the one to open the door.

He isn't, but it's one of his brothers I recognize, and before I can ask where he is, Benny shows up behind him.

I smile wide, and then, without saying a word, I scoop down and sling Benny over my shoulder.

"What the fuck?" He almost knocks my hat off in his struggle, but I hold it down with one hand and pin him to me with the other. Benny's heavier than I thought he'd be, and I regret carrying him after only a few steps, but I'm going to make it to the goddamn truck if it's the last thing I bloody do.

"You all right, Dalton?" his brother asks, not making a move to help.

Benny sighs. "Just being kidnapped. Nothing to see here. Carry on."

The front door closes behind us, and I laugh as I set him down by the passenger door, holding off the temptation to rub my shoulder.

"Lucky you weren't actually being kidnapped," I say, tucking his hair back behind his ear.

He startles at the touch, suspicious glare aimed my way. "I doubt a kidnapper would have the guts to walk up and take me like that. Besides, I'm strong enough to save myself."

"Sure you are." I resist patting him on the head because I want to tease him, not have my hand bitten off. Instead, I tug open the door for him and slap him on the ass. "Get in."

His glare softens. "Couldn't have written back to a single text? Nothing to let me know you were still coming?"

I close the door behind him and round the truck to get in. "I told you I was coming, didn't I?"

"Yeah, but people usually say shit they don't mean."

While I think his cynicism is cute most of the time, I also wonder if there's something deeper that's made him so jaded.

"Talking about anyone in particular?"

"Why? Are you trying to head-shrink me?" he mocks.

"You're impossible to talk to."

"And yet most nights, you won't shut up from messaging me."

"Not my fault you reply to everything in about a second."

He's mock offended. "You're not supposed to call me on it, asshole."

"I think it's cute."

He whips around. "You take that back."

"Very, very sweet."

Benny gets me in a nipple cripple. "Try again."

"Sorry, sorry." I laugh. "You're the baddest of all bad boys I've ever met."

"Better." He moves back to his side of the car, but seeing him smile, even the small one he's wearing, warms my whole chest.

"Where are you taking me?"

"Can't you just let me surprise you?"

"I hate surprises. The last time I got one was when my parents never came home. Surprise, we're dead!"

I roll my eyes. "You were a kid. There's no way that was your last surprise."

"This is where you're supposed to give me sympathy, then feel bad and spill all your secrets."

"So cute. So, so cute."

"I've changed my mind. Take me home."

My good mood dulls a notch. "You really are extra grumbly tonight. Everything okay?"

He props his elbow on the door and starts chewing on his thumbnail. "I ... It's nothing."

"I know we fuck around a lot of the time, but you can talk to me about the real stuff, you know?"

I feel him look at me, and his voice is softer than usual when he replies. "I know."

"Then ..."

At first, I think he won't talk, but when he finally lets it out, it's like he needs to.

"There's not a lot I can say. I'm just ... I'm worried about ... my brother."

"What's wrong?"

"I think he's keeping something from me."

"People are allowed their secrets."

"Yeah ..." I don't like the way he's holding it all in, but it's not my place to force him to talk. "We're super close. I can't remember us ever having secrets from each other, but every time I try to ask him what his plan is next, he changes the subject."

That does sound hard, but if I know one thing, it's that you can't know everything about another person. No matter how close you are. "Maybe it's not that he's keeping a secret. Maybe it's that he's working through it himself. I'm sure when he's ready to talk about it, he will." If anyone can relate to that, it's me. I've wanted to talk to Benny all week, but until I had the words, I couldn't. It's not that I wanted to keep anything from him, more that I want to be sure before I open my big mouth.

We reach campus, and I pull up in the parking lot near the science buildings.

Then, I turn in my seat to face him. "I know you try to hide it, but you're a really good guy. I love having you for a friend, and if you're this good of a friend, I imagine you must be the best brother. Sometimes things that feel like they're about us really aren't."

One of the corners of his lips twitch, just for a second. "That was very wise."

"It's the red hair. Gives me superpowers."

"And red pubes."

I snicker because that's the last response I'm expecting. Then I lean over, pop his door, and push it open for him.

With our faces hovering right next to each other, so close I could tilt my head and bring our lips together, I say, "Play your cards right, and you might even get to see them again."

16

BENNY

Awareness tingles from my scalp to my toes as I follow Harrison up the staircase. My gut is in knots, and I'm trying really, really hard not to think about what he just said to me, but it's filling my brain anyway.

He might want to hook up again. It's the nightmare scenario Em gave me, only it's here and it's real, and I can't just *pretend* to think about it anymore. I have to make a choice.

My throat is all tight as I swallow and drag my gaze down his back, landing on his ass, which is just below eye level.

Make a choice.

That's hilarious.

Somehow, I've turned into a fucking simp for this guy, and I hate him for it.

Then, Harrison throws a well-timed smile back over his shoulder at me, and that knot in my gut loosens and tightens all over again.

Why, *why* the fuck does he have to be so sexy?

We reach the rooftop, and the cool night air is a welcome relief from how heated it was getting in that stairwell. I can make out the stars through the bright campus spotlights below, and even with the noise from the dorms past the math buildings, it's kinda peaceful here.

Harrison ignores the giant greenhouse in front of us and moves to the side of the building. I join him, standing side by side like that night at my party, and we watch the few people pass on the path below.

"You showed me your favorite place. I'm showing you mine."

It figures that his favorite place would involve plants, and somehow, it makes me love it even more.

Harrison is just Harrison.

It's getting uncomfortably mushy in my chest, so my dumbass frat side comes out instead.

"Is it because you can see straight down the chick's tops?"

Harrison shoves me and moves away. "You're a dick."

"You're the one who likes titties. If you were on the stairs above me and I could see up your shorts, I can't guarantee I wouldn't take a peek."

"Yeah, but I've got a good-looking cock, so I couldn't blame you."

"Aren't you supposed to let other people tell you that?"

"You already did, but if you want to tell me again ..." He watches me expectantly.

I grin. "You want me to tell you that you've got a pretty dick?"

"Couldn't hurt."

I lick my lips, knowing that I'm shooting myself in the foot with what I want to say, but it comes out anyway. "To do that, I might need a refresher though."

Harrison's exhale is heavy, and one of his large hands comes up to cup my chin, thumb running the length of my bottom lip. "I had this whole plan to show you my plant babies, have a picnic, and then maybe get up the courage to kiss you again."

"Oh yeah?" The tension is seeping so deeply into me I feel like I'm going to snap. "What changed?"

"I really want to kiss you now instead."

Fuck. My heart is trying to pound its way out of my chest, and that stupid little voice in my head is warning me to step back, to say no, but I've never been all that into self-control and protecting myself, and every part of my body wants this. Aches for this. Has been dying for it to happen again but not trying to get my hopes up.

My hands curl in his shirt, and I pull him to me.

Our lips meet, and pure bliss courses through me. Freedom. So much fucking happiness. There's none of his initial hesitation. Just confidence. His kisses are sweet, light, and I indulge in this weird moment where we're both drinking each other in without giving over to the frenzied want I'm fighting back.

Harrison snaps first. His fist curls in my hair, and his mouth opens, tongue pressing into my mouth as he brings our hips together. I press against him, wanting to be closer, wanting to be naked and get a chance to enjoy every delicious inch his body has on offer.

His thick thigh presses between my legs as he backs me into the greenhouse wall, and I ride the friction it gives me, rubbing my cock against any part of him I can reach and loving the way his hard length is pressing against me too.

I'm average height, but Harrison is huge, and when his body blankets mine, it's consuming. I fucking love feeling overpowered like this, especially from the kind of guy who's pure sweetness and light the majority of the time.

Then, his large hand grabs my ass, hauling me tighter

against him as he lets out a feral growl. Oh, yeah, I like this side of him.

Balances me out in the streets, matches my passion in the sheets.

I'm in so much fucking trouble.

I kiss him harder anyway.

His grunt is frustrated as he pulls back, but he's still so close our noses touch. "I've never been this addicted to kissing someone before. I can't get over it."

"It's not your fault I have a magic mouth."

A tiny smile. "Of course you do. But ..."

"Yeah?"

"Makes me wonder what it might be like to ... kiss you somewhere else."

My dick twitches. "Like ..."

Harrison squeezes my ass instead. "Right here. I want to kiss you right here."

"You want to rim me?"

"Can I?"

"You'll never hear me say no to that." I hurry to undo the front of my pants. "You sure?"

"If you're ready for it, I am."

Thank the hookup gods for my very thorough shower before he kidnapped me.

I shove my pants down my thighs, and Harrison takes my waist and spins me so I face-plant into the greenhouse wall. It's mostly dark inside, spots of light hovering over some plants, but still enough that I'm confident no one is inside about to watch me come all over this motherfucker.

"Quick question," I throw back as I hear him drop to his knees. "Does coating the greenhouse in my cum count as defacing school property? Because it's definitely going to happen, and I just wanna know if I'll end up expelled after."

"Don't worry, there aren't any cameras up here."

"Should it worry me that you know that?"

He chuckles, spreading my ass cheeks. "If there were, I would have been caught a long time ago."

A sludgy feeling fills my chest. "You bring lots of people up here for sex, huh?"

"Do you want me to use my mouth to talk about my history or for this?" Then, he makes the irrefutable argument of running his tongue over my hole.

I pound the wall I'm leaning against with my fist. "You win. Keep going." Because when he starts eating my hole, there's no room for anything else to occupy my thoughts.

All I can concentrate on is him licking and sucking the sensitive skin, his tongue teasing my hole and making my cock leak.

"You're criminally good at that," I moan.

"Maybe me being straight for so long has its advantages ..."

He can claim any sexuality he goddamn likes if it means I get to reap the benefits of it. I'm panting, it feels so good, especially when Harrison presses his tongue harder against my hole, testing the resistance as I relax and let him press inside.

He groans, and the sound races through me, making my head float. Someone could step out on this rooftop right now, and I wouldn't stop riding his face.

"More," I beg.

His tongue fucks in and out of me faster, deeper. I could have taken one hundred wagers on where the night was going, and I would have lost every one of them because there's no way I would have picked this. My forehead rests against my forearm as I reach my free hand for my cock. He's making me unravel way too fast for my liking, and I know I should tell him to stop, to give me a minute, but there's no way those words are coming out of my mouth. The only thing coming will be my dick.

I'm wet and sloppy and toeing the edge of my orgasm when Harrison stands up suddenly. He presses against me, and I get the incredible feeling of his heated cock smearing precum over my ass cheek.

"Someone was enjoying himself," I say, desperately wanting him to finish the job.

He hums into my ear. "I wanna fuck you so bad."

My knees almost give out, and I want to cry in frustration. "I don't have a condom."

"Fuck. Me neither." He ruts his cock over my ass. "God, you turn me on something fierce."

I grip my cock and swipe the gathering precum from my tip. Then, I reach back over my shoulder and slide my finger into his mouth. "Taste how close I was."

He sucks like his life depends on it, grinding harder against me. It gives me an idea.

"Spit on your dick."

"What?"

"Get it nice and wet, then slide it between my thighs."

Harrison pulls back, letting my finger slip out as he gives himself a few tugs.

"Hey, don't take away my fun, asshole."

He laughs, then I hear him spit before he repositions and slides his cock along my taint. He's long and thick, nudging my balls, and a shiver ripples along my spine as I clamp my thighs around him.

"Fuck, that's tight."

"Hockey thighs," I reply without thinking.

He grunts and pulls back before pushing in again. His hips meeting my ass almost have me face-planting against the glass again, so I brace myself with both hands on the wall.

One of Harrison's hands covers mine. He links our fingers

together, and he grips my hand in a fist. It anchors me, and I love and hate the way I grip him back.

"Fuck, Benny, you feel so good," he says, panting into my ear. Each thrust is smearing precum between my legs, making it easier for him to move. I'm so fucking sensitive everywhere that when he slips his free hand under my shirt to brush my nipple, I have to grip my cock in a vise.

"Touch me," I beg.

His hand slips from my chest to wrap deliciously around my length. He strokes me to the rhythm he's pounding out against my ass, dick rubbing against my oversensitive balls. They're tight and full, wanting to release, but I'm fighting it.

My whole body feels like it's floating, unable to wrap my head around that this is happening, and Harrison's the one who instigated it again. Will it be the last time, or will he want more? Will I?

Fuck, I don't know, but my gut is swimming, and my chest feels full, and I need to come as desperately as I'm trying to stop it.

He straightens behind me, fucking my thighs faster, each thrust punctuated by a grunt, and my gaze catches his reflection in the glass. Hat backward, face angled down like he's watching as he fucks me. His arm muscle is working overtime to jerk me off, and his hand around mine is tight. So tight.

Zaps are building up deep inside of me, filling my cock and vibrating out to my limbs. I feel filthy and used and sweaty and high and like sex will never be this fucking hot ever again.

Almost as soon as I have that thought, I lose it. My dick throbs as the first rope of cum streaks across the glass, and Harrison keeps stroking me, milking my cock dry until he's got every drop.

"Motherfucker," he moans, but it's not until my orgasm rush

is seeping out of me that I notice the sticky wetness over my balls and running down my inner thighs.

He's panting, forehead resting on the back of my neck while he catches his breath, and my eyes drift closed, letting the coolness of the air reach my senses again.

Harrison lets out a long, slow groan that morphs into a laugh. "Well, shit."

"Exactly my thoughts."

Instead of letting go of my hand, he pulls it back and presses a kiss to my palm.

My heart fucking stops.

He releases me and steps back, tugging his pants back up his thick legs. "I swear, when you're around, I just lose my damn mind. Anyone could have come up here."

"Two people did *come* up here."

"You're the fucking worst."

"Good." I'm glad that weird little moment is over. "You're learning."

Harrison reaches into the bag he brought with him and pulls out some napkins. He hands some to me to clean up and wipes down the wall himself.

I'm still sticky, and my pubes are going to give me hell later, but at least I'm mostly cum-free by the time I pull my pants back up.

"God, you had a lot of cum in you," he says, taking the napkins and tossing them back in the bag before pulling me to him by my hips. "Take it you had fun?"

"Obviously. But I still didn't get a good look at your dick."

He grins, bright and confident, as he looks down at me. "Next time."

"Next time?"

"Yes."

I'm caught off guard by how much I like that he's sure.

"M-maybe I can finally give you that blow job?"

"Maybe." He kisses me gently. "But for now, food. And I have some friends for you to meet."

I narrow my eyes at him. "Do these friends have stems and roots and are kinda green?"

"Damn, you know me so well."

"Yeah." I pause at that thought. "I really do."

Harrison takes my hand and grabs his bag, leading me into the greenhouse.

I hate holding hands.

I don't know why we're even doing it, but it doesn't occur to me once to let go.

17

HARRISON

"Rich has been causing me a world of headaches these last few weeks," I tell Benny. "Keeps getting sick, the poor thing, but I think we've gotten it under control."

"I'm sure that's a huge relief." His voice is dry.

"You being punny?"

"What?"

"You know, re-leaf. Relief."

He blinks up at me like I've lost my mind. "No."

"Well, that's lucky. We don't need me accidentally falling in love with you."

That breaks through some of his guardedness. It's bonkers to me that we could have sex, and now he's turned all … weird. But maybe he's still processing the straight but not-quite-straight aspect of our friendship, so I'm okay to give him time with it.

"That one's Stacy. She's the fire lily I told you about. We

love her, and she's been such a good girl with growing big and strong this year."

To his credit, he leans in like he's interested. "This is the one that can kill me, right?"

"She is poisonous, yes."

"Cool. It looks like fire."

"*She* does. It's where she got her name from."

He gives me a sly smile. "Cute how much you love them."

"No reason not to. We owe a lot to the environment."

"It's just … no offense, and this is so not directed at you, but learning about grass and rocks and things is just …"

"Boring?" I say it so he doesn't have to. It doesn't stop him looking guilty though. "I know. I mean, it isn't to me—I really don't understand how people don't find it fascinating and awe-inspiring. But I know that most people think trees are boring, and there's the whole tree-hugger stereotype of the dirty, smelly hippy. I'm not any of those things. I just come at it from the viewpoint of if we look after the environment, it'll keep on looking after us."

"But you're not an animal person?"

I shrug. "It's not that I *don't* like them. They just get enough attention, and it makes me a bit shitty. No point saving all the animals if they run out of things to eat."

"That's true." He squints his eyes and tilts his head to the side. "I just don't see that opinion ever changing."

"Well, that's what I'm working on." I plant my hands on my hips, that familiar fire of indignation burning in my gut. "I'm going to do it. I just need to work out how. And I *will* work out how."

"You don't let anything stop you, do you?"

It's not really a compliment, but it gives me a boost anyway. "Things don't have to be complicated. A problem to be solved, sure, but it can be solved. Everything can."

Not looking at me, Benny steps closer. He hesitantly wraps his arm around me and headbutts my shoulder. "You're so positive."

"Determined."

"That too. I really should hate it."

Should is a fantastic word. "But you don't because you can't because I'm amazing. I know. I get it. I'm obsessed with me too."

His puff of his laugh hits my arm, and I ease back a little so he has to look up.

"What's going on?" I ask. "You're quiet."

"Yeah, no. We're not talking feelings. I won't fall into your trap."

"Feelings, huh?"

"What? No. No feelings. No one said anything about anything."

He looks so stressed that it's impossible to smother my amusement. "Fucking relax. We're not going to talk about anything you don't want to. All I want is for us to have dinner together, maybe kiss some more ... oh. And I want you to tell my plants you love them."

"You *what* now?"

"Kiss some more. I really like kissing you. Duh."

He holds up a hand to make me stop talking. "That part's a given. Go back to the plant thing."

"What plant thing? I want you to tell them you love them. No biggie."

"I'm not doing that."

I gasp the biggest gasp. "Benny Roger Phillip Frankie Dalton—"

"None of those are my middle names—"

"Do you really want my babies to think you don't like them? Rich has been sick. It's been a hard time for us all."

"Anyone ever told you you're a drama llama?"

I smirk. "Anyone ever told you you're a grumpy lumpy?"

His cute nose wrinkles up, and it hits me again how fucking gorgeous he is. "I won't say it."

"Come on. Just once. For me."

Benny throws a quick look over at them.

"Just one time," I push.

"You're such a pain in the ass."

"Eh. Didn't hear you complaining before."

"You weren't in my ass before. So, I was definitely complaining."

I love hearing how he talks about sex. No embarrassment, just exactly what he wants. And he wants it from me, which I'm still struggling to process. I have zero self-confidence issues, but Benny is ... I don't even have words. I just know that the more of him I get, the more of him I want. He takes away my ability to breathe, to think, to function like a normal human. It's on the tip of my tongue, heart beating out of my chest, to ask him to come home with me after this. To spend the night. Maybe get more naked time in.

Fuck, I'm craving it.

I don't ask though. I'm still feeling this thing out, and the last thing I want is for us to go full pelt into sex and some kind of relationship, only for it to fizzle out. I don't want that with him.

I pull Benny in front of me so we're both facing my plants and wrap my arms around his waist.

"Say it."

I can feel the reluctance radiating from him.

"Like you mean it."

He huffs and drops his head back against my shoulder. "I love your plants. They're the prettiest flora I've ever seen."

"Aww ..." I headbutt him this time. "I think you just got Stacy pollinated."

He belts me in the shoulder, and I laugh, pulling him out of the enclosure and closing it up behind us. We still have a lot of night left to spend together, eating in the Zen Garden under the stars, but I'm already dreading the night being over.

I'm just going to take each moment together one at a time and hope he's right there with me.

I GRAB my usual green tea and hot chocolate and hightail it to class. I'm running later than usual due to Austin being slammed at Bean Necessities, but I still have plenty of time to make it before Professor Brooks locks the doors.

The second I see Benny, hood up and pretty eyes darting around the class, the smile that breaks out across my face is out of control. The other night was … wow. And every text message since has made me confident I'm falling for the guy, which is something I'm still trying to catch up with. It's one thing to be attracted to him sexually, but to start having feelings, to be thinking about more than just hanging out and getting off? It's been a process.

I jog up the few stairs between us, careful not to spill our drinks, and plonk his hot chocolate down in front of him.

"Good morning, cutie."

Benny scoops up his drink. "You're in a good mood today."

I dump my bag and drop into the seat next to him. "No more than usual."

"Just more … obvious, I guess."

"Well …" I give him a sly look. "Fun nights out will do that to a guy."

He laughs easily, obviously catching my drift. I still can't shake the feeling that he's different in class though. Definitely not as grumpy and cynical … maybe he's trying to make us look more platonic than we are while other people are around.

I don't care if they guess though, but I've never actually told Benny that.

"I'm assuming you're busy after this?" He always is, but it's worth checking.

There's regret in his eyes as he says, "Study."

"Of course."

"Sorry."

"It's okay. I know."

I think he's going to drop it at that when he turns to me suddenly. "I just want you to know that I would if I could. I don't have a whole lot of friends, and being able to talk to you, it's just … less lonely. That's all. I have to study. But I really like that we're friends."

I nod, but I don't have an answer for that. He likes that we're *friends*? Is he trying to drive home where I stand? And what does he mean that he doesn't have friends? He has an entire house of frat brothers he talks to; he has his family, we message nonstop. And *lonely*? Did Benny just talk feelings to me? Without me having to push?

Everything about that was … weird.

Discomfort creeps along my spine. I can't pinpoint what causes it, but it has me agitated for most of class. Benny is back concentrating, I'm back watching him, and something is … off.

The feeling's been coming on for a while, but while we're in class, statistics is usually our main source of conversation. That out-of-left-field apology type of thing is new and … not Benny.

He doesn't feel like Benny.

The thought is fucking ridiculous.

I shake off the discomfort. I'm reading into things. Being hot and cold is sort of Benny's thing, and if I thought hooking up again would change that, I'm an idiot.

"Want some gum?" he asks.

"Yeah, thanks."

He holds out the stick, and I take it, gaze catching something on his hand. "What's that?"

"Huh?" He opens his hand. "Ah, just a scar. I've had it since I was little."

It's a good one too. Raised and shiny white, stretching across his palm.

There's only one problem.

I kissed that hand.

That palm … didn't I?

I stretch my memory back, trying to remember exactly which hand it was. The more I think, the more sure I am.

"That … that wasn't there before."

He snatches his hand back. "What?"

"The other night. Maybe …" I laugh and run my hand over my face. "I think I'm going crazy, but I swear that wasn't there when we … you know. Don't worry, my mind is just playing tricks on me."

Benny looks confused as hell for a moment, and then his face morphs. "H-Harrison?"

"Yeah?"

"Oh, *fuck*."

His voice is so loud it draws attention from the people around us, made even worse when he scrambles for his bag.

"What's going on up there?" Professor Brooks calls, making yet more people look.

I drop my voice. "You okay, Benny?"

"Fine. I'm fine. I just … I have to go. Not feeling well." He holds up a hand—the non-scarred one that's currently lodged in his pocket—to Professor Brooks. "Sorry, sir. Feeling horrible. Gotta run. Class was great. Everything was great." He keeps rambling all the way down the stairs to the front of the class, and then when his feet hit solid ground, he bolts.

I'm left staring at the door swinging back closed behind him, feeling like something is very, very wrong.

18

BENNY

I have a screen full of missed calls and texts from Em when I climb out of the shower, and my heart shoots into my throat. They're a mix of "I fucked up" to "I'm sorry," and now he isn't answering, and I'm starting to freak out.

Towel clung to my hips, I make for my room, trying him again, while I remind my heart to just *stop* for a fucking second until I find out what the hell is going on. Those messages don't automatically mean he's in trouble. They don't. He's still fucking alive, so the rest we can deal with.

I make it to my room and rip through my drawers to find a clean pair of underwear to pull on. Anything has to be better than trying to handle a crisis in a towel.

My phone goes off, and I dive for it, hoping for Em and finding a text from Harrison instead.

Everything okay?

What the hell is going on?

Normally my default is to reply to him instantly, but the twist in my gut makes me wait. Em's freaked out about something, and Harrison wants to know if I'm okay, which clues me into the fact that maybe something happened between them. Did Harrison spot him in class and think he was me? Did they kiss? Fight?

"*Fuck.*" One hand rests on my head as I press my phone to the ear with the other, listening to it ring and ring and cut out again. "Fucking shit fuck."

My window thumps open, and Emmett all but falls inside. He struggles out of his bag and pushes to his feet, eyes wildly meeting mine.

Just the sight of him calms me.

"Dude, what the fuck? Why are we panicking?"

"Benny, I'm so, so sorry. I didn't know."

"Know what?"

"That Harrison is Bowser."

I stare at him for a beat. "What?"

He presses his face into his hands and lets out a short, raspy scream. "Okay. So. I kind of fucked up."

"Get to the point. Faster."

"Right." He bares his teeth like he really doesn't want to continue, but he fucking better because I'm about to strangle it out of him. "You know how we've always had that sort of loose kind of rule about not talking to anyone in classes and pretending to be the other person for real?"

My gut sinks. "Not a *loose* kind of rule. An actual rule that we've always been super careful to stick to and I always, *always* did for you."

Em looks like he's going to cry, and it takes me aback. My brother never cries. He might be the sweet, kind one out of the two of us, but as close as we are, as much as we've been through, since we hit preteen age, he's only ever cried once from what I can remember. Whereas whenever I get frustrated, I can't see through the fucked-up, angry tears that won't leave me alone.

"*Em?* What the fuck does Harrison have to do with this?" Because if he's figured it out, if he knows there's two of us, not only could he report us for cheating and have me thrown out of college too, I ... I might lose him. The fact I don't know which option is worse is a real fucking problem.

"I'm *lonely*, Ben. Okay? I'm sorry. This year's been kind of fucked-up, and that first day of class, I almost missed it, and there weren't many seats, so I sat near him. He started asking questions about the class, so I answered them, and then ... He was really nice. He sat next to me every time, I didn't go to him, but he's a talker, and it's so hard not to talk back, and ... I liked him. It was nice to have a friend again. Someone I could talk to who wasn't you."

"Please tell me you're not falling for him?"

"*What?*" He scrubs at his eyes. "Of course not. I don't even know him very well. But when he's around, I ... I don't feel so lonely."

Holy shit.

Everything makes so much sense now. The way Harrison approached me that first day of class. How he knew I'd planned something with hockey, even though I'm sure I've never mentioned it. Him calling me *Benny*. No one calls me that except Em, and if that's how he introduced himself ...

I drop back to sit on the side of my bed, head fucking spinning. My phone is still lighting up with messages that I can't answer, and my brain is flooding with indecision. I'm pissed at Em for breaking our promise, but as much as yelling would make me feel better, I just ... can't. Because I had the same thought, didn't I? The same moment of getting to have a person who wasn't my twin. And I at least have my frat brothers, but who does he have?

I let out a frustrated shout, just something to get all this burning energy out of me.

It would be so much easier if I didn't love my brother. If we could fight and I could tell him to fuck off and that'd be it, but I know that it doesn't matter what happens here—if Harrison ditches me and I'm thrown out of school, we have each other. Forever.

Fighting with him ends quickly because we both end up feeling so damn sick over it.

"I'm *so* mad," I choke out.

He looks terrible.

"Fuck, Em." My voice breaks. "I actually really fucking like this guy."

"I know. I swear, I had no clue it was him. None. Like I said, we don't talk about much that isn't schoolwork."

"Then how did you figure it out? Does *he* know? We need to stop and go back. Tell me exactly what happened."

Em's teeth sink into his lip, and he opens his hand, showing off the scar he got when we were kids. "He saw it and said it wasn't there the other night. Hinted about something happening between us, and that's when it clicked."

If he saw the scar, we're fucked. There's no way to cover up that we're separate people. I've already attempted my own matching scar, and all it got me was a scolding from West, a sore hand, and a cut that healed over too fast.

The thing is ... I don't *want* to lie to him. I don't want Harrison talking to Em and thinking he's me. I don't want to try and hide it all from him or deceive him or whatever. It's bad enough that it's happened already, even if it wasn't on purpose.

Which means, apparently, I have two choices.

Walk away from Harrison and avoid him like the plague.

Or tell him the whole truth.

Everything.

Including the cheating and hope like hell that he doesn't turn me in.

"What do we do?" I whisper, not really expecting an answer.

"Drop the class? Shave our hair? Move to Mexico?"

"That isn't funny."

"I'm not joking." He sits next to me. "It'd help me out with Asher and West too."

"If you think they can't hunt us down in Mexico, you don't know our brothers."

He sighs, looking out my window. "Do you ever sometimes think that school isn't for us?"

"What do you mean?"

"Well, we both suck at it."

"Says who? We've always had top marks."

"Except that one year we were put in all the same classes."

I try to forget that year. I almost had to retake math, and his English results were in the hole. We had to make up this whole lie about spending too much time together and always fighting, which meant we had no time left to study. Somehow, everyone bought it.

"Okay, so maybe we're stupid about some things, but it doesn't mean school isn't for us. Is that why you don't want to go back? You think you're dumb?"

"Something like that …"

"You're not dumb. Quit that. And also, why won't you just let me be mad at you? It would be a lot easier right now."

He laughs and tackle-hugs me to the bed. "Because I know you don't want that. It always makes us both feel shit."

"Stupid twin stupid bond. Aren't we supposed to have superpowers?"

"I don't think it works like that."

I gaze up at my ceiling, following the patterns in the cracked paint with my eyes. "Do you think he looked at you and pictured you naked?" I ask Em.

"What?"

"Eh. Nothing." It's not something I've ever considered before. That someone I'm with might be equally as attracted to my brother because I've never actually cared. If you'd asked me, I probably would have thought it was hilarious, would have loved it, because Em and I share everything, and we love that people can't tell us apart.

I think this is the first time ever that I don't love it so much.

The fact Harrison has this whole friendship with Em that's caught me by surprise makes me uncomfortable. I hate that he couldn't tell the difference. Hate that if something happened to me, it wouldn't matter because he has a backup guy. A replacement.

Fuck, my thoughts are getting dark.

"I need a drink," I say.

"No, you need to talk to him."

"Can't."

"Why?"

I turn my head to look at Em. "What if he never talks to me again?"

"What was going to happen if you started dating? If things got serious?"

"He's still figuring himself out. I don't see that happening."

"You suck at hypotheticals. Just try for me."

"*If* we dated, we would have dated. What kind of question is that?"

"And you would have had to tell him about me."

"Obviously. But he never had to know you were in class with him. I would have just been all, 'Here's Em, who has never been at all around this area, and you definitely haven't met him before.'"

Em laughs. "Ah. So, you'd start your relationship on a lie."

"Don't be an asshole."

"Well, stop being chickenshit."

I huff and ignore my phone lighting up again. The dread curls deeper in my stomach every time I think about facing Harrison. We'd been all date-y the other night, and it low-key freaked me out, even as I loved it, but now that there's a chance he might get angry with me? It's driving home how much I want him.

"He'll be okay, right?" I ask Em. "It was a simple mix-up. And technically his fault. He approached *us*."

"Yeah, I suggest leaving that last part off."

"Fuck."

"You can do it."

But that's the thing. I really, really, really can't.

19

HARRISON

I'm confused and worried, and I only get more confused and more worried as the day wears on with no contact from Benny. My gut is telling me something isn't right, but I don't want to jump to theories or conclusions without getting a chance to talk to him.

Classes are a write-off, so I head home rather than over to the DIK house. If Benny isn't texting or calling back, he doesn't want to talk, so forcing him into a corner won't do either of us any good. He needs to come to me, and he needs to explain what's up with that goddamn scar.

"You okay?" Felix asks when I walk into the kitchen and pull out the bottle of vodka.

"Fine. Just too much thinking going on."

He watches, amused, as I throw back a shot. "So, the cure to overthinking is killing brain cells. Love it."

"What else would you suggest?"

"Talking it out is a good alternative."

I grunt and take another shot. What do I say? I think the guy I've been hanging out with and having sex with might be hiding something from me, and that something is a whole-ass person?

Urg ... my head aches.

Because if the theory I'm trying not to think about is actually true ... I don't know who I've been seeing anymore. I don't know if it was all some joke they do for a laugh.

They.

Fuck.

I take another shot before Felix rescues the bottle from my hand and puts the lid back on it.

"Now that we have the drinking out of the way, we're going to try the talkies next."

"I have no idea what to say, Fe. I'm confused."

"Well, first of all, you could tell me you had sex with your gorgeous new friend."

I frown at him. "Marshall told you?"

"No, I overheard you two talking, so I kept my distance so you'd have your privacy. And you *still* haven't told me. But I figured it was relevant to this conversation, so you don't need to worry about some big coming-out moment. I love you, I'm happy you're figuring yourself out, blah, blah, blah ..."

"The funny thing is that I haven't figured anything out at all."

"Oh. I assumed you were having some big bi moment?"

"Maybe ..." I scratch my chin, not really having room in my brain for this too. "I know that I'm drawn to Benny. Super hot for him. Everything is ... easy with him."

Well, it was. Until now.

"Think you could be demi like Marshall?"

"Nah, but it did occur to me. I've never not wanted to have

sex with someone just because I didn't know them though. Sex is great. People are attractive. But ..."

"What?"

"Well, it's that whole wanting more thing that doesn't always hit me. But with him, I think it might be. Sex is just an addition to that."

"Hmm ... maybe pan?"

That would probably make sense. I wasn't immediately sexually attracted to Benny, but I did like him. More than friends. That feeling has only intensified the more time we've spent together, and it's gotten to a point that I don't care if he has a pussy, a dick, or a fucking tentacle between his legs, he just makes my cock all the way hard. Getting him off is one of my favorite things to do.

Figuring out that little lightbulb moment doesn't make me as relieved as I'm expecting though.

I'm just ... sad.

I want to talk to Benny.

But do I even know him at all? He's helped me figure out this huge thing about myself, and what if everything I thought I knew about him is a lie?

A knock on the front door immediately catches my attention, and Felix and I exchange a look. Marshall has his own key, and we don't have a lot of visitors.

"I'll get it," I tell him, hoping like hell it's Benny and he has the scar and he really was just sick this morning.

Only when I open the door and meet his guarded hazel eyes, the truth sinks into my gut.

Whoever that was in class wasn't him.

I knew it, long before the scar; his eyes are a dead giveaway. Looking at them now, the way they always seem so wary and like they're looking too hard, reminds me that whoever I sit next to in class is never like that.

I step aside and hold open the door.

Benny doesn't say anything, just walks inside and heads straight to my room.

Normally all the plants in here send off happy feelings through me, but I'm on my guard too. On edge, waiting for what the hell he's going to say, and the way he's so stiff, the way he's inspecting the pots by my window instead of me, tells me I probably don't want to hear whatever is coming next.

He finally talks. "I hear you met my brother."

And there it is. Confirmation. Just thrown out like a casual statement and not the kind of thing making my head spin. Sure, the alcohol isn't helping, but I didn't drink that much. I still heard every word.

"H-how? Are you a—"

"Twin?" He shrugs, hands in his pockets. "Yeah. Obviously."

"Obviously." I snort because this isn't funny. "Why the hell is he pretending he's you?"

Another shrug. "Just something we do."

"Yeah? And how often do you fucking do it?"

"Don't yell at me."

"Then start goddamn talking because I'm spinning out here. The guy I'm into suddenly isn't who I thought he was, and now I have no fucking clue which parts were real and which weren't. Was it only you I had sex with?"

He finally looks at me. "I don't know, *did* you have sex with Emmett as well?"

"How the fuck am I supposed to know that?"

Hurt crosses his face. "It wasn't on purpose. It's not like we tried to trick you or anything."

"Well, that's a relief." And even though my voice is heavy with sarcasm, there's a part, deep down, that acknowledges it really is. "Why did he tell me he was you?"

"He had to." Benny scuffs the toe of his sneaker against my carpet before lifting his head, determined. "He's taking the class for me. He had to pretend he was me, just like I've always done for him. It had nothing to do with you, and I'm really sorry you had to find out that way."

"Would you ever have told me?"

"Of course," he snarls. "Goddamn it, he was never supposed to talk to anyone. This should never have been an issue, but apparently, you had a big effect on the both of us."

"This is my fault?"

"Did I say that?" His gorgeous face is splotching red. "I'm shit at this. I'm shit at talking. You know that."

Know that? At this point, I have no clue what I know. "Do I though? How the fuck do I know what's you and what's … Emmett?"

"He said he's never talked to you outside of class."

"And you believe that?"

"He's my brother. He'd never lie to me."

"Except you just said he was never supposed to talk to anyone. Did he tell you he was talking to me? Is this the same brother you said had a secret? Who you were worried about?"

"That doesn't matter."

I scoff. "How do you know that secret wasn't me?"

Benny glares, and even though he does that a lot, it's not with this kind of intensity. "Em would never, ever lie. If he says he only talked to you in class, he only talked to you in class. That's not up for discussion."

"How is it that *I'm* the one who was played by *you*, and yet you're getting angry with *me*?"

"I never played you."

"Oh, yeah?" I step forward until we're toe-to-toe, actually letting myself feel the hurt now. Actually, looking at him and overlaying the face in front of me with the face in class. The subtle differences. The subtle changes in how they made me feel. The guy in class never made my heart race the way the one in front of me does. "I was falling for you, Benny. Goddamn turned stupid over you. And now ... I don't know who you are. You say you're a twin, and you say all those moments outside of class were ours, but ... how do I trust that? How do I trust you? Fuck, you're *cheating* in class. You're talking about it like it's some kind of normal thing, but it isn't. Who *are* you?"

His eyes are watery through his glare. "Clearly not the person you thought I was."

"Clearly."

He clears his throat, suddenly looking confused about why he's here. "I'm sorry. I just wanted to say that. I'm sorry. Everything I've said today was the truth. Em and I never played you. We didn't even know the other knew you."

"So, you didn't tell him anything about me?"

"Of course I did! I talked about you constantly. I'm one step away from being obsessed with you, but you told him your name was Bowser, and I only knew you as Harrison."

That makes sense. He randomly started to call me by my name that day we hung out after class. Was that the first time it was him?

"I ..."

"Look, I shouldn't have come over. I'm sorry. We'll just ... get the hell out of your life, I guess."

I grab his arm as he tries to step by me, but even I'm not sure why. All I know is that I don't want him to leave, but I'm not ready for this conversation.

"Look, I'm confused, and I'm hurt, and ..."

He nods quickly.

"I don't know, Benny. I don't know what to say."

"I get that."

"You've just made it so hard to trust you."

He sets his hand on my chest.

Before he can say anything, I lift it off and turn his hand over, revealing his completely clear palm. The solid proof that this is really happening. My face twists, and he snaps his hand closed again. This whole thing is just too much.

I step back, trying to arrange my thoughts in a way that makes sense.

When Benny walks out of my room, I let him go.

20

BENNY

This party blows.

I hate it.

The beer tastes like piss, and the music is too loud, and this guy grinding up on my lap is only making my dick softer. Not his fault I'm in a shit mood, but I'm getting irritated at him anyway.

He had *one* job. Take my mind off Harrison. But like my dick, my brain is doing the opposite of what it's supposed to.

The guy runs his mouth along my neck, and it actually makes my skin crawl.

I tap his thigh. "I've had enough. Get off."

"If you wanna get me off, you've gotta give me something to work with."

"No. Get off as in vacate my lap. Now."

He scowls and climbs off me. "You're such a fucking dick, Dalton."

"Duh." I roll my eyes and watch him walk away. He's hot, and it won't take him long to find someone else who thinks I'm a dick, and then they can bond over blow jobs.

I, however, see no blow jobs in my future.

I pour the rest of my beer out onto the floor and toss the Solo cup after it. I'm in peak dick mode, but I can't stop myself. Sure, I'm not the most pleasant person most of the time, but my bad moods usually pass quickly—Em helps with that—but this time, it's clung on like herpes. Instead of distance from my fight with Harrison making things better, it's only getting worse. I still feel like shit for snapping at Em over food earlier, and I've reached the point where I don't care if anyone spots us both here together.

Harrison hasn't responded to my message the day after our fight either. I've typed about a million since then too, all I was too chickenshit to send. I should be studying. I should be focused on school. I should be partying my heart out and getting the best of my college days under my belt, and I should be helping Em figure out what's next, but no.

No.

My stupid brain, which is apparently resistant to alcohol tonight, is determined to think about one person and one person only. Fuck it. I hate it.

Instead of spending any more time at this party, I climb the ladder to the attic and watch them all from the window there. Of course, it makes me feel shittier than ever, but so does everywhere, so fuck it.

I pull out my phone, trying not to be too depressed over the lack of messages and unable to stop myself from opening our texts. All amazing and cute and flirty right up to the radio silence. It's not fucking fair.

I'm typing before I can stop myself.

Sure, don't write back. Ignore me and act like
I'm a total stranger. Real mature.

I give him a few minutes, and when there's still nothing, I
kick the wall and try again.

I said I was sorry, what the hell else do I have
to do?

Nothing.

You're acting like it was on purpose and it
wasn't! Dammit, Harrison. This isn't fair.

The more I write that he ignores just brings on my frustration. I bite my fist as I smother a scream and plead with myself
not to write anything else. Of course, I'm a dickhead and don't
listen to that good advice.

Clearly weren't falling for me after all, were
you? Why'd you have to go and fuck up my
whole life, huh?

My phone vibrates, and the way my gut flips should put me
in the hospital.

Are you drunk?

I glare at the three words, rage building that it's all the
response I get.

ME:

No, I'm not fucking drunk.

HARRISON:

Have you been drinking?

ME:

Yes, but it didn't work.

HARRISON:

I'm glad you think that. Go to bed.

Those stupid tears are pricking my eyes at being talked to like a kid. He's not interested. He's not going to give me what I want. Apparently, I'm an even bigger mess than I realized because I'm out of control with my next message.

ME:

Can't. Gotta go get my dick sucked. Night.

He doesn't reply.
I can't even blame him.

MY RINGTONE IS PIERCING, and I forgot to close the blinds last night, so the sunlight is burning my motherfucking retinas. Apparently, the alcohol eventually started to work because I don't remember passing out in bed naked.

I also have a hangover, which means ... I squint at the mattress on the floor and find Em gripping his head.

"Ow."

I grunt. "Me too. Thanks for that, asshole."

"Right back at you." He hugs a pillow to his face. "Answer your fucking phone!"

I grumble and reach for it, heart dropping when it's not Harrison's name on the screen. It's Asher's.

"Fuck."

I answer immediately because unlike West, Asher will call until he gets through to us. And considering hockey season has started, the fact Asher's calling means something is up.

"Who's dead?" I groan into the phone.

"Your brother."

I jerk upright. "Wait. Actually?"

"Not actually." It's like I can hear him rolling his eyes at me. "But he will be if he doesn't answer West's fucking calls."

My gaze flicks toward Em and away again. "Ah, yeah. Rhys is *so* bad at that—"

"You know I'm not talking about Rhys. Where's Em? What's going on?"

"Em ... Em ... Remind me again—"

"Pretending not to know who he is. Cute. Also how I know you're guilty."

"Guilty of what?"

Asher grunts. "Covering for whatever reason he's avoiding our calls."

Fuck. I'm too hungover and mopey to deal with this today. "Now, are you sure you're calling the right person?"

"I know how to press a contact in my phone, thanks."

"I'm just saying, how do you know this is Ben? Maybe you've called Em."

"Because Em doesn't make my brain itch the way you do."

I hum, wanting to wind this up. "Your brain is itchy? You'd think with Kole being a doctor, you'd avoid STDs. Though maybe it's a BDD. Brain Dumbass Disease. I hear there's no cure for that."

"Delightful as always, Ben. I know you've seen Em. Now, get him to fucking call West before our brother starts having kittens."

"But kittens are so cute," I deadpan.

"This act isn't. Serious talk, do we need to be worried?"

"About what?"

"About *Em.*" Good. He's starting to get frustrated, which means he'll hang up soon.

"Who. Is. Em?"

"Your idiot twin brother. Look in the mirror and quit playing this game."

"Wait. I'm a twin?"

"Fucking hell."

"Question: how do you know I'm a twin?"

"We're not doing this."

He's so close now. "How can you be sure it's not just me? That you haven't been hallucinating this whole other person? I don't remember a twin. Do you love me that much that you need more of me in your life? I've gotta say, Ash, that probably worries me more than the hallucinations. You should get it checked out. And the brain itch. I hear losing your parents at a young age can make you kinda fucked—"

The line goes dead.

I fall back onto my bed, wanting to be a whole lot more relieved than I am.

"West has been calling you?" I ask Em.

"Can't talk. Hungover."

"You're getting us both in shit. I can handle West and Asher over the phone, but if they come here—"

"They won't."

"How the hell do you know that?"

"You can really see Asher missing a game or West skipping out on work as the season's just starting?"

He's got a point there. As head coach of a Division One hockey team with multiple Frozen Four wins under their skates, West is busy right from the start of the semester.

"What if they send Jasper?" I ask.

We pull identical *we're fucked* faces. Jasper is West's husband, and because he's a world more put together than any of my siblings, he's always felt like the adult in our household.

We both love and fear him because when Jasper gets angry, he doesn't pitch a fit like a Dalton does.

He goes quiet.

Some of the most terrifying moments of my life have been sitting across from Jasper as he stared me down, waiting for me to cough up all my sins. As a tenured professor at CU and head of the math department, our cheating wouldn't just disappoint him—it'd kill him. I'm worried Em being expelled will do the exact same.

"Jasper has work," Em says. "They took all their vacation leave this summer."

"Don't underestimate them. You know West is good at going for the low blow."

"Too. Hung. Over."

"Fine, but you need to figure out something to tell them. I can't pretend not to know who you are forever."

"Maybe I *should* disappear, and we can test out that theory." He moves the pillow to grin up at me, but it does nothing to make me any happier.

I hate worrying and stress. Actually, I hate everything right now.

I rub the building ache in my sternum, wondering when the hell it will fuck off already. "Maybe you're right. Running away to Mexico is getting more and more appealing."

"Wouldn't work."

"Why?"

"Because the thing you're running away from is something that can't be left behind."

I'd ask what he's talking about, but I already know, and the last thing I want is for him to say it out loud.

"Well, moping isn't working. Texting isn't working. Hiding out from everything and running away aren't the answers. So, what do I do?"

"Go see him. Talk to him."

I groan as I think about what I sent him last night. "He'll probably punch me in the face."

"Eh. At least then you'll have something new to complain about."

"Fuck you, I don't complain."

"Not out loud." He kicks his sheets off. "But your face is loud, and I'm sick of listening to it."

"Hey. I just took on Asher for you."

"As you should. You're my twin. Deal with it."

I scowl as he pulls a T-shirt on. "I thought you were disappearing. Can you do that faster?"

"Nah, because then I'll miss your disastrous love life."

"I don't have a love life."

Em pushes the window open. "We might look the same, but I'm so glad we weren't gifted with matching attitudes."

"You'd be lucky to be as delightful as I am, pyro."

He laughs. "That was an accident!"

"Sure. Tell your old dean that."

"Whatever. Just put some damn clothes on. I see our dick enough on my own, thanks."

He jumps out the window, heading fuck knows where, but it's not like it matters. I'm not planning on leaving my room today.

Everyone on campus can think Emmett's me.

Hey, maybe Harrison will run into him first and yell at him instead.

I can only hope.

21

HARRISON

Entering statistics, I'm still not entirely sure what I'm going to do. It's hard to believe that it's been a whole week since I've seen Benny, and I'd be lying if I said I didn't miss him.

What happened is so far out of my normal life, and now I'm supposed to get over it and move on.

Hell, *he* has.

My teeth snap at the thought of him being with someone else, but I haven't given him reason to think there's still anything between us, so I can't blame him. It's a shitty situation the whole way around.

Which is why, when I see his face a few rows up, I falter. I *want* to go up there, want to sit with him and try to talk. Because I really do want to put this whole thing behind us, but I just don't know *how*.

But then our eyes meet, and my heart sinks.

It's not Benny.

It's his brother.

We watch each other for a moment before I change my mind about going up there and duck into the row beside where I'm standing instead. I can still feel his unfamiliar gaze on the back of my head.

"Hey," I say vaguely to the guy I've sat beside.

He flicks me a wave and goes back to his laptop.

I glance back, but Emmett has his laptop out as well now and is concentrating hard on the screen, so I try to do the same. The whole time I'm waiting for Professor Brooks to start, I keep picturing what would happen if I went back there. If I confronted him. Benny says he trusts his brother, but I don't know him. I'm not so sure I know Benny either, and the thought that the guy I really fucking like isn't who I thought is too much for me to handle.

But his brother ... his brother I could corner. Could make talk.

"Everything okay?" the guy beside me asks.

"What?"

He chuckles awkwardly, like he's not sure I am okay. "You keep looking around."

"Oh. That. Yeah ... nothing. Just, umm, avoiding someone."

His smile lights up his sweet face. "That sounds like a fun story."

Urg. Fun. I wish. "Just your standard straight boy falls for his first-ever guy crush and then finds out guy crush is actually a twin, and straight boy doesn't know who the fuck he's been seeing."

The guy laughs and holds out his hand. "Jordan."

Judging by his FU Kings baseball hat, I'm guessing he's on the team. "Harrison."

He adjusts the cap, still smiling, still cute, and a very evil side of me hopes that Emmett is watching. That maybe he goes home and tells Benny I was talking to a cute guy. Two can play at that game. "Now I've heard all that, my girlfriend issues don't feel so bad. A twin?"

I rub my face. "The whole thing is stupid."

"Sounds like a melodrama to me, man. I mean, does it matter that he's a twin? That's not something he can help."

There's a whole lot more context I'd need to give him for him to understand, but as much as I'm annoyed, I'm not going to rat them out for cheating. "Let's just say I know both of them, but I didn't realize they were two different people. I feel like a fucking idiot."

"Wow. Low move that they didn't tell you."

If Benny's to be believed, I can understand why they didn't. Doesn't make me happy about it, but it definitely makes me less mad. "Maybe I should have stuck to women ..." I mutter.

"Trust me, they're no easier."

I shoot a quick look his way. "You've dated both?"

"Uh, no. I have two dads, and they've told me enough stories to know that whether you're straight or queer, dating is a pain in the ass."

"This is why I never date."

"You weren't dating the twin?"

Him saying it like that makes my head throb. "Who fucking knows? I'd been planning to take things slow and see where it ended up, but we fell in with each other fast, and now we've had some distance ... I don't like it."

"You said he's the first guy you've ..."

"Yeah." It's weird saying the next part out loud. "My roommate thinks I'm pansexual. Makes sense since I don't really care what's between someone's legs. I've never been that interested in dating so I've never pushed myself for a label much, but with him, it's different. Which doesn't make any sense when we're nothing alike."

"My dads are nothing alike either. Sorry, I don't have any advice for you. My sexuality is sort of up in the air, too, so I'm not exactly bursting with advice." He tears a strip of paper from his small notepad and scribbles something down. "Happy to talk about it though. Or you can use that to give me updates."

"Updates?" I take the scrap of paper with his number on it. "Such a nosy bugger."

Jordan's laugh is half-embarrassed and very cute. Look at that. I do find other guys attractive. He's not Benny though.

We're quiet during class and even though I've just spilled my guts to him, I don't ask for his help. It's not until we're packing up that a presence catches my notice. I look up into the familiar face, thrown at it being Benny-not-Benny.

"Yeah?"

Emmett shifts to his other foot. "You got a minute?"

"Nope. We're grabbing something to eat."

And in the worst cover-up in history, Jordan has my back. "Ah, yeah. Food. We're going now."

Don't laugh don't laugh don't laugh.

"A second, then," Emmett says dryly, sounding a whole lot more like my Benny. I hate it.

Jordan looks to me for what I want to do.

The thing is, I'm curious, but this is between me and Benny. Not us and his brother. Emmett has had enough of a role, but other than being the guy who sits next to me in class, he doesn't owe me anything.

"You're not who I want to talk to."

"Good." He plants his hands on his hips. "If you want to talk to him, then do it."

"Yeah, but I get the feeling he has no interest in talking to me."

"Was it the multiple obsessive messages that gave you that impression?"

I snort, because that actually gave me hope. "No, it was him sleeping with some other guy that gave me that impression."

Emmett slumps. "Did *he* tell you that?"

"Yes."

"I'm gonna kill him. My brother is a dumbass, but I'm assuming you know that already since you've spent more than five seconds with him. He said that to hurt you because he's hurting, and he has no idea how to be a normal person and deal with his shit properly."

Jordan's still eagerly listening in, and I don't blame him. We exchange another look.

"You ghosted him!" Emmett snaps. "He just wanted your attention."

"That's ridiculous."

"From where I'm standing, you're both ridiculous."

Jordan tries to hide his snicker. "I'm getting that impression too."

I narrow a glare his way. "Jumped ship fast over there."

"I'm entertained. Sue me."

Emmett turns his glare on Jordan instead. "*You* shouldn't even be here. Bowser isn't going to use your number because he's perfect for my brother, and my brother is perfect for him."

"Whoa." Jordan throws his hands up. "I wasn't hitting on him. I don't even like guys like that, and I have a girlfriend, or at least I do for right now."

Emmett takes another few seconds before his glare lets up. "In that case ... umm, sorry?"

"You're okay," Jordan assures him.

Emmett shakes his head and turns to me. "No, sorry to you. I texted Benny. He's waiting outside, and he's kinda pissed."

"Jesus fucking Christ."

"I *said* sorry! But I thought you were moving on, so I freaked out. I've never heard him talk about someone the way he talks about you. It's so cute."

My heart does this weird little stutter thing. "It might be cute, but telling me he was getting a BJ from someone else isn't okay."

"Yeah. That was a dick move."

I glance over at Jordan. "What do you say? Want to help me teach my maybe future boyfriend a lesson?"

Emmett bounces on the spot. "Boyfriend?"

"You keep quiet. I'm still unsure what to make of you."

He mimes locking his lips, and I turn to Jordan.

"Help?"

"I'm invested now."

"Good." I pack my stuff up and sling my bag over my shoulder, then place a hand on Emmett's shoulder. It's creepy how he feels exactly like Benny. "You stay here for a minute before you give us away."

"You have sixty seconds, then I'm coming out there."

"Deal."

I lead Jordan down and outside. Since Benny thinks he's coming here because I've been all flirty with some guy in class, I'm going to let his imagination do the talking. No need to be holding hands or playing it up. I'm unsure whether to believe that Benny didn't actually hook up with someone, but thinking he did made me feel like shit, and maybe I want to give him that one tiny moment of what I felt as well.

Benny isn't right outside like Emmett said, but once we step out of the science building, I immediately spot him. He's under a tree a few feet away, arms crossed and looking murderous. The second he spots me, he beelines right for us.

"Don't do it" are the first words out of his mouth.

"Sorry, do what? Get my dick sucked? I thought that was what we do these days."

Jordan makes a choking sound beside me.

"If you want someone to suck your cock, I've been begging for weeks. He can't even breathe without choking. Can you imagine him trying to deep-throat?"

"Oh my god." Jordan smothers his laugh, and okay, maybe dragging him into this wasn't the smartest choice.

I step toward Benny and tug him away a few steps. "You can hook up with someone else, but I can't?"

"I—"

I wait him out, eyebrows raised. "You what?"

His jaw clenches, and I can't stop from reaching up, taking his chin, and forcing him to meet my eyes.

"You better finish that sentence, or Jordan and I are going to have some fun."

He glares.

I wait him out.

"I didn't hook up with anyone. I can't. You're the only one I can fucking think of, and I hate it. Happy now?"

I thought I would be. I thought it would be this huge relief, but it's ... not. My thumb smooths over his jaw. "I miss you, Benny."

"Yeah." His voice goes small. "I broke my phone."

"You broke your phone? Why?"

"Because it didn't have any messages from you on it. Apparently, glass screens don't like being thrown."

Fucking hell. "That's insane. You know that, right?"

"I know." The anger drains from him. "But I can't stop thinking about you. Which is also insane because we hooked up twice, and sure, we were friends, but I shouldn't be this upset about you wanting nothing to do with me."

"It's not ..." I drop my hands so I'm not touching him and turn to Jordan. "Sorry. It was cool of you to have my back, but I think we need some privacy."

"Not going to lie, it was getting kind of awkward." He backs up. "Text me, yeah?"

"I will."

I swear, Benny growls.

"That's enough from you," I tell him, pulling him away. "It's not that I didn't want anything to do with you, but imagine if I told you that I'm not Harrison. I'm some other guy. You'd probably need a minute to adjust, wouldn't you?"

His confused frown makes it obvious that's not the right question.

"Never mind. You're used to the twin thing. But it's sort of a big deal for me to suddenly find out that there's *two* of the dude I like. I needed time."

"You didn't text me back though. At all."

"Yeah, that's what needing time is."

"Okay, so ..."

"So ..." I'm still not all the way there, but it's obvious I still feel something for him. "I want to give this another go, but we're going to have to talk about some things. The cheating in class ... It's uncomfortable. And I need to know that you and Emmett aren't going to be switching things up on me or lie about anything."

"I wouldn't lie to you."

"Except about getting your dick sucked."

His face falls. "Shit. Yeah. That."

"You also omitted a pretty big thing."

"Fine, so my track record isn't great. I get it. But I want to try. I ..." He sucks in a long breath. "I like you a lot, and I don't want to push things. I don't know where you're at with men, and maybe you *do* want to sleep around and try out this new side of you, but I want to date you. For real. So, if that's something you want ..."

I lean in and press my lips to his, the connection making

everything inside of me full again. "I want. I want it so fucking much."

He holds my face gently. "Good. Because I really didn't want to have to kill that guy back there."

"You're so stabby and cute. Not going to lie, jealous Benny is a real turn-on."

"Good, because I'm not used to dating, so I get the feeling he's going to come out a lot."

I don't hate that anywhere near as much as I probably should. "Then I guess we need to clear some things up."

22

BENNY

Harrison has faded freckles beneath his eyes. They're more obvious in the sunlight, same as the way his light brown eyelashes fan out over them when he blinks.

If I'd been asked what my type was, I wouldn't have described him, yet here I am so painfully attracted to him that I can't keep my thoughts in order.

It's annoying and distracting.

We walk side by side across campus until Harrison speaks.

"Sorry I went MIA."

"Yeah. Sorry for ..." How do I say everything without sounding dismissive?

"Nah. You already said that. A lot."

"I know, but I'll say it as many times as I need to."

"The thing is you were right. You weren't intentionally shitty toward me; it was just one big clusterfuck. Also, what you guys are doing ..." He throws me a look. "Not the kind of thing you just confess to random strangers."

"Exactly."

He stops walking right at the edge of campus. "I can't turn a blind eye to it. I'm sorry, I can't."

I swallow thickly because this is what I'd been expecting. The moment he makes me choose between him and him reporting me.

"We'll stop," I whisper. "I don't care, whatever. No one was supposed to get hurt. Hell, no one was supposed to know at all."

"I'm not sure that makes it better."

"Probably not, but do you know how many twins do it?"

He laughs. "Not an argument that would hold up in court."

He's right, and it's not an argument I want to be making at all. This whole situation is fucked-up, and I should easily be able to tell Em to stop taking my class, especially since he has no classes for me to take in return, but every time I think of statistics and numbers, I want to throw up.

Who knew that avoiding math since elementary school would mean you know shit all about it now?

He steps closer, turning me to face him. "Why'd you do it? You're smart, Benny. You're acing your classes. You're going into fucking journalism, for fuck's sake. Do you even need statistics?" His face falls. "Tell me this is the only class Emmett is taking for you?"

"It is," I hurry to assure him, and then I start walking because I can't look at him while I give up the details. "When we were younger, we met another set of twins at hockey camp. They were a few years older and had been switching places in school for basically ever. Em and I already liked to switch it up and prank people, but we hadn't considered the school thing. The thing is ... we tried it. We got away with it. It was all fun." I bite my lip, not wanting to spill this next part in case it sounds like a cop-out, but we really did fuck ourselves over. "Problem with that is … it became a bit of a habit. We missed a ton of school when our parents died, and then home was a fucking mess with our older brothers at each other's throats while they desperately tried to hold things together. It was too much. Em and I were kind of forgotten about. Not intentionally—there were just a lot of us, and our brothers were dealing with their own shit." I kick at the loose gravel by the road. "I hate math, so he did my work. He hates English, so I did his. We already had so much other shit to deal with, it was our way of giving ourselves a chance to breathe. In high school, we decided to stop being shithead kids. We were scared about being caught and making things harder on our brothers if we were kicked out of school, and it seemed like the sort of thing we *should* do …"

Harrison fills in the silence. "But it was too late."

My good mood at being with him crashes. It kills me that shitty choices when we were kids have messed us up *this* much. Em hates having to read; I don't understand simple math. "Yeah." My voice comes out all rough. "The thing is, I'm going into sports journalism. Statistics is something I have to know, but I grew up around hockey my whole life. I know that shit. I learned it all through doing, not through numbers. This class is a checkbox—it's why Em's taking it and not me." My whole chest feels like it's trying to close over at the thought of sitting through that class again, where the professor talks too fast and it feels like he's speaking another language.

"I'm sorry," he mutters. "That's really rough, and you're right. It puts you in a shitty position now."

"Yeah, but that's my problem, isn't it?"

"Yep." He reaches for me, and as soon as the warmth of his palm fills mine, I cling to it. All fluttery and excited in the gut while I'm still heavy with the knowledge of what I have to do. "But like I said, you're smart. You can do this without Em. I'll be there to help you, and I'm sure your brother will be too. You'll be okay."

I try to look confident, even though I'm not at all. He's making it sound simple, like I can walk into class and study the work and it'll be fine. He's completely overlooking the way none of it will stick in my brain. How I don't know basic measurements. Break out into a cold sweat whenever I have to pay for something with cash.

I smile his way. "Piece of cake."

"Exactly." He squeezes my hand. "It'll be hard, but it will be worth it."

I've never dreaded anything more. "And if I do it myself, you won't rat us out?"

"I won't. It crossed my mind a few times when I found out, but I understand why you did it. Sometimes you can get so caught up in something you don't see what's happening until you look at it from the outside. Now you know it isn't okay, all you have to do is give it a good go, Benny. We're halfway through the semester, you've already scored highly, and even if you have a couple of rocky scores, you'll still get through."

Except if I go from my usual high scores to a big fat zero, it's going to wave a red flag in Professor Brook's face. I'll deal with that when I deal with it. *If* I deal with it. Because if Harrison and Em are there to help me, I'm going to work my ass off to learn as much as I can just to get me through the tests. After that, I can let all of it go, no problem.

Tests. Simple.

Oh, wow. There's that urge to throw up again.

"I hate that I even have to say it, but please don't make me regret this."

I glance over and find him already looking at me. "What do you mean?"

"If you and Em switch again, I'll know. If I keep quiet and

find out you're cheating again … it'll kill me. I'll feel like an idiot."

I'm quick to shake my head. "I swear we won't. I promise. I know that you wouldn't know even if we did, but it won't happen again."

"Of course I'd know."

I roll my eyes. "We're twins, Harrison."

"And?"

"And we're identical. Even our brothers can't tell us apart most of the time, unless they make us show them our hands, and I really don't want to have to high-five every time I see you."

Harrison makes a noise that's a cross between a laugh and a groan. "I also don't want to live in constant mistrust of you either. I'm not going to be demanding to see anything. I also don't have to."

"What do you mean?"

He's quiet as we approach the DIK house, but I'm burning with curiosity now.

"What do you mean you don't have to?"

"I'm worried it will come across a bit intense."

"After everything I've just told you, I think you'll be okay."

"Fine." He steps closer, hands on my hips as he looks down at me. "It's your eyes, Benny. The whole time we were in class, I couldn't figure out why I didn't have the same reaction to you. I was happy to be with you and excited to see you, but there was nothing deeper. There were none of these nerves, and honestly, you just didn't get my dick hard. It's like I could sense it wasn't you. Then after I knew, I took one look at Emmett in class and figured it out. You both have different eyes."

"No, we don't. They're hazel. Exactly the same hazel. We are literally identical."

"Maybe, but I'm not talking about the color. Yours make you look older. His make him look younger."

That fills me with a vicious kind of happiness. I'm not even sure how to explain it, only that for the first time in my entire life, I feel like my own person. I love Em, I love being a twin, but this? Harrison being able to tell us apart? If he's telling the truth, the man has just made me fall in love with him.

"Ha. Maybe I was right about him being younger, after all."

"What do you mean?"

"Well, I'm the baby of the family, but I told Em there's no way to really know he came out first. Who's to say we didn't get mixed up all the time as flesh monkeys?"

"Somehow, I don't think parents do that."

"If I had twins, I definitely would."

"Noted. No children for you."

I pull him up the stairs to the front of the house, then turn my back to the door before we go inside. "Good thing you can't get me pregnant."

"True." Harrison steps in and presses me against the door. "I've really, *really* missed you, Benny."

I melt against him. "I've missed you too."

"Please tell me you have condoms inside."

I nod so fast I'm surprised my head doesn't fall off. "As many as we need. I'm not above raiding the other guys' rooms."

"Let's just start with yours and see how we go."

My dick likes the sound of that.

23

HARRISON

We reach Benny's room, and I kick the door closed behind us. I wasn't lying when I said I missed him because our whole time apart, there's been this deep ache in my chest telling me it's not right.

Am I happy about the cheating? No. But I get how he got to the point he did, and now all I can do is take him at his word that he's going to change.

And be there to help him do it.

Until then, I tug him against my body and lower my mouth to his.

It's immediately electric. The type of high that feels like my body is expanding with helium. When Benny kisses me, I can shut the whole world out because there's nothing more important than the way he clings to me. The way I can still need him so deeply even though he's right here in front of me.

"How do you want it?" I murmur, not wanting to break my lips from his. Not wanting to be further apart than we need to be.

"I don't care. I can do whatever. Top, bottom, side, I'm good with it all."

Okay, that makes me pull back. "What the heck is a side?"

"A man who doesn't like anal. Sure, I like it, but if you don't, it's not a deal breaker for me."

I cup his sweet face in my hands. "Good to know. But I've done it before, and I'm more than ready to do it again."

"Oh, really? You a big ol' top, are you?" His pillowy lips curve evilly, and I can't stop myself from biting into the bottom one. His little gasp is fucking musical, and I love how plump his lip feels as I drag it through my teeth.

"I'm good for whatever too. But I've never been fucked before, so I don't know what to do."

"What have you eaten today?"

That question takes me by surprise. "Ah ... just breakfast. So far. Fruit and granola, why?"

He presses tighter against me. "I bet you're a natural bottom. It's like you knew you had to prepare for me."

"So that was a good choice?"

Benny turns and pushes me down onto his bed. "Best choice. I wanna fuck you, if you're cool with it."

"Yeah." I have no clue what to expect, but my dick is apparently ready to find out. "Definitely."

He strips off his shirt, sending his blond hair wild and giving me the most delicious view of his toned body.

"I want to see you naked. Completely."

"I will if you will. Just ..." He reaches for his phone and fires off a text. "Need to give Em the heads-up to stay away unless he wants to see my bare ass."

"I ..." There's so much I want to ask. Does Em come here often? Are their asses also identical, and if it is, would he really care about that? "Never mind." The last thing I want when I'm with Benny is to be remembering there's a fucking clone of him out there.

He unbuttons his shorts, shoving them down and kicking them off to the side. He's right. He does have hockey thighs. And a hockey butt.

Damn, Benny.

Now all I need is for those boxer briefs to go so I can see the cock straining against them.

"Somehow, I'm more turned on than I've been in my whole life," I say, hurrying to yank my shirt off and wriggle out of my jean shorts. "Fuck me." I give myself a quick tug before going for my underwear.

Benny reaches out and places his hands over mine. "Let me."

The rasp in his voice goes straight to my balls. It's an incredible sound. I let go and lie back, tucking my hands under my head and lifting my ass a bit to make it easier for him.

His gaze is locked on my groin as he curls his fingers under the elastic band and slowly pulls them down.

Shit, it's hot. The way he's staring at me. His chest deepens with every exhale, and then his eyes flutter closed, and he leans in and wraps his lips around my tip.

Ah, damn.

He doesn't try to suck me off, just gently flicks his tongue over my slit like he's tasting me, and I can't stop myself from freeing a hand and burying it in his hair.

"Keep that up, I'm going to be fucking your face in a second."

He pulls off. "Baby, that's not a threat with me."

"Baby, huh?"

He looks ready to roll his eyes. "The shit I say when I'm horny will not be held against me, got it? And you make me so —" He kisses my balls. "So—" The crease of my groin next. "Horny." He runs his tongue along my V. I'm nowhere near as defined as he is, but he doesn't seem to care.

"These cum gutters are going to be the death of me. I can't wait to see you fill them up while I'm fucking you."

"Then stop talking about it and do it." Sure, I might sound more confident than I feel, but I'm also getting way too horny for his teasing as well. Especially when he cradles my balls in his fingers and drags his tongue over the sensitive skin.

"So, tempting to just climb up and sit on you," he says.

I grunt. "Don't tempt me. I'm too curious."

"You wanna feel what it's like for me to be in your ass?"

"Sure do." I know it's apparently supposed to feel good, but I don't know how it could.

He finishes tugging my underwear off, then stands and strips his briefs off in one go. He kicks them to the side as he grabs something from his nightstand and gives his rigid cock a rub.

I can't keep my eyes off it. I'm transfixed. His head is an angry reddish purple, two veins straining the side of his long shaft. He's not too different in size to me, which is surprising, considering I'm taller and wider, and I think the only way we'd know for sure who's bigger is by lining them up, side by side, just like our first time together when I was too distracted to compare.

He flicks open the lid of his lube. "Gonna have to spread those legs open."

I shift them apart, letting my knees roll to the side, and when Benny's attention drops to my ass, I'm torn between turned on or wanting to ask him if he's sure.

Thankfully, I don't get to sit with that doubt for long

because Benny climbs up over the top of me and seals his mouth to mine. He tastes like my cum, which floods my brain with possession, and I'm so distracted by the kiss it takes me a moment to realize his fingers have slipped into my crack.

Huh. Okay. That actually feels better than I expected. My balls are all tingly as he rubs my hole, bringing the nerves there alive. It's the strangest mix of want and being resistant I've ever felt, but even though my ass is telling me no one's supposed to be down there, I know what I want. And what I want is to ignore that stupid little voice and have Benny sink into my ass.

"Am I ready yet?" I ask, holding his face close so he can't stop kissing me.

"I haven't even gotten one finger in you yet."

"Hurry up then. You're being a fucking cocktease."

He pushes one in, and it burns more than I expect it to. His gorgeous eyes are narrowed in challenge as he strokes his finger in and out. "Hurt, did it?"

"Only ... only a small bit."

"I'm not going to fuck you if you lie to me."

"Fine. It hurt. But I'm fine."

"I know you are." He drags his lips over mine. "But now you know that it'll hurt if I go too fast. You need to relax."

"That's a whole lot easier to say when no one is poking at your back door."

His husky laugh is felt in my gut as he takes my hand and reaches behind him. "Do it, then. Poke."

I brush my fingertip over his hole. "Need lube."

"It's right beside us."

I scoop it up as Benny drops his mouth to my neck and sucks his way along it. I try to relax as he fingers me, try to breathe through when he adds a second. To his credit, it doesn't hurt nearly as much as the first time, even when he bites down on my shoulder and works to stretch my hole open.

It's a completely different position to what I normally take in the bedroom, but the longer I settle into it, the more I like it. Lying back, spread open for him while he prepares my body for his cock.

Once my fingers are lubed up, I reach for him as well. It's hard to concentrate on following what he did to me when Benny has my whole body tuned in to him and the lust coursing through me, but I start out rubbing, waiting until he's loose enough to press inside.

"Shit yes," he rumbles against my throat. "Gimme two."

"Can you take that?"

"I've been playing with my ass a long time. I've got this."

Two it is, then. I add the next finger as he does the same, and as I fuck them into his ass, Benny writhes on top of me. His steely cock grinds against my leg, leaking precum all over my skin, as I loosen enough for him to fuck his fingers in and out. "You're ready," he says. "But hold on."

He leaves his fingers buried deep as he straightens, forcing mine to slip out. He reaches for his nightstand again, and after tossing condoms beside us, he pulls something else out.

"A butt plug?" I ask.

With an evil grin, he tosses it to me. "Shove it up my ass, then put on a condom. I'm going to fuck you until I come, and then I'm going to bounce on your cock until you do." Benny leans over me again, face hovering just above mine. "You don't know what you prefer yet, so let's figure it out at once."

"I don't know how the hell I'm going to hold off coming if your cock feels anything like your fingers."

"You have no idea. Put it in."

I reach down and have to feel my way toward lining it up with his hole. Once I've got it there, I push the metal plug forward with little resistance.

He moans and moves his fingers again, pressing them harder

and faster this time. We don't kiss; he just stares down at me the whole time I'm filling him with the plug. It sinks in until the exact moment his ass swallows it, leaving only the flared base sticking out.

"I can't wait until that's your cock," he says.

"I can't wait either. Literally. I don't think I can."

He presses a quick kiss against my lips, then pushes up on his knees. His fingers leave my ass, and I hate how open I feel. How empty.

I watch Benny tear a condom off the strip and toss it at me, then grab one for himself.

"Put that on, then grab the lube and keep jacking yourself until I'm inside. It might get a bit uncomfortable since you've never taken a dick before, but it shouldn't hurt. Stretching or a small ache, good. Burning fiery pits of hell, bad. Got it?"

I roll the condom down my dick. "Just fuck me already."

"Don't need to tell me twice." He takes my thighs and pushes them back, spreading them further in the process. Then, he knee walks closer until he can press his cock to my hole. Nerves and excitement spike at once.

He gestures toward my neglected dick. "Give him some love."

Right. I fill my palm with lube, and it's instant relief as I stroke myself.

Benny uses my distraction to push forward. He's right—it is borderline uncomfortable, but it doesn't hurt. He goes slow, which probably helps, stopping every inch or so to pull back slightly and go again. Over and over until I swear he must be close because I feel like I've been split in half.

And I don't hate it.

My dick is still hard and leaking, and once Benny's pubes meet my ass, it's like everything clicks into place. His thrusts are slow and shallow, but I love the feel of him so deep inside me.

"You should feel the way your greedy ass is sucking me in," he says, rolling his hips in a way that hits something amazing.

I let go of my dick. "Whatever you did then, do it again."

He chuckles and does, and that same rush of pleasure shoots through me. It's indescribable the way my balls tighten every time Benny hits the spot. Some of the awkwardness is still hanging on, but it's quickly dissolving the more confident Benny gets.

His hold on my thighs is strong, and his abs are contracting with each thrust, and when the weirdness finally disappears all together, I push back to meet him.

Benny is the sexiest fucking sight I've ever seen, and even though I've been curious about sex with a man, I never thought it would be like that. To be hungry for it. To be begging him silently to go harder. Faster. To fight my instincts to strangle my dick and get myself to the finishing line.

His eyes are hooded, lips parted, and I'm on the same level. The little crease between his eyebrows drives me wild, and I want to bite it. I want to pull him closer and taste myself on his tongue again, but Benny's pounding the life out of me, and I'm too afraid that if I touch him, he'll stop.

He can't stop. Not now.

He's owning my body. I've never had that sappy connection from sex, but I'm getting it now. Heart too big. Balls too full. The intense need to hold him down and make him come. To do anything I need to for him to feel good.

The thoughts in my brain are all soft as I watch him, but the thoughts in my dick are hot as fuck. His pecs, his abs, the sheen of sweat over him. The light strip of chest hair I didn't know he had but definitely fucking appreciate from my position looking up at him.

Benny flicks his wild curls over to one side, and the sight of a random one sticking to his neck takes me back. To the Jell-O wrestling, and the flirting, and the feel of his slick skin against mine.

"You better fucking hurry up," I beg.

He's panting when he replies. "I can slow down and draw it out more. Give us a chance to breathe and calm down."

"No." I shake my head hard so he knows I'm serious, my cap digging into the back of my neck. "I need to blow. Come on, Benny. Please. Fuck. I want to come in you so bad."

"Shit." His fingers grip tight as he picks up the speed, making his bedposts bounce off the wall with frenzied thuds. The sound is so hot I reach for my balls, gripping them tight and trying to keep my mind off the pleasurable ache building near my spine.

Benny cries out and stiffens, cock twitching where he's buried inside me, but before I can check if he came, he pulls out, straddles my waist, and pulls the butt plug out. There's no hesitation as he sinks down on my cock and almost makes me see stars.

"Fuck, you're tight."

"Yeah? How do you think your virgin hole just felt?" He laughs as his mouth covers mine. The kiss has my toes curling into the mattress.

I tilt my head again, and again, my damn hat digs in. I grab it to toss it across the room when Benny takes it from me instead. Then, he holds my gaze and flicks it backward before pulling it down over his hair.

"Shiiiit," hisses between my teeth, and I close my hands over his hips to steady him as I get to take my turn. I thrust up, cock so full and balls so tight that this really isn't going to take long. He's clamped tight around me, hockey thighs helping him bounce frantically on my cock. His spent dick is still half-hard, bobbing between us, and I can't get over how sexy I find it. How sexy I find him.

Hovering over me, wearing my hat, all that muscle and cock on display. Now he's gotten off, his smirk is back as he watches me fuck him, chasing my own high. I can't get enough. Can't decide if I even want to come, but the pressure building in my gut makes it clear that isn't my choice anymore.

It's inevitable.

So close.

Building.

Higher.

"*Nrg fuck.*"

It crashes into me, and my head drops back as I close my eyes against the room and blacken out everything but the way orgasm takes over. I'm coming for ages, then just when I think it's done, aftershocks take their turn.

I'm panting when I'm steady enough to open my eyes.

I'm expecting more cockiness, but Benny's face is soft.

"God, I loved seeing you come."

That makes me laugh.

"I wanna do it again."

I pull him down to crush him against my chest. "Give me a minute."

"Only a minute?"

"Or two. Jesus."

He's already hard again as he snuggles his face into my neck.

"My hat looks good on you." I trail my fingertips down his spine.

"And my cum would look good on you. We never did make use of those cum gutters."

I slap his ass, then slide the condom off him. "Go on, then. Show me what you can do."

So he does. Benny jerks off until he paints my stomach with his cum and then collapses on top of me, finally soft.

The whole time he's touching himself, all I can think is that I nearly lost this.

And I never want to do that again.

24

BENNY

I'm kicked back in the greenhouse on the foldout chair I brought with me. There's a class on across the other side, but Harrison is working hard on whatever it is in front of him, and I tagged along because I'm a moron who has a boyfriend, and apparently, that makes me a little obsessed.

"Why don't you play anymore?" Harrison asks without looking up from the notebook he's scribbling in.

"Play what?"

"Hockey. I'm guessing you played for a while to get the body you have."

"Basically my whole life."

"So ..."

I make a farting noise with my mouth because I goddamn hate talking about it. "I'm sort of a ... legacy. My two older brothers played, and Asher was cocky enough to win the

Stanley Cup in his rookie year. You think I'm a pain in the ass? You should meet him."

"It sounds like you had a future there, then. What happened?"

"I hated it."

Harrison looks up at last. "Why'd you play for so long, then?"

"It's not the sport I hate. It's the pressure. The media. The way they treated my brothers, especially Asher, was fucked-up, and then I went back and saw some of the things they wrote about West before he left to look after us. My brother was wild, but it went too far."

"I'm really sorry."

"Me too."

"If you don't like the media, then why are you looking at sports journalism?"

"It's easier to change things from within than without. Those fuckers need stricter guidelines."

"Yeah, but they don't have those guidelines because the more sensational what they're reporting, the more it sells."

"I know that, but ..." I bounce my foot where it's rested on my other ankle. "There has to be a better way. I hate that they can hurt people and get away with it. When Em and I were headed for the draft, they dug up everything about our parents. It's all we heard about. If we think they're proud of us, how they'd feel if they were alive. How the fuck were we supposed to know that? We were eight when they died. We barely remember them. Em felt guilty about that, and every time some fucking reporter asked some variation of the same question, he died a bit inside. It's why I got us the fuck away from there. I got tired of seeing my brother drowning." And I got tired of drowning myself. The constant doubt about whether I'd have any skill at all without Em was eating at me.

Harrison smiles my way.

"That was supposed to be a depressing story. Why the fuck do you look so happy about it?"

The bastard is smug as fuck when he says, "You talked feelings to me again."

I cross my arms. "I'm gonna cut my tongue out."

"Not allowed. I have too much fun with that tongue."

He sure does. I finally got his dick in my mouth the other day, and he was begging by the time I was done with him.

"We could be having fun with it now, but you're all wahh schoolwork."

"Sorry I don't have a twin brother to do it for me."

"Fuck you very much. I went to class today, didn't I?"

He hums and looks pointedly toward my bag on the floor. "And you're supposed to be reviewing it."

Reviewing it isn't going to help when it's like reading another language. My brain was screaming at me the whole time I tried to note, word for word, what Professor Brooks was saying. None of it makes any sense.

I'm well and truly fucked, but I can't tell Harrison that.

"If you're not going to study, want to help me so we can get out of here?"

"To fuck?"

"To go to the *library* and study."

I pretend to die in my chair.

"Come on, Benny. You'll feel better once you've wrapped your head around it."

All lies, but I pull my ass up anyway and head his way. "What first?"

"I'm going to do some pruning, and I'll get you to make up some more baking soda spray. All the shit we need for it is down there." He points toward the lower shelf of a metal cart.

I duck down and glance between the mix of unfamiliar things.

"Grab the spray bottle," he says.

I pick it up.

"How much is left in there?"

I look from him to the bottle and back again. Then I lift it higher so he can see. "Ah ... this much."

"It needs to be a liter. The measurements are on the side, so check what's in there and top it up."

My eyes go unfocused, brain chugging along at a snail's pace. "What the fuck is a liter?"

"Metric system, baby. Just under ... about a quarter of a gallon."

"A gallon." My cheeks are getting hot, and my tongue feels too fat to swallow. Right. I know what a gallon is. We constantly had milk in the fridge growing up. So, if a gallon is *that* and this spray bottle is this size, and then it needs to be a quarter ... it means ... it means ...

I toss the spray bottle back on the cart with a forced laugh. "No way am I doing that while you get to massacre a tree. Budge up, I want a turn."

"We're not *massacring* my babies."

I lean in to inspect Stacy. "That leaf looks kinda brown."

"It's not."

"How do you know?"

"Because she's perfect. Seriously, I just need the spray to keep them safe from bugs. These guys need to be perfect."

Shit. Distract, distract. "Why do they have to be perfect?"

"Because I want to show people how beautiful plants are. How they thrive with the proper care. If we look after them—"

I let out a loud snore. "Tell them about the poison."

The look he gives me is all indulgence. "Not every plant is poisonous."

"Look, you know I adore you, and Stacy is my most favorite girl ever." I blow her a kiss. "But I'm sorry, if you want people to care, you have to talk about cool shit."

His whole face morphs into confusion. "But plants *are* cool!"

"Yeah, of course they are. I know." I'm totally fucking lying. "But you have to make them cool for *other* people."

"I'm trying."

"Are you though?" I throw a look at Rich. "Zero shade to Rich, but who hasn't seen a rose before?"

"Women love roses?"

"No." I gesture at Stacy. "Women love death. Women want to hear stories about carnivorous plants out for revenge. Ones that slowly strangle the lives from their partners."

Harrison gives me a blank look. "You really know nothing about plants. Or women."

"Maybe, but find me a woman who wouldn't rather learn about how to make poisons for their enemies from plants."

He grunts and pets Rich. "Women are weird."

"Hey, you're the one who's attracted to them."

"So, if that's what women want, what do men want?"

"Sex."

Harrison's gaze runs hotly over me. "For you, maybe."

"Every single, allo man wants sex. It is what it is. Why do you think it's so well known in advertising that sex sells?" I prod Stacy. "Think you can conduct a pollination porno? That'd get people interested."

"I don't think it'd be anywhere near as sexy as you're imagining."

"Ah. Damn. Then I'm out of ideas." Although ... "Maybe *we* do the porno ... on *top* of plants. And you ramble a whole bunch of plant facts while you fuck me. Screw having a charity event— just put it up on OnlyFans and rake in the money. If you dress up as a plant, it'd still be hot as fuck but *also* weird as hell, which would target two markets. Then I'm sure there's more weirdos like you with a plant fetish—*Ooh!* I could dress up as a bee. Your Benny-Bee. Mmm ... pollinate me, Harrison."

He laughs so hard at my ingenious idea that the class on the other side of the greenhouse looks over our way.

"I take it that's a no, then."

He's wheezing. "That's a please never put that image in my head again. Oh, god. All I can picture is one of those flowers from the *Alice in Wonderland* cartoon, doing the creepy caterpillar. Fucking hell, Benny-Bee."

"Ah, but you like the nickname."

He sighs when he catches his breath. "That was fun, but you actually have given me an idea."

I light up, but he quickly shakes his head.

"*Not* porn. No costumes."

"Then ..."

"People want the weird shit. Death and sex and whatever. I know weird shit. Mother nature is *full* of weird shit." He starts excitedly tapping away on his laptop. "Look at this."

I move beside him to see the screen and the little purple flowers on it before reading the title across the top. "The naked-man orchid—*what?*" My face almost hits the screen in my hurry to look, and sure enough, the purple flowers look like little men wearing flower hats with something unmistakable between their legs. "Look at their little peens."

"Cool, right?"

"Very. This is the shit people want to know about. What else you got?"

And that's how we spend the afternoon with Harrison excitedly telling me about plants.

I don't even have to pretend to be interested this time.

25

HARRISON

My Benny is a fucking genius. I have a list of the weird and wonderful as long as my arm, and now that I have some direction for my capstone project, I'm jumping into stage one. Seeing if this idea holds water before I begin my project next year.

The excitement buzzing in my veins tells me that I'm on the right track. Learning about plants stimulates me, interests me, and I can never shut up about them. This idea though, it's next-level, and I can't wait to put it into practice.

"Okay, so." I pace my area of the greenhouse, loving that Benny is hanging on to my every word. That's a good first sign. "How do we test this hypothesis? I'm going to need some kind of sample audience. A control group and a test group ..."

Benny's eyes glaze over.

"Don't judge me!"

He holds up his hands, clearly trying to look awake. "No judgment. I'm super interested."

I walk over to where he's sitting on the table next to my laptop and step between his legs. "Thank you."

"For?"

"Being fucking incredible and interested enough to try and help me with this?"

A little of his snark melts as he wraps his hands around my neck. "You're cute when you're being nerdy."

"I'll take that as a compliment."

"Why would it be anything else?" He smiles so innocently I pinch his side.

"You know, I can tell the difference between you and Em, but sometimes ..." I hesitate. "I might need to start checking your hand whenever I see you as my insurance policy."

"You really think we'd switch places on you?" He looks hurt, so I hurry to clarify.

"No, like, if I want to just walk up and kiss you or grab your ass or something, I don't want to accidentally get the wrong guy. That's all."

"You mean you *don't* want to be the meat in a twin sandwich?"

My face twists. "What? No. Do you do that?"

Benny snickers. "Never. But we've been asked a lot, and I wanted to make sure that wasn't on your mind."

"Ah. Well, no. You're safe." I lean in, brushing my mouth over his before pushing my tongue inside. Fuck, it feels good to be able to kiss him when I want to. I'm still waiting for that moment to hit, the one where I realize being in a relationship isn't for me, but thankfully, nothing yet. Every day I'm more excited to see him than the last one. With our class work, and Benny's frat duties, and spending time with our friends, we don't get to catch up every day, and on the days I don't see him, it makes me grumpy. Full days like this are rare.

"As soon as we're done here, you're coming home with me," I tell him.

"Finally!" Benny goes to jump off the table, but I hold him firm.

"Not now. When we're finished. I'm not finished."

Benny makes a sound of protest before giving in. "Fine. What are we doing?"

"Figuring out a way to test your sex-sells theory."

"Isn't me being a thousand percent more interested proof enough?"

"Nope. Sorry, babe, but it's a thing in science. You need a decent sample size, otherwise it could be a fluke." Still between his legs, I slide my laptop around to face us, then type in "group research ideas."

Benny looks around the room instead. "Why don't you do something here?"

"What do you mean?"

"Well, it's a greenhouse. Sure, pictures of those things are cool, and you could show people a slideshow all day long, but imagine having them actually here?"

"The plants?"

"Yes! Those ones that smell like a decaying body would be a real draw card."

I laugh into his shoulder. "Or make everyone evacuate the scene."

"Come on. Seeing them in person would be so much cooler."

"You have a point." I rub my jaw. "I'd have to source them all though, then organize the event—what kind would I even do? Like an expo type of thing?"

"A dinner."

I blink at him. "That sounds like a lot of work."

"Maybe, but people love them. The NHL does it all the

time. A charity dinner to get people in the door, charge them a per-plate cost, and then get them to empty their pockets."

That sounds … ambitious. "I was thinking more two groups, one shown everyday plants and one shown the kinds we looked up today—"

He makes a buzzer sound. "How do you measure that?"

"A simple 'does this interest you' quiz."

"While that sounds sufficiently stiff and boring, you're better than that. Your whole appeal is your personality—"

"Thanks."

He waves me off. "You're hot too, *obviously*, but you're the kind of person people are drawn to. You want people to care about plants? *You* need to be the one making them. And how better to make people pay attention to what you're doing than by money? Money talks. I see it in hockey all the time. They plaster dollar figures all over their social medias, like those numbers mean anything."

"So, I have a dinner for an environmental charity?" I'm not really asking, just talking through it. "I could reach out and see if anyone is interested in helping. Try to get plants here. Hit up Professor Nottering to see if I can hold it in the greenhouse. Maybe I can get a not-for-profit on board …"

"See?" Benny squeezes me. "You're way too much of a personality to do some basic test."

"Only problem is that for this to work, I'd have to throw *two* dinners. Otherwise, the results are inconclusive."

"You're telling me there have never been charity events for the environment before now?"

He's right. Maybe if I can match up what I'm doing with one of those, it'll hold enough weight for passable results. After all, this doesn't have to be a perfect experiment. It's preliminary, a way for me to test whether this is the thing I want to be completing my capstone project on.

"This is good," I say. "This is *really* good."

I want to ask him if he'll help me with it, if he can be a part of my team with getting this organized, but I hold off. Benny has more than enough on his plate with his schoolwork, and that was before he had to take statistics for himself.

If I'm honest, it's something I do feel bad about. It's clear he struggles with it and isn't happy, but it's not like I could pretend not to know while he gets a degree thanks to his brother's hard work. It's unethical. Even if I really, really hate seeing him struggle in class and want to fix it all for him.

I move toward a pad of paper and a pen to jot myself out a list before I forget it all.

"How long have we been here?" he asks, looking toward the wall at where the sun is sinking in an orange display.

"Not sure. What's the time?"

"My phone's died." Considering he only got it back from being fixed a few days ago, I'm not surprised he forgot.

"Clock's over there." I point toward the far wall behind me.

Benny doesn't answer, and after a couple of moments, I glance up to find him staring toward where I pointed. He looks confused, but when I follow his gaze, the clock is right where I thought it was.

"You okay?"

He snaps out of whatever that was and grins. "Be better if we were back at your place already."

As much as that distracts me, I also can't shake that something ... isn't right. "What time is it?"

Benny points at the clock. "Right over there, remember?"

My gaze swings from him and over to the clock again. Is he ... No. There's no way Benny doesn't know how to tell the time. I'm torn between pushing him to read it out for me and letting it go, but it all comes down to the fact that I don't want to make him uncomfortable.

"Silly me," I say, trying to shake the feeling. But the clock reminds me of the baking soda spray and the measurements for our dinner. I know Benny said he struggles with math because he's never had to do it, but *that* much? Time is something you learn in, like, second grade, right?

Benny's behind, but he's not *that* behind. I can't imagine there were a lot of opportunities to switch classes in primary school.

Most likely scenario is that he zoned out.

"Past seven," I mutter, and Benny nods like he knew that all along. I can't shake the feeling that I don't believe it though. "We got here around two."

"Cool."

"Then we've been here ..." I don't know why I do it. Trail off like that. Like I can't do a simple subtraction, but I wait for Benny to fill in the blanks.

He doesn't.

Just gazes at me like he's waiting.

I swallow, feeling like I've taken a wrong step somewhere. "Five hours. We've been here five hours."

"Oh, shit."

The genuine surprise in his tone doesn't help things.

"I had no idea it had been that long." He jumps off where he's sitting on the table. "I've gotta study for this stupid test tomorrow."

"The one in statistics?"

"Yep." He doesn't sound like he's dreading it, so that's promising.

"Want some help?"

"Nah, you have your own stuff to do. Em will be home, so he'll help me go over it all."

I hate that I took up all of his time though. "Fuck, I'm sorry.

You shouldn't have been here helping me when you have your own stuff going on."

"Yeah, no." He steps closer, wrapping one of his hands around mine. "I like helping you."

"That sounds like a lie."

"Normally it would be, but if it wasn't for you, I wouldn't know about the vagina plant."

I beg for patience. "For the last time, it's called a Hydnora."

"I can guarantee if you call it a vagina plant at your dinner, the men will suddenly develop deep pockets."

"And now I'm picturing someone trying to stick their dick in ..." I shudder at the imagery.

He pecks me on the lips. "My work here is done. Enjoy."

"You're really going to leave me like that?"

Benny rubs his hand over where my dick is, shamefully, a little hard. "You really *do* love plants."

"What do I see in you?" It's a rhetorical question, but of course, he answers.

"A hot guy with a big cock."

I catch him before he can leave, feeling all fluttery with him beside me. "You are so much more than that."

26

BENNY

Sweat prickles its way down my back as I stare at my notes, begging for any of it to make sense. I'm not stupid, I'm *not*, but this is really making me think I might be. How the hell does anyone understand this shit? How the hell does anyone remember what the fuck all of these numbers mean?

"Benny?"

I jump at the dining room table and find Em leaning over me.

The house is dark and quiet, but I still look around to make sure none of my frat brothers see us.

"What are you doing?"

"Wondering where the hell my brother is."

I frown. "What do you mean?"

He smiles softly and taps my phone screen, lighting it up to show it's 3:00 a.m.

"And?"

"You've been at this for six hours."

"I *have?*" Jesus. No wonder my brain feels like it's been pressed through a strainer.

"You started at nine."

"I'll take your word for it." Other than being tired though, it's like no time has passed at all. I could spend days on this, and it wouldn't make any more sense to me than it does now. Tears press at the backs of my eyes. Why can't I do this? Why the fuck do numbers have to be so goddamn hard?

I press my fingers into my eye sockets, holding back the urge to scream. "We fucked up, Emmy."

"What do you mean?" The chair scrapes as he pulls it out to sit down.

"We never should have started this. We never should have ..." I swallow back the panic. "I can't do it."

"It's confronting, I know that. I get it. But I'm here. I'll help with whatever I need to. It'll all be okay."

My laugh is bitter. "I still count on my fingers, Em. That's not normal."

"You just never learned. It won't take you long."

"I can't tell the goddamn time! Who do we know who can't tell the time?"

"You *just* told the time."

"Off of my phone. An analog clock makes no goddamn sense to me." I don't know why I'm voicing this. Don't know why all these insecurities are leaking out now, but I can't stop them. I've always been so careful to build up my copying strate-gies—life cheat sheets, in a way—to make sure the things I struggle with stay hidden. Harrison almost picked up on it today, though, and I've never felt more sick in my life. "I can't do the most basic shit, and I'm supposed to be able to understand all this? I don't even know how many times I've read this page, but I don't remember any of it. I have a test tomorrow. I'm going to fail."

"Stop. Breathe."

Kinda hard to breathe when I'm launching into a full-blown panic attack. I can't do this, and he's not listening. He doesn't get it. It'd be like me learning to speak fluent Japanese by tomorrow. By next week. Fuck, even this year.

I know why Harrison made this request. I know why he doesn't want us cheating. I've never regretted anything in my life more than I do this, but it's gotten to a point where I need it. Without passing my classes, there is no degree. No future. My brothers are going to kill me, and I'll be facing the repercussions of this choice for the rest of my goddamn life.

"It'll be hard," Em says. "But you'll get there. You're smart. Learning ten years' worth of stuff at once won't be easy, but a lot will be intuitive. I'll help you. Bowser will help you."

"I'm not going to him for help."

"He'd—"

"No. Goddamn it."

Emmett sighs, and sure, he thinks I'm being ridiculous—I can read it off his face—but I'm not going to the guy I've just started dating and being all, "Hey, I probably couldn't even pass a third-grade math quiz, but that's cool, yeah?"

How fucking embarrassing.

"Fine." He pulls my books and laptop toward himself. "Let's do this."

BY THE TIME I get to class, I'm feeling one tiny bit more confident about my test. Harrison meets me at the door, and I try to return the happy smile he gives me, but I'm not sure I pull it off.

"Hey, it's just one quick test. It'll be over before you know it, and I bet you do better than you think."

I try to hold on to his confidence. "Yeah, we'll see, I guess."

I'm just trying hard to hold on to Em's voice in my head as he explained everything to me. Step by step, take my time, I've got this.

"I'll be waiting for you right out here when you're done."

"Why don't you have to take the test?"

"I'm auditing this class. I've already been through the tests, but none of the information really sank in, which is why I'm going for round two."

"That's a long way to say you like to punish yourself."

He laughs and gently nudges me toward the door. "I'll see you soon."

Probably too soon. Not having him here to sit next to me is both shit because I could have used his support and a blessing because he won't get to see me crash and burn in real time.

As soon as I sit down, Professor Brooks locks the door and sets his timer. He says, "You have an hour and a half to make it through. No talking, please."

An hour and a half?

Tests are one of the things I hate most about school. Even in subjects I know, it's a panic to make sure I get it done in time, and an hour is trackable; an hour and a half is not. With the analog clock up in front of the room, I can visually track a full circle, but anything over that leaves me lost.

He calls start, and the second he does …

Blank.

My whole brain is blank.

I try to set all the work out as I go, but I'm hyperconscious that time is slipping away. Pressure weighs down against me as I try to make it through. Most of the math-heavy ones I skip, but there are a few more logic-focused ones that I can muddle my way through. The working out is hard, and my calculator and notes are my best friend, but my chest keeps getting tighter and tighter every time I try to figure out how long I have left. It has to be close to running out. Half of the test is on paper, and the other is through the computer, which completely loses me before long.

I finally submit the computer side and glance around at everyone still working. The room is hushed; only muffled coughs and the rustle of papers and fingers frantically typing away on their computers keep my thoughts company.

It's tempting to get up, hand in my paper, and leave. I've done what I can, but I don't want to draw attention to being done early, so I turn back to the start of my paper test and try again with the stupid questions that don't make any sense.

This is all the Greek's fault. Probably. I think they're the ones who came up with math. Or maybe it was Cleopatra. She seemed like a smart chick.

Either way, whoever it was can suck a big one because math sucks. It's stupid and useless, and who even needs it anyw—

"Time's up."

My exhale is less relief at this being over and more resignation at the big, fat F coming my way. I stay sitting right where I am as everyone breaks into conversation, grabbing their stuff and making their way out as fast as they can.

The room is emptier when I stand and pack my shit away. I'm not looking forward to handing this in. I'm not looking forward to facing Harrison. Technically, if I didn't hand it in, I'd probably score about the same. My gut is in knots as I drop the paper on Professor Brooks's desk and hightail it for the door.

Harrison's exactly where he said he'd be, and I can't bring myself to drop that happy look from his face. "How was it?"

"It was a test."

He chuckles, taking my bag from me and slinging it over his shoulder.

"I can carry that."

"I know. But you've had a stressful morning, and I can do it just as well as you can."

Instead of being a dick and arguing the point, I let it go. "I ... I don't think it went well," I force myself to say. The last thing I want is for him to have hopes that I'll pull off some miraculous pass when there's no way in hell that will happen.

"I always feel that way after a test too. It's all the stress. But it usually turns out okay, and if not, you can always retake it."

That isn't the reassurance he thinks it is. The thought of having to go through that again makes me want to throw up.

My phone vibrates in my pocket, and I grab it as a way to avoid this conversation. But it's another one I don't want to face.

EM:

How did it go?

I groan and shove my phone away.

"Who was it?" Harrison asks.

"My brother."

"Then why the groan?"

Okay, I guess I'm not avoiding this conversation, then. "He also asked how it went, and it's not something I want to think about."

"In that case, I'll shut up about it, but one more thing."

"Yeah?"

"I'm really proud of you. Sure, you made some shitty choices that got you into this mess, but you're working to fix them. That's important. Maybe more important than people give credit for."

"Does it still count when the only reason I'm fixing my mistakes is because you called me out on being a cheater?"

Harrison thinks about it for a moment, pushing the door at the end of the hall open for me to pass. "It depends. How do you feel now you're not relying on Em?"

"Stupid."

"Benny ..."

I roll my eyes at him, not liking that he can already read me. "Fine. I'm glad I've taken that pressure off him. And, sure, maybe now that I've realized just how behind I am, deep down, waaay deep, under all the fear and self-doubt, I'm kinda glad I'll be working on it. Better late than never and all that."

"Good." Harrison gazes at me with a type of look I don't deserve.

I ignore it. "Can you please feed me now?"

HARRISON

"So, you really never go out together? Ever?" I ask.

Benny and Em exchange glances, and I cannot stress enough how weird it is. I'm in tune with Benny—he feels like a different person to Em—but there's no denying they're completely identical, and seeing my boyfriend's face on another guy is a bit of a head fuck.

"Sometimes," Benny says, tossing a chip up and catching it in his mouth.

"Careful, you'll choke."

He's lying on my living room floor while Em occupies the armchair. They do that exchange look thing again, only this time, they're definitely mocking me.

"Sorry I care."

Em laughs. "It's cute. But no, we don't really get to hang out socially together anymore. The most we do is go to a club a few towns away."

"But I assume everyone knew about you both in high school, so why all the secrecy?"

"Two reasons," Em says.

"We wanted to avoid the usual questions from people about whether we swap identities and classes and share partners—" Benny starts.

"And we didn't want anyone to put together that we're the Dalton duo. The chaos twins."

That was creepy. "You regularly finish each other's sentences?"

"Yep," Em confirms. "Don't worry, I'm sure you and Benny will learn that skill soon enough."

"Right. So, who or what is the Dalton duo?"

Benny throws Em a glare. "Don't."

Thankfully, Em doesn't listen. "Us. It was our nickname in hockey circles."

"That's cute. I got myself a chaos twin."

Benny smothers himself with a cushion.

"What's up with him?" I ask Em.

"He hates being reminded of those days." Em raises his voice. "Back when we were a sure thing for the NHL and everyone loved us."

"Loved us?" Benny throws off the cushion to glare at his brother. "They constantly said we'd be nothing without each other and that we wouldn't be half as good if we were on separate teams."

"We both know they were wrong."

Benny doesn't look like he knows that at all, and as much as I might like finding out more about him and his brother, I also don't want to be talking about subjects he clearly doesn't like.

I'm not sure where else to take the conversation though. I can't ask Em what he's studying because that'll only bring up the expulsion and how worried Benny is about it. I can't ask about his future plans because as far as I know, he hasn't even talked to his brother about them. Who would have thought it would be so hard to talk to someone who looks exactly the same as the person I like most?

"Awkward ..." Benny sings, and Em kicks him.

"Sorry," I laugh. "It's just bizarre trying to wrap my head around being friends with Em but dating you. I'll get there, but give me a minute."

"It wasn't on purpose, you know," Em says.

Benny and I have been over that. It's obvious that nothing they did was malicious, but if they hadn't done it to begin with, no one would have been confused. Still, it's all been set right now, which is the main thing.

"Harrison was saying the other day that he was going to grab you on the ass," Benny says, and I want to hit him with that damn cushion.

"I didn't say that. I said I have to be careful that it doesn't happen."

"He likes hockey butts."

I raise my eyes to the ceiling, but he doesn't stop.

"Bet he couldn't tell the differences between our asses in a lineup. Should I be offended?"

"You should stop talking," I point out.

"Yeah, Benny, stop talking." Em hits him with the cushion I'd wanted to, and then Benny tackles him, and I'm left watching them wrestle on the ground. How do I love this guy?

Jesus, he—*wait*.

Waaaait.

Love?

My thoughts snap to a halt because no way should I be there yet. We've only been together officially a few weeks. There's still a lot we don't know about each other, but as I watch him pull Em's hair as Em tries to get him into a headlock, all I do is smile. Warmed at the sight of him so happy when he's been in his head a lot since he took that test in statistics.

It also shows me where he learned those skills he used against me in the kiddie pool.

But somehow, I can't shake the L-word from my brain.

IT GETS EASIER to talk to them, and by the time Em leaves a few hours later, it's not *completely* weird anymore. Only a tiny bit.

"Sure he'll get home okay?" I ask from where I'm sucking on Benny's balls.

He flicks off my hat and runs his fingers through my hair before directing me back to his dick. "He'll be fine."

I swallow his cock, and the sounds he lets out has my balls high and tight. We have sex at every opportunity, but it still isn't enough. I crave him, whether it's a quickie in any private place we can find on campus, long, teasing sessions where we make each other as horny as possible, or times like now. No rush to get off, just enjoying each other's bodies. And fuck am I enjoying this.

I love being between Benny's strong thighs. Love the taste of his skin and the feel of his balls under my tongue. The texture difference from his tight, hard sac to the silky-smooth skin over his cock to the glistening tip. Getting to touch and taste, to be able to swallow him down and keep him in my mouth, all of it makes me so hard I can barely see.

The tunnel vision gets me good.

His gravelly sigh is music to my ears, and I double down on my efforts, wanting to make him feel as good as possible.

I'm only new to sucking dick, and I've only sucked this one, but I can't help but think that's a good thing. No other dude could measure up to my Benny. It wouldn't be fair on them to come after him.

"Put my balls back in your mouth," he begs. "Both of them."

I pop off him and do exactly what he says. My mouth wraps eagerly around him, and I run my tongue from one rounded side to the other.

His chest is rising and falling under harsh breaths as he releases my hair and wraps his hand around his cock instead. Each stroke is slow, smooth, with a grip that makes his knuckles stand out.

I want to be the one to do it, but as I watch him touch himself, it's too much for me. I have to strangle my own cock with some much-needed strokes, otherwise I'd probably come all over my sheets.

His cock is leaking, so I swipe some of the precum with my free hand and reach back to rub it over his hole. I haven't topped him again since the first time, both because of our schedules and because a lot of the time, we're so horny we don't get that far. I'm not in any hurry though.

"Fuck, Harry," he moans, back arching from my bed. "I'm so close you're gonna make me come."

I release his balls and run my tongue over them. "That's what I'm aiming for here. But I'd prefer if you did it in my mouth."

"Better hurry up, then. I'm gonna shoot."

He doesn't need to tell me twice. I'd keep his cock in my mouth always, if I could.

I suck him deep, still getting the hang of this deep-throating thing, but the way his grip returns to my hair makes me think I'm on the right track.

"Yeah, right ... now ..." His cum floods my mouth, and I drink it down greedily. Once he's done, I grab his hip and flip him onto his front, then jack myself off over him. All it takes is gripping one cheek and spreading it open to see his hole, and then I'm coming.

I release into his crease, loving the way my cum runs over his hole and reaches his balls. Then, I rub my cockhead over the mess, using it to rub my cum into his skin.

When I'm done, I lean down to press a kiss between his shoulder blades. His legs twist back, ankles linking over mine, locking me in place.

"Can't go anywhere now," he says sleepily into my pillow.

"Good." I nuzzle behind his ear. "I have no plans to."

Benny passes out not long after, but I'm still wide-awake. I lie there and watch him, the way the moonlight through the trees outside creates patterns on his face, his slightly parted, pillowy lips, the dark eyelashes on his cheeks.

When he sleeps, he's finally relaxed.

And it's in the dark that I can well and truly acknowledge that it might be fast, but this is definitely love.

28

BENNY

Leaving Harrison naked and alone in bed is a crime I don't want to commit. I love lying there and tracing his freckles, finding where one tanned shade blends into the next before tapering off to his stark white ass.

"Where are you going?" he mutters, half-asleep. It won't be long until he's up for his morning jog, but I want to get home and ready for class so I don't miss anything. There's also a rumor we're supposed to be getting our stats grades today, and I don't want to be around Harrison when they come in.

The last thing I'm going to do is tell him that, though, because he's always so endlessly positive about it. Poor guy doesn't realize how shitty that makes me feel.

"Home. Gotta shower before class since *someone* decided to give me a cum bath last night."

"What can I say? It looks good on you."

I smirk as I step into my shorts and T-shirt from yesterday.

Even after a few years in California, it's still odd to be mid-October and not need a jacket.

"What do you have on today?" I ask.

"Going to work on your charity idea. Think it could be fun, and I had some ideas last night."

"That's awesome." I lean down to kiss him goodbye, but all it does is make me want to crawl back into bed. It's stupid how quickly I've become addicted to this, and it scares me. Going all in with someone, giving them the power to hurt me, it's not something I do lightly. Emotions and feelings are something I avoid for exactly that reason. I loved my parents, and look where that got me.

I might not be able to remember a lot, but I'll never forget how it felt when they were gone.

I'm sure Harrison isn't planning on dying on me in a hurry, but deciding he's done with me and my shit, that's a real possibility, and I'm constantly having to remind myself to play it cool.

No matter how desperately I want to be around him.

I pull away and stuff my feet into my flip-flops before heading to the door. "I'll text you later."

My phone beeps in my pocket, but before I pull it out, I glance back over at him, finding his phone in his hand.

"Beat you," he says.

I act like I'm embarrassed by him, but the second I step outside of his room, I grab my phone, open the message, and almost die at the heart hands emoji he's sent me.

I'm in so much fucking trouble.

I don't think my heart has ever felt like this before.

My bossy GPS gets me home, and just as I've pulled up in one of the vacant spots out front of the DIK house, my phone goes off again. I'm assuming it's Harrison, so when I find a notification for the student portal instead, my good mood takes a rapid nosedive.

Fuck.

This has to be my result.

I stare at my phone without seeing it, no clue how long I sit there, debating with myself over my next step. If I don't open it, I'll never know how bad it is. Living in delulu-land sounds like a fucking perfect decision to me because it comes with Harrison and orgasms and no knowledge of just how much I've fucked up my degree.

If I don't open it, does it even exist?

I think no. Not so sure Professor Brooks would agree with me, but *so what* he's a qualified professor? That doesn't mean he's right.

I'm on the verge of opening it when I swallow, shove my phone away, and climb out of my car instead. I know I've failed—there's literally no way I could have passed—but it doesn't stop that hopeful little voice that's crying out for some miracle here. And that hopeful voice feels nice.

Opening this stupid result puts an end to that.

The first thing I do is creep into my bedroom, where Em is sleeping, grab some clean clothes, and then shower. I'm done faster than I thought because the house still has that pre-dawn stillness to it, and it's not until I'm done making a shake that people finally start to appear. Brothers come in and out, getting ready for their day. Even though we don't exchange many words, I still like this, the being around people. The company gives me a boost, even if I don't do anything with it.

Until Big Wally walks in and grabs me in a headlock. "Dalty-boy. Make me breakfast? You shouldn't have!" He swipes my shake and drinks half of it in one go.

What was that I said about liking people?

I pump my eyebrows at him. "How'd my boyfriend's cum taste?"

"What?"

"Gotta get that extra protein in early."

Wally looks from me to the shake and back again, skin slowly tinging green. "You're fucking with me."

"Okay. You gonna drink some more and call my bluff?"

He scowls and sets my cup down, looking disgusted when I pick it up to finish off. Fuck him. That'll teach him to swipe something from me again.

"Boyfriend?" he finally says when he looks like he's not going to be sick anymore. "Is that why you've been all sunshiny and shit?"

"What?"

He laughs. "You've been a real Miss Congeniality lately."

"Fuck off."

"The guys and I were talking about it the other day. Happy looks good on you, Ben."

It sinks in that they're not talking about me at all. Em has obviously been spending some time with these doofuses and ruining my street cred. I'll have to remind him that if he wants to be me around the house, he's going to have to learn how to scowl more.

Still, I can't find even a shred of annoyance that Em has been hanging out with my friends as me.

I kinda like it.

He needs more people to be around.

I just wish he could do it as himself. Maybe it's time to revisit the college conversation. I'm still struggling to believe my brother lit a fucking fire, even as an accident, but mistakes shouldn't ruin your whole life. I mean, shit. I'm getting a second chance to make mine right.

With that thought comes the reminder of my test results, and my gut crashes through the floor again.

"Still." Wally pulls out some cereal. "Can't believe you're

settling down with someone. Who the hell wants to be crippled by commitment junior year?"

"Well, that's not something you need to worry about. No one wants to commit to you."

"Thank fuck. I couldn't imagine anything worse than being locked down. Campus is big, but it's not that big, y'know. Imagine trying to pick up at Shenanigans and your ex is there?" A shudder ripples through his body.

"Just because you've fucked half of campus and regularly get drinks thrown at you doesn't mean we all do."

"Be real, Dalton. Relationships at our age don't last. So what's the point? College is all about sowing your seeds, and boyfriends will just get in the way of that." He nods at me like he's just given life-changing advice. "You know what I'm saying."

"Sure do." I'll say anything at this point to escape, and once I've dumped my shake cup in the dishwasher, I swipe a banana and leave.

Emmett's awake when I get back to the room, still in bed, though, and scrolling through his phone.

"What are you doing?" I ask.

"Just realizing that while I might have hung out with a bunch of these people, I was never actually friends with any of them. I thought you were supposed to make college besties and whatever?"

"Kinda have to be in college for that."

He blows me a kiss, courtesy of his middle finger.

Normally that kind of shit would make me tackle him, but between Big Wally's life lessons and this test result hanging over my head, I'm deflated.

I drop onto the side of my bed, and Em's immediately on high alert.

"Why are we sad? What happened? Do I need to kill Harrison?"

I snort and kick him. "No. It's fine. I just ..."

"Yeah?"

"College relationships don't last forever."

"What the fuck are you talking about?" Em screws up his nose and lifts his phone, showing off a picture of Asher, his boyfriend, Kole, and their fur babies. "You gonna tell them that?"

"They're the exception. Not the rule."

"Ah. So, you're just going to freak out over something that hasn't happened yet. Makes sense."

It's my turn to flip him off. "Big Wally's an idiot. I don't know why it's sticking in my brain."

"Well, that's easy—you like him. Harrison. Not Wally. I like him too, by the way—even before you started dating—and Harrison isn't the kind of guy to play games."

I give Em a dry look and wave my hand down the front of myself. "It's not him I'm worried about. Kind of a hot mess over here."

"This better not be about the math thing again." He sounds at the end of his patience. "He doesn't give a shit about that."

"Yeah, but maybe I do. I got my results."

Em goes from exasperated to wary. "How did you do?"

The worry in his voice matches what I'm feeling, and it's a relief that he's not pretending to be optimistic. That voice in my head is already too far out of line.

"Haven't opened it yet."

"Then do it now."

"I don't want confirmation of how badly I did."

Em's back to being exasperated, and he climbs up beside me and takes my phone. He opens it with his own face—smart-ass—and logs in to the student portal. "You ready for this?"

"Nope."

"Too bad."

The sharp intake of breath doesn't tell me anything, only that the result is a shock. Fuck, did I get a *zero*?

I snatch my phone back and take a second to look at the grade on the screen. *Thirty-two percent.*

The sinking feeling in my gut tells me it's not good, but it's also not a zero. I just don't get what thirty-two means. "How ... how bad is it?" I ask.

"It's ... it's an F, Benny."

An F. *F.* I'd been pretty sure it was coming, but being faced with the reality ... *fuck.*

"I was really hoping—" he whispers, but he's drowned out by the ringing in my ears.

The test was open fucking book. Open book, and I still failed big-time. It doesn't matter how much I blink back the frustrated shimmering in my vision, the numbers don't change. Just get bigger, brighter, taunt me that I don't even understand one stupid fucking grade, yet I somehow have to pass a math course to get my degree.

I unstick my throat. "Think they have first-grade math on the curriculum?"

"Don't joke."

"Why not? I am one big fucking joke."

Like it's timed, a message from Harrison comes through.

> I saw the email go out that results have been posted. How did you do?

All I can picture is writing back that I got an F and seeing his face fall. Seeing how disappointed he'd be.

I close out of the message, knowing I can't reply.

I don't even know how I'll face him after this.

29

HARRISON

The fact Benny doesn't immediately write back to my message tells me this isn't good. The fact he hasn't written back by that night tells me it's really, really *not* good.

It's hard not to feel guilty. It's hard to know the guy I've fallen for is struggling because of a limit I set. I'm almost tempted to message him and just tell him to have Em take the class, but I won't.

As much as I hate knowing he's probably failed, I can't support cheating.

The clock thing from the other day keeps coming back to me, and at this point, it's not even completely about the cheating either.

Benny needs this. Emmett probably too. They've never had to stand on their own before, and while I'd never want to split the twins up, it's more about getting them not to rely on each other so much.

The other night when I saw them together, it was clear that when one struggled, the other would save them. As soon as I had that thought, I was tuned in to every little thing that was out of the ordinary.

Struggling with a word? The other one would jump in.

Bored? The other was their entertainment.

When dinner came, I asked how we were splitting it; Em jumped in before Benny could and worked out their part.

When we were talking about an article, I went to hand my phone off to Em to read, but Benny grabbed it and read out loud instead.

If Benny's struggling with math stuff, it makes me curious whether Em has his struggles too. He wasn't confident with his typing in class, for one thing. *Jesus.* Just how much have they made everything harder on themselves, all because they took the easy route for so long?

I'm fucking stressy over the lack of contact. He's read my messages—I can tell because his read receipts are on—but even after dinner, when I'm considering smothering myself in bed, there's nothing. The longer it goes on, the more anxiety tries to take hold.

Then an upsetting thought hits: does he blame me?

That both makes me feel guiltier *and* mad. Sure, *I* feel like it's my fault, but I also rationally know it's all bullshit. That thought comes from wanting to fix things for him when I can't. If *he* blames me, that's a whole other issue. They're the ones who got themselves into this, and I'd be devastated to know my wanting him to do the right thing was what came between us.

But what the fuck else could it be? Why would he be ignoring me?

It'd be just my luck to know I've fallen in love with him right as he broke up with me because he failed a test. And I get it. That's scary shit when you're talking about a degree and your future, but here I am wanting to be in this, to see where it goes for as long as possible, and I have no fucking clue where Benny's at.

Fuck. I've gone from feeling guilty and worried about him to being convinced he wants to break up with me. There's something seriously wrong in my head.

I force myself to bed after midnight, the smell of him on my sheets just making me feel worse. My sleep is shitty and broken, and even though I crash hard sometime after three, I'm back up at five, scrambling for my phone.

There's still nothing.

Obviously.

He's probably asleep.

I toss my phone beside me, wondering how I'm supposed to handle this. He left me on read. All day. That's a clear sign he's pissed, but that's my job. I'm allowed to be shitty with myself; it's not fair to get it from him too.

I'd really hoped he'd pass. Really fucking hoped this would have been a success story. It wasn't a midterm or a major assignment; it was a low-weighted test on the subject matter we've just covered, so surely Benny could retake it? Surely he could do something extra to boost the grade, just enough to scrape a pass.

As much as I just want to believe he's out celebrating a good grade, I know Benny better than that.

I'm up earlier than usual for my jog, hoping it will rid Benny from my brain, but it doesn't. When I stop at my usual coffee cart, Austin asks me if I want the usual, and I hesitate.

"Harrison?"

"Actually, add two hot chocolates to that."

I've given Benny plenty of time to blame me and sulk. Now, it's time for us to talk whatever this is out. I can't get through classes today without speaking to him first.

Someone's on their way out of the DIK house when I get

there, so I let myself inside and make for Benny's room. I'm sure Em will be there with him, hence the second drink, but hopefully the hot chocolate will butter him up enough to give us a private moment.

Or maybe Benny won't want that. Guess I'll have to wait and see.

There's commotion inside his room when I knock, and a moment later, the door cracks open the smallest amount, and Benny's wary eyes peer out through it, then widen comically.

"Harrison?"

"Hot chocolate?"

He hurries to step back and open the door so I can slip inside, which I take as a good sign.

Doesn't stop me being nervous though. Facing Benny has my heart thumping loudly because his eyes don't light up like they usually do.

I turn to Em for something to do. "For you."

He takes his drink with a huge grin, and it's ridiculous how I didn't pick it straightaway. "This is perfect, thank you."

"Would have gotten you coffee if I knew what you drank."

"We don't drink coffee," Benny mumbles. "Tastes shit."

He looks so small and defeated I want to wrap him in a hug and never let go. His hair is wild from bed, big lips poutier than usual, and his stunning eyes have deep depressions under them. Every one of my protective instincts goes wild for him.

"I'm gonna go before you start fucking," Em says, hopping up from the mattress on the floor. "Benny, don't leave the room until you text me. I'm getting breakfast." He steps out into the hall and closes the door behind him.

I point to the door. "Your brothers know about you two?"

"Of course not. They just assume he's me."

Similar to how I did. Though, Em actually introduced himself as Benny to me, so maybe not the same thing.

"What are you doing here?" Benny's voice is gravelly, and as hot as this look is on him, I can also imagine how shit he feels. Hell, I had bugger all sleep as well.

"You didn't text me back."

"I needed to think."

"All day?"

His forehead flexes under his frown. "Was it all day?"

"Yeah. I messaged you yesterday morning."

"Huh."

"Benny ... do you need me to remind you what happened when I was the one not writing back? You threatened to sleep with some other guy and broke your phone."

"Can't help but notice your phone is in one piece," he snarks, not looking at me. "You weren't that upset about it."

"Or maybe I handle my emotions like a normal person."

Benny takes his hot chocolate, then swings his desk chair around and sits on it backward. He's hugging the back as he says, "I failed."

I brace myself for him to point the finger.

"And now I'm really embarrassed about it and stressed because I'm running out of ideas. It was an open book one, and I still couldn't do it."

I wait for a moment. "You're not mad at me?"

Benny's mouth drops. "What? Why would I be?"

"Because it's my fault Em isn't taking the class for you anymore."

He stands up, looking like a terrifying Chihuahua. Benny might have a hockey build, but he doesn't quite reach my nose. It's his attitude that makes him appear bigger than he is.

"That's not your fault. You didn't turn me in, are you kidding? I'm so fucking relieved you're on my side and pushing me to do better. It's why I'm so mad with myself that I can't."

"You just need—"

"What? Time?" He looks a second away from pulling his hair out. "What the fuck even is time? Earlier, later, soon. Five hours from now? It might as well be a year. Or a minute. I don't get it. Any of it. These books?" He grabs the stats book from where it's resting on his bed. "Why do they even bother writing this shit in English? I don't have enough fingers to count shit out, and when I use my calculator, it's great until they start throwing in words like more or less. I can't do it, Harrison." He stalks closer, breathing loudly. "I. Can't. Do. It."

There's so much blind panic on his face that it cuts off my automatic reply of taking it easy on himself until he learns. Because he will learn. Right?

My voice is a whisper when I answer him. "Do you need Em to go back to doing it?"

He shakes his head hard. "That's not ... No. Taking the easy way out is what got us into this mess—I'm not getting upset over that. I don't want to rely on him. I want to know this stuff, want it to make sense. But I'm worried it never will. My brain won't remember any of it."

I eye him for a moment. "Any?"

His jaw sets. "I can memorize just about anything in most of my classes. I wrap my head around it, take it in, understand it. With this ... there's something wrong with me."

I watch him blink back tears, that same niggling from the greenhouse taking over me. Then I grab my phone, find my clock app, and hold it up to him. "What time is it?"

His eyes fly wide. "I don't ... what are you ..."

"Take your time."

"Read it yourself."

"I want *you* to read it."

His glare feels like he's trying to make my head explode.

"What time is it, Benny?"

He huffs and looks back at it. "Seven ... something."

"Seven what?"

"It's too small to tell."

I take a deep breath. "What's four times five?"

His whole face goes white, hazel eyes and black circles under them the only things standing out on his face.

I step forward and grab him, tug him into a hug that's so tight it's like I want to transfer my pain onto him. I didn't know. I didn't understand how deep this went, and that he stepped up and tried anyway blows my mind.

He sniffs and wipes his eyes on my shirt.

"Don't know why you're hugging me," he mumbles.

"I needed one."

"Why?"

"Because I'm worried you'll get mad at what I'm about to say."

That makes him pull back. "Are you breaking up with me?"

"What? Fuck no. I just …" How the fuck do I word this? "Have you ever been tested?"

"For STDs? Obviously."

I stare him down because I'm not at all surprised he's trying to deflect. "For a learning disability."

"You think I'm stupid?"

"Don't use that word." I try to sound as stern as I can. "It has nothing to do with intellect. Some people need extra assistance, some just learn differently. It's obvious you need help with math, and I think talking to someone at the disability and accessibility office on campus might be a good first step."

"No way." He backs up. "I can't tell them I'm having issues when all of my tests have been near perfect. They'd throw me out of school if they knew what Em and I had done."

"Fuck. Okay." My mind is whirling. "Maybe not here, then. Maybe get a referral somewhere. I might be wrong, but we won't know that until you talk to someone."

The laugh he lets out is bitter. "My eldest brother is married to a math professor. My nerdy brother is a fucking math genius and graduated college four years early. You want me to tell them that not only do I not take after Rhys, but I'm probably going to fail out of college because of the subject they love so much?"

"There has to be something."

Benny's lips press together. "You should probably go. You didn't sign up for this."

I straighten, planting my feet firmer to the ground. If he wants me out, he'll have to wrestle me from the room, and we know who won the last time we tried it. "No."

"But—"

"*You* are who I signed up for. All of you. And I'm not going anywhere."

30

BENNY

Acknowledging that I might need to be tested for a learning disability is confronting. Trying to convince Em he might need to do the same is near impossible. His suggestion of me also dropping college and then neither of us having to worry about it just earns him an eye roll, but I'd be lying if I said it doesn't look like the only out.

The thing is, if I'm tested and something comes back, what do I do about it?

Tell the school? Ask for a waiver or assistance? That's only going to open up questions about why it's never been a problem before now. *Hoo boy*, the shit I'd be in if I admitted to cheating.

It wouldn't just be Em who's expelled.

"How'd it go?" Harrison asks the second I get back to my room from my doctor's appointment.

"I have a referral."

When he reaches for me and pulls me into his big arms, I go

eagerly. I'm not used to this. The whole being vulnerable thing fucking sucks, and I know why Asher fights it so hard. I want to fight it too, but unfortunately, there's no running away from my brain. It's still a struggle to believe this is happening to me.

"Now we wait," he says.

I drop my whole body into the hug, sagging against him and loving the way he holds me up. It's hard not to get in my head about everything, but he's been really good at distracting me. Not only with sex, either, but just … everything. The Halloween party we went to on the weekend as a tree and Poison Guy-vy was so fun, and helping him plan his plant dinner over these last few days has been perfect for redirecting my focus.

And surprisingly fun.

"I hate waiting," I remind him.

"I know. I don't think I've ever met anyone more impatient than you are, but suck it up, babe, because you've only taken the first step."

I press my face to his shoulder. "And if I don't take any more steps?"

"Then you struggle. I'm not going to tell you what to do."

"Be easier if you did."

He laughs, shoulder moving under my face. "It's not my place. I'll give you my opinion and my support, but the rest is up to you. Not gonna lie, it's probably going to get really bloody hard from here on."

"You're not supposed to be truthful," I grumble. "You're supposed to tell me it will all be okay and then feed me ice cream."

"Ice cream, I can do."

"And the rest?"

Harrison pulls away. "It *will* be okay, but that doesn't mean what you want it to mean."

I scowl and kick his shoes across the floor toward him. "Fine. I'll settle for the ice cream."

Harrison fist-bumps, and I'm tempted to knock his hat off his head. I don't, but only because he looks hot as fuck with it on.

"Any luck getting Em to go with you?" he asks as he pulls his shoes on.

"Nope. He says he doesn't need it."

Harrison shakes his head, but he looks indulgent. "You Daltons are a stubborn bunch."

"You've only met two of us."

"About that ..." He clears his throat, adjusting his cap a bit. "I thought, maybe if you want to, that we could talk about Christmas."

"Christmas?"

"Well, it's next month, and it's the only time I fly home during the year, and you'll probably also be going home, but ... well ..."

A sly grin spreads across my face. "You want to spend it with me."

"I know it's a long shot, and maybe not the actual day if we can't swing it, but something would be cool. Even if we just celebrate before we both leave. Or you ... fly to Florida, maybe?"

I blink. "You want me to meet your family?"

"It will happen eventually, right? So why not?"

"Why not?" I'm sure my face is blank because I'm fucking stunned. Harrison tells me he's serious all the time, he tells me he's not going anywhere, but that doesn't mean I believe him. Not all the way deep down. This though ... it's serious. It's more commitment than I would have expected, but then I look into his earnest eyes and feel my heart do that squishy thing it does around him.

"If it's too soon—"

"It's not." I sound like a fucking fool with how fast that comes out. So much for playing it cool. "Christmas Day, I have to be with my family, but ... what if you come home with me? Then fly out Christmas Eve to head home, and I'll meet you there the day after? Would ... would that work?"

His sweet, brown eyes are wide as he nods. "It's kind of perfect. You'd be okay with that?"

"Very. Besides, my family aren't going to believe that someone likes me enough to put up with me unless I have you there for proof."

He pinches my chin gently. "I'm not sure even having me there is enough to prove that to them."

"Dick." I slap his hand away but press a quick kiss to his lips anyway.

Harrison is so damn incredible he makes me sick sometimes. Insults as a love language?

Marry me already.

"HOW ARE YOU FEELING?" Em mutters from where he's sitting next to me. It's going to be a long-ass day being head shrunk, and he wanted to be the one to drop me off and sit with me while I waited. As much as I would have loved Harrison to be here, I'm glad it's Em.

"Like I'm about to have to talk to people about this shit."

"That is why you're here."

I glance over at him. "Sure you don't want to come in?"

Em raises his hands to ward me off. "This is all you."

"It's just ... embarrassing, you know?" I hate constantly going over this, but I can't get past it. I know what people will think, and it fucking sucks. "Rhys was probably born understanding more about math than I ever will."

During the two weeks I spent waiting for this appointment, I've given Google a workout. All it took was typing in *problems with math* to stumble across dyscalculia and match just about every fucking symptom like it was a checkbox exercise. I didn't realize that it wasn't only numbers that I was struggling with—directions have never been my strength, and when Coach would shout things like "Take it up the left," I'd have to check which way everyone else was going before I'd know what he meant. No wonder I had a reputation for going rogue.

Near, far, soon, later—those words mean absolutely nothing to me.

My sensitivity to the criticisms that Em and I wouldn't be as good if we were split up was valid because they were right. I looked to him way too many times, and I hadn't even realized I was doing it.

I'm so confident that's what's going on with me that if these guys come back to me and say everything's fine, I'll start questioning *their* degrees.

"We really fucked ourselves, didn't we?" Em asks.

I glance over at him, hazel eyes heavy with guilt under my Franklin U cap. "We didn't know."

"Yeah, but if I hadn't been covering for you all these years, it probably would have been picked up when we were kids. You might have gotten help and been able to—"

"No maybes." I'm firm about that. "I'm sure it would have been picked up sooner, but it's just something I'm going to have to live with. It wasn't your fault, Em. I never talked to you about any of it."

"But I knew you were struggling, and I thought I was helping. Making things easier for you."

"Yeah, but by the same reasoning, we could say similar about you. Your English skills are shit."

"Maybe, but I can still read. Write. It might be hard, and I might not like it, but—"

"At least you can work out change," I say mockingly.

He flicks my leg. "Shut up. I'm being serious. I feel like shit."

"Well, you can quit it with that because it's my turn. Be supportive or something."

He smiles and bumps me with his shoulder. "I think you're very brave for doing this."

While Em is normally the nice one, he's not usually sweet to me because he knows I'm allergic. He must sense I need it now though. "That's ... thanks. It's gonna be shit, but—"

"Wait, you think I'm talking about the test?" He gives a forced laugh. "Benny, that'll be the easy part. I mean having to tell West, Jas, and Asher."

"Who says I'm telling them?"

"I fucking won't be."

"Just leaving me to it, huh?"

Em cuffs my shoulder. "Like I said, super brave. Well done, you."

"I already know what they're going to say."

"Cheating only cheats yourself?"

I sigh because that's exactly it. We're grown adults; they can't exactly give us a lecture, even though West will probably try. The thing is, they'd be right. Em was right. Cheating was the easy way out, and because that's the path I chose, I'm fucked now. Look at me.

It's a decision I'll have to live with for the rest of my life.

Em's always been my crutch. My safety net. I always thought it went both ways, but if he's right in that he doesn't struggle as much as he makes out, then I was wrong. It's been Em looking out for me all this time.

Emmy and Benny.

Benny and Emmy.

Completely identical.

Basically the same person.

The identity I loved for so long has gone sour, and as much as I hate to admit it, I think it's time Em and I really made moves to figure out who the hell we are.

For real.

I glance over at him, hoping he's not going to hate me for this. "Will you pick me up after?"

"Obviously."

"Good. While you wait, there's something I want you to do for me."

31

HARRISON

I let Benny know I'm proud of him today, but I hold off my burning urge to text him and check in every few seconds. From what he was told, the initial meeting will have some assessments and a chat with his psych about what he's experiencing and what it could mean.

I'm desperate to know how it went, but I force myself to focus on my own shit. Organizing a whole-ass charity dinner on top of my regular coursework is a lot to take on, but I'm excited about it. That kind of frenzy building in my gut tells me I'm on the right path with it all.

I've found a local conservation group who are interested in what I'm trying to accomplish, and they've jumped in to help out with the agreement that the funds I raise will go to them. Claribel is the rep I've been talking to, and she's been a goddamn angel with finding some of these more obscure plants I'm after.

"I'm so excited to see how it all turns out," she says over the phone. "I am floored you got your hands on a ghost orchid. *Floored.* I want to be there just to see that thing myself."

I chuckle, still proud of myself over that one. Living in Florida and volunteering for different organizations over the summer definitely came in handy. "Well, I think we're ready to start selling tickets. I don't want the plants to be here long before returning to their homes, but I also don't want to rush things."

"Did you get your branding worked out?"

"I think so. The art department came in handy there."

"What tagline did you end up going with?"

"Everyone loves a good root. Root is British slang for, uh, *bedroom stuff* but also works for plants. Fits with the sex-sells aspect."

"Bedroom stuff." Claribel laughs. "Love it. Now ..." She hesitates, which immediately grabs my attention. "One of my bosses got wind of your project. They had me run through what your plans were, and they're interested."

"Oh." I don't know what she's getting at, but it's cool to have interest from people higher up. "Tell them thanks."

"Tell them yourself. I assume you're cataloging data for how this event goes. They want to read your findings when you're done."

I blink at my laptop screen for a few moments. "That's ... awesome. Thanks." Any contacts I can get at this stage can only be helpful, *if* they don't think I'm full of shit. Making plants fun has been done before, but those people didn't have a Benny who's happy to tell me exactly what people need.

While *I* think it's mind-blowingly cool to read up about soil health and photosynthesis, apparently, those topics are out. I need to be light on the education and heavy on the cool facts. Finding that balance hasn't been easy, but I've been putting all my time and effort into it.

Benny has been so patient as my sounding board.

A presence presses against my back, immediately chasing away the worry and bringing a smile to my face. I can't get off the phone with Claribel fast enough.

"I'm wrapping up for the day, but I'll let you know if there's more progress this week."

"Can't wait. Talk soon."

We hang up, and I turn to grab Benny in a bear hug.

"Should I be worried about late-night phone calls with strange women?" he asks, teeth tugging on my earlobe.

"Claribel *does* really like plants."

He growls, and it does all these weird, happy things to me. "Which one was a good poison again?"

"You don't need to worry about her. You *don't* like plants and act interested anyway. It's why I love you."

I'm expecting snark back when Benny goes tense in my arms. "Stop. Repeat."

"What do you mean?"

"That last damn thing you just fucking said to me."

What ... oh, *fuck*. "Ah ..." I swallow. "Plants ..."

"You love me?"

"Love? What? There, umm, must be some amnesia—hallucinogenic—pollen in the air. Very strong. I think I stroked out for a minute."

Benny narrows his eyes. "Say it again."

"Say what?"

"You know what."

Well, fuck. Looks like he's not letting me get out of this. I want to say it was a slip of the tongue, but I've gotten so used to thinking that about him lately that I look at him, and it's all I see. I've wanted to tell him so many times, but we're both so busy with everything that it's never the right moment.

Looks like my malfunctioning mouth has decided the time is now. Whether I want it to be or not.

My nerves are going wild as I swallow and look down into his gorgeous face. He's waiting, eyes watching me carefully, and I can't read whether he's going to say it back or think I'm jumping way too ahead for even thinking it.

I let all my nerves out on a sigh. "I love you, Benny. Your lips, your snark, your big dick. The whole package. I love everything about you."

"E-everything?"

"Everything. Especially your brain."

"Kinda cannibalistic and creepy, but okay." He can try to lighten the mood all he likes, but I heard the way his voice got all caught up.

"What about you?"

"Me?"

I smirk, loving that I get to put it back on him. "You forced me to talk feelings. Now, it's your turn."

"That doesn't seem fair to me."

"Benny ..."

"Look, I got a tattoo!"

I do a double take at the bandage on his forearm, and he almost has me. But I shake off the distraction and focus. "If you don't say something, I'm going to assume it's not returned. If it isn't, that's okay—it doesn't change anything for me. I'd just like to know for sure."

He huffs, cute nose wrinkling. "Fine." His voice drops and turns muffled. "Kinda, sort of love you or whatever, I guess."

"Louder."

I swear steam shoots from his nose. "I love you."

"Louder."

Benny snarls and grabs my jaw, pushing onto his toes until he's right in my face. "I fucking love you, and I'm pretty sure I'm obsessed with every dumb thing you do because I can never stop thinking about you and talking about you, and if Em kills me, it's all your fault because he's sick of how disgustingly schmoopy I am." He makes a horrified noise and backs up a bit.

"You're schmoopy?"

"It's a sickness. I'll recover."

"Cute you think I'll let you." I link my finger into his belt loop, and even though he tries to act annoyed, he can't get to me quick enough. I kiss slowly along his hairline, over his cheekbone, and down to his jaw. My chest is so damn light I can't stop smiling the entire time.

"You're perfect," I whisper.

"You'd be the only person alive who'd think that."

"Bet I'm not."

"Ohhh, I'm not falling for your bets again." He pulls back. "Fine. Everyone thinks I'm perfect. I don't care as long as I don't get stuck on lawn duty again."

"Oh, baby, there is still so much lawn duty in your future."

"Worst boyfriend ever."

"So ..." I run my hand along his arm until I reach the edge of the bandage. "A tattoo? What prompted that?"

"While I was waiting for my appointment today, I really got to thinking. I've used Em as a crutch for so long, and truthfully, I don't trust myself not to do it again. And so ..." Benny peels off the bandage, revealing two linked triangles. "We booked in with Remy at Indelible Ink and both got one. Mine on my left arm and his on his right. The added bonus is that it might help me with directions ..." He squints at the tattoo. "It's weird. I know this is left, but my brain keeps trying to say the wrong thing." When he looks up, his grin is happier than I've ever seen it. "It also means the man who loves me isn't going to get me confused with my brother ever again."

"Damn. No sneaky butt grabs?"

Benny thumps my shoulder, which is fair.

"Seriously, that's amazing. That was a big step for you both."

His fingers twist through mine. "Yeah. I almost chickened out, if I'm honest. A few times."

"But you didn't. I'm so impressed."

"Thanks. I guess I was kind of boosted by today."

I'd been hesitant to ask, but now that he's given me an opening, I can't hold my question back. "How did it go?"

"I want to say good, but ... not the right word. Promising? Depressing? All of the above."

I chuckle. "They're not usually words that go together, so you might want to explain some more."

"Okay, so, even though this was just the preliminary meeting, we had a good chat, and he went over some basic tests with me. He said the testing is needed for a definitive diagnosis, but he's confident in what the results will be."

"Dyscalculia?"

"Yep." Benny frowns for a moment. "I don't think I'm upset *about* it. More that I should have known a long time ago. It's ... frustrating."

"But you also said promising?"

"Yeah. He said because there's more known about it, there are more coping mechanisms than ever." Benny takes a deep breath. "He said when it comes to dyscalculia, there's no magic fix. I'll probably always operate, naturally, at an elementary school level. So that fucking sucks."

I squeeze Benny's hand harder.

"Numbers don't just magically become understandable. I won't suddenly learn my left from right, and I'll probably never be able to look at a clock and read it without counting it out or even understand what the time means. *But* he said there's also no reason to think I couldn't pass statistics with extra time, a calculator, one-on-one assessors, and the ability to take notes in with me. I might not remember it after, but I'd be able to remember the steps for figuring everything out."

"That's amazing."

Benny doesn't look excited though. "All that is done through learning support. And to get that, I have to declare my diagnosis."

That's what he's most afraid of. "What are the chances it'll go under the radar? That they'll grant the support without looking at past history?"

"I really don't know. I don't know how they do any of that, and the thought of risking my degree is terrifying."

"So, what do you do?"

"For now … I've decided to drop stats. At least for the rest of the semester until I've been through this process. Once I have my diagnosis, I can think about it more clearly." He swallows. "I did have a thought. Something that would probably work, without risking my degree, but it would mean transferring to Vermont. My brother-in-law is head of the math department there … they'll be so fucking angry at what Em and I have done, but …"

"You'd still graduate."

"Exactly."

We stand there, not saying much, even as my fucking heart is hammering out of my chest. We've just told each other we're in love, and now there's a very real future where he might leave me. One that I wouldn't even hold against him because it makes the most sense.

"Whatever you need to do."

His scowl creeps back in, and I hurry to add, "Vermont is known for its greenery."

Benny peeks up at me. "What are you saying?"

I'm running on pure instinct, gambling that this isn't

pushing too hard for what he's ready for, but when it comes to his degree and the choices he needs to make, I don't want to be a barrier for him. He has enough of those already. "There'd be a lot of plants there for me to study."

"You'd come with me?"

"As long as you want me there, you wouldn't even need to ask."

His sweet face lights up, and I'm desperate to kiss him, but I hold off. "Holy shit, I think today just became perfect."

"I'll take that as a yes, then."

"Fuck yes."

"Okay." Fuck. Looks like we might be headed to Vermont. "I can probably wrap my master's up in a year if I pick up some more units next semester. I'll be busy, but I was already thinking about it, so does that give you enough time?"

"I'd be able to go whenever. Even if it means taking an extra semester there." His face turns determined. "But I'm not giving up on here yet. That's a last resort because I don't want to have to keep relying on my brothers to fix my problems for me. I want to at least try and do it for myself."

It's probably the best thing he could say. The fact he wants to try, even if it means he could fail, is more important than he knows. Not even to me, but to him.

If we end up in Vermont, at least he'll know he did everything he could before he reached out for help. It sounds like it'll be a first for him, and I'm so glad I get to be here to witness it.

32

BENNY

I'm glued to Harrison as we back into his room, feeling all bubbly and high from today. Not gonna lie, it was emotionally exhausting to go over everything, to admit my failures and the things Em and I had done. Once I got it all out to the doctor and we talked in depth about dyscalculia and what to expect, it eased some of my questions. My talk with Harrison eased the others.

His tongue glides across mine, and while I love the softness sometimes, tonight, after all that emoting and love, I need a good hard fuck.

"Take my clothes off," I manage between kisses.

Harrison immediately reaches for my shorts. He's efficient with stripping those and my underwear off before breaking our kiss to tug my shirt over my head. I'm not cold, but goose bumps rise across my skin anyway.

He steps back, takes a moment to drink my body in.

I pull my dick a few times to dim the ache building there. "You wanna fuck me?"

My man nods slowly, jaw set and eyes hooded. His seriousness does something to me that sends a ripple down my spine.

"How?"

"Bend over the bed and hang on for dear life."

Now we're talking.

Harrison strips off, then grabs a condom and lube while I bend over the edge of the bed. When he steps up behind me, he tosses them onto the sheets, then runs his hands from my shoulders down either side of my spine to my ass.

"You're so hot, Benny."

"Look who's talking."

He wipes his leaking tip over my hole. "I swear I want to nut instantly when you're around."

"Then stretch me open, suit up, and get to it. Horny as fuck over here."

He chuckles, leaning down to press a kiss to my tailbone before he picks up the lube. Feeling the cool liquid drizzle down my crack immediately makes my hole twitch. I'm so ready for it. So ready for him to fuck me hard enough that I forget about everything else.

Harrison's fingers dip into my crease and drag the lube up and down my skin before pressing gently to my opening. His other hand reaches between my legs and cups my balls, causing me to fall face-first onto the bed. I'm a shameless slut for anything and everything he does to me. The combination of him gradually entering me and the way he rolls my balls in his palm is enough to make my legs weak.

"I don't know which is better," he says. "Fucking you or you fucking me."

"That's because neither of them are better. They're completely different. Sometimes one is what you need, and sometimes it's the other." The stretch in my ass is delicious as he gets his two fingers inside. "Sometimes I don't want either. And other times, like right now, I want you to fuck me so hard I forget my name."

He chuckles and squeezes my balls lightly. There's a hint of pain that takes the edge off how horny I am, but damn, I want him to touch my cock. I fold my arms, resting my forehead on them, using all my willpower not to reach for it instead. No way am I coming until I've taken a beating, but my man knows how to work me up; apparently, telling me he loves me is one of those ways.

"I always forget how tight you feel," he says, stroking his fingers in and out. "It's such a tease. I need my cock in there. You make me so hard, Benny."

Pure lust rushes from my head to my toes. "Prep me faster, then, damn."

He releases my balls, and I hear him tear open the condom wrapper. "I'm not going to hurt you just so I can get off."

"Maybe I'll like it."

"Yeah, but I won't."

My heart feels like Jell-O. "Anyone ever tell you you're disgustingly considerate?"

"Only this guy I know who likes to pretend he's allergic to feelings."

"I don't pretend."

"You totally pretend." He leans down and kisses my spine, turning me to mush. "See? You crave it."

"I hate it."

He removes his fingers and steps in, feet beside mine, his hot thighs flush with my skin, dick snuggled between my ass cheeks. Then he tugs me up, and I almost fall back against him. He holds me tight, big arms encircling my torso until I feel so completely owned, I'd agree to anything from him right now.

Harrison ducks his head until his lips hover in front of mine. "Don't kiss me, then."

Fuck. "Easy."

"Not even a little bit." My lips tingle as his brush against them.

Fuck, he's close. Smells so good. That mix of his deodorant and soil is becoming my favorite thing. My heart is beating out of my chest with the proximity, and even when his lips curl with a smile, I can't force myself to pull away.

"You're the worst," I grunt before surging forward. Our mouths meet, and I can't hide how much I love it. I sink into our kiss like nothing else matters, just wanting more of everything he'll give me.

He kisses me back as forcefully while he reaches down between us and lines his cock up with my hole. His knees bend, and I arch up onto my toes as he pushes inside. I'm not stretched enough, but I lean into the slight sting, loving the way it makes me feel owned inside and out by him. Sex isn't something that holds a lot of emotion for me, but with Harrison, it's instantly different. The urge to get off is still strong, but the closeness, the clawing need to feel connected, is new and different and terrifying. I shiver as his lips find my neck, and it takes me a moment for it to really sink in that he's mine.

The scratch of his pubes meets my ass, and he holds still there for a moment, waiting for me to adjust to the fullness I've been craving.

"As much as I'd love to do it like this," he says against my shoulder, "we're going to end up on our faces. You're going to have to bend over for me, baby."

I grunt, not wanting to separate, but when he guides me forward, I go easily.

"You ready?"

"Yes." I grind back against him. "Stop making me wait for it."

The first thrust is everything I need. Harrison's cock pummels me, lighting up the nerves in my ass and filling me with bliss. I push back into every movement, seeking more. My prostate is oversensitive, and his balls are brushing mine in a way that has my cock leaking. The steady grip he has on my hips anchors me in place, even as we send his bed knocking against the wall with a steady *thunk thunk* that makes me vaguely glad his roommates are out.

"Aw, Benny," he gasps, and I can feel in his voice how good I'm making him feel. It's heaven. Amazing, lusty heaven.

I'm stretched tight around him as he fucks me so hard it's making my brain scramble. My teeth knock. My ass tender with the beating it's taking, and I'm greedy for it. Hungry for how consumed I am by him.

One of my hands bunches tight in his sheets while I give in to the need to touch myself. I jerk off in time with his thrusts, punishing my dick with how desperately I want to come. Harrison makes me feel like I never have before. I'm warm from my head to my toes. Panting and sweaty. Balls pulling high and heart feeling like it's going to fill out my chest and keep going.

How can everything feel so much with him and still leave me wanting more?

I groan, deep in my chest, as my cock thickens in my hold. It doesn't give me much warning before the pressure releases, and my orgasm crashes into me. I pulse in my fist, cum landing on his bedspread, arms and legs sapped of the energy I need to hold myself up.

Harrison cries out and presses in deep, twitching as he empties into the condom before he sags forward against me.

His added weight sends us both crashing onto the bed.

I'm ready to pass out after that.

"You sure know how to keep a guy happy," I say.

Harrison chuckles, pressing his hips tighter against me to try to keep inside. "Hopefully always."

"Not possible. We're bound to fight at some point."

"You mean we haven't fought enough already?"

I grin into the sheets, even though he can't see me. "You're dating a Dalton. We're known for boneheadedness, so you should probably prepare yourself for that."

"I'm prepared."

"It's okay. Once you meet Asher, he'll make me look like a saint."

"No one can make you look any better in my eyes."

I groan and turn my head to the side. "No saying cutesy things around him either. He'll never let me live it down."

"Be extra sweet and mushy. Got it."

"I'm really starting to doubt the whole you loving me thing."

"That's okay." He rubs his nose behind my ear, and I wish I didn't love it so much. "You deserve all the love and affection in the world, Benny-Wenny."

Oh.

Fucking.

No.

"*Shit.*"

"What's wrong?"

"I really am like Asher."

Harrison waits me out, but I don't even want to say the words. I can't just leave it there though.

"My brother. He has a safe word. But not for sex, for affection. Because Kole likes to amp it up to embarrass him."

Harrison pulls out and flops down beside me, wearing a smirk that looks annoyingly similar to the one Em and I share. "Let me guess. I'm a Kole."

I pretend to sob.

"You're in love with your brother-in-law."

"Shut up."

"You Daltons really *are* messed up."

"Fuck off."

Harrison hauls me against him. "I cannot *wait* to tell your brothers this story."

And I don't doubt for a moment that he will.

33

HARRISON

My palms are damp, and I've already changed my shirt once, but as the people for my event filter in, Benny throws me a thumbs-up from where he's checking tickets. We sold fifty, which was all I could do for this space, and I'm overwhelmed we even managed that.

Since Benny dropped stats, I've been sitting with Jordan, and the sneaky guy bought a ticket without even telling me. Benny looked like he'd chewed on rocks when he saw Jordan's ticket and checked it about three times.

My snarly man just makes me love him more every day.

There are a few other familiar faces here too. It's blown my mind to be getting so much support from not only Claribel's team but from people here on campus too.

Professor Nottering reached out to some people who might be interested in helping, and a newer FU transfer, Ryan, jumped on the opportunity. He's quieter, but we've bonded over video games and wouldn't have had everything set up on time if he wasn't so efficient. Then there's Dex, who's a poli-sci major and was really interested in what I was doing.

The thing about charity work is that people want to help. I was hesitant to reach out at first, but between Claribel and Professor Nottering helping me with contacts, and some local organizations in San Diego, I've been able to pull together people for audio/visual, catering, setup, and plant maintenance.

I tug at the button-up I'm wearing. It's a cooler December night, but the greenhouse temperature and my nerves aren't the best combination.

"Hey," Jordan says, approaching me with a champagne glass in each hand. He holds one out to me that I wave away. There's no way I'm drinking before I have to run this evening.

Jordan looks doubtfully at the glass. "Guess I'm going to have to choke down two, then."

"Not a champagne guy?"

"If champagne's the vibe of the evening, I'll go with it, but damn, it tastes like piss."

I laugh and take both glasses before setting them down behind me.

"Your boyfriend growled at me," he says.

We both turn and see Benny done with the tickets and glaring our way. I blow him a kiss and love the way he tries so hard to fight the smile he wants to let out. "That sounds right."

"He's kinda cute. You said he has a twin, right?"

I'm still unsure how much of that to talk about, but Jordan *has* met them both, and he's never said anything. I change the subject instead. "What about your girlfriend?"

"Ah. We broke up."

"Damn."

"Still unsure how I feel about it."

I look Jordan over again. "Is that maybe the reason for this sudden bulking up?"

"It felt like the time."

Benny pops up beside us. "Yes, yes, Jordan is so hot and muscular and whatever."

Jordan gives an adorable laugh and nudges Benny's shoulder. "Relax. I was just asking Harrison about your twin—"

"Off-limits."

It's my turn to laugh.

"Well, damn. Still no clue if I'm queer, but you guys have nice genes. Thought it was worth a try."

"I'll give you a hint," Benny says, less bite this time. "If your go-to is 'nice genes,' you probably don't want to fuck the guy."

"Right. I'll leave you guys to it." He claps me on the shoulder. "Good luck."

"As far as I'm concerned, the night's already a success," I say, looking around at the people reading the cards on each plant. The naked-man orchid has gotten a few snickers and closer looks, Stacy has understandably gotten a lot of attention, and even Rich—with the whole history of roses laid out for people to read—has gotten the respect he deserves.

"You are so clever," Benny says, wrapping his arm around me as Jordan leaves us.

"You're the one who gave me the idea."

"Yeah, but an idea is only an idea. All of this is fucking impressive."

"We're a dream team, baby."

"Hells yes we are." He holds his free hand up, and we high-five in front of us. "I'm proud of you."

I press a kiss to his curls, holding him for a beat longer than I mean to in order to try and absorb his strength. Even when Benny is struggling, he's one of the strongest guys I know, and I want to channel his confidence. I know this shit. I *love* this shit.

Tonight is just another night where I get to talk to people about the things I love.

On one greenhouse wall, I have a mini stage set up with a projection screen behind it for my talk later and eight tables facing it. They're all decorated fancy with as much local flora as I could get my mitts on.

After everyone has taken a good look around, we let them know dinner will be served soon, and then I'm on.

"Think I'm gonna be sick, Benny."

"You were made for attention. Once you start talking, you're going to convert every person in here to a plant fucker."

"Not my aim."

"Eh, agree to disagree."

The fact he doesn't understand this stuff and is so viciously supportive anyway just gets me in the heart.

"Time to do this."

I leave him, feeling a smidge more confident than I did a minute ago. It doesn't help that once tonight is over, my nerves don't end there. I'll be flying to meet Benny's family in a few days once break starts, so this is just the start of my torment.

But I'll be myself there, and I plan to do exactly the same here.

With a massive breath, I power up the projector, and Benny flicks off the main lights.

"Thank you so much to everyone for coming. I'm Harrison Dunn, and this might not be the most professional event you've ever been to, but I'm sure as hell going to try and make it worth your time anyway. Starting by letting you all know that animals are my mortal enemies." There's some confusion, and I shrug. "True story. Who's this?" I bring up a photo, and people call out Steve Irwin's name. "And this?" I play a clip, and David Attenborough's voice is immediately picked. "Those two men are *also* my mortal enemies." I laugh at the shock that passes through the room. "See, these two have done more for animal conservation than arguably anyone else in the world, but with the focus on those critters, no one is giving a shit about the plants. The trees. The ugly-ass shrubs and grasses that are keeping everyone alive." I grin over getting literally everyone offside already. "Ooh, tonight's already *so* controversial. But I have your attention, don't I?"

Benny whoops from somewhere at the back of the room.

"What's your first thought when you see this?" I ask, flicking over to a picture of an adorable koala yawning.

There's a beat of silence, and then Jordan has my back. "Cute?"

"Wrong! Chlamydia." I bring up the next image of a diseased koala and get the response I was hoping for. Disgusted noises and expressions pass through the audience, with a few who look mildly interested. "If those charity ads showed you pictures of *this* guy, I can't imagine too many people would be rushing to donate, can you?" I bring up the cutesy photo again because I want people to be able to stomach their dinners. "This is what sells. This is what empties your pockets. Unfortunately, my photosynthesized friends don't have the luxury of a widdle tail or fwuffy ears." There are a few snickers, which helps give me a boost. I bring up an image of a scraggly-looking tree with dried leaves that looks on its last legs. "Believe it or not, this baby is most well-known for keeping your diseased little beasties alive. The eucalyptus tree might not look like much, but got a cold? Bam! Eucalyptus to the rescue. Respiratory problems, dental care, wounds, and fevers—even goddamn bug repellant. Want a supercharged immune system? Eucalyptus is coming in hot with the assist. But it's not pretty."

There's a lot of silence in the room, but from what I can tell, people are still paying attention.

"What about this guy?" My next picture is of a rainbow eucalyptus tree, and that catches people's attention.

"There's no way that's real," someone says.

"You're correct." I flick over to an image that hasn't been saturated to high hell. The bright pinks and purples fall away, but it's still impressive. "People think they need to create something over-the-top to catch attention, but *look* at this guy. The yellows and greens and oranges and red that are coming through in the bark as it ages. And that's just *one* tree. We've got corpse flowers." New photo. "Monkey cups. Tree tumbo. Birthwort. All ugly as hell but also *cool* as hell. The really sad thing is that these ugly guys just aren't being studied as often as the pretty flowers that catch people's attention." I go through more facts and cool images and slip in a couple of plant dad jokes that help lighten the mood. But most of all, I have fun with it. I'm so swept up in talking about the things I love that I almost forget I'm talking to a room full of people. Do I want to score a bunch of money to help research? Hell yes I do. But tonight is an experiment, and while I'll give it my all, the results will be the results, and I'm interested to see where we land.

I wrap up to applause and leave the screen going with facts and tidbits that everyone can read or not read while they finish eating.

As soon as I leave the stage, I all but swamp Benny with a hug. "I'm sapped."

"Haven't had enough of the tree puns yet, huh?" he asks.

"I have no idea how that went."

"I might have snuck around with the donation QR code and set it down while people were eating. If I had to guess by the number of people who immediately grabbed their phones to donate, it was a lot. Most, probably. I hate to even admit this, but it was fucking interesting."

"You're my boyfriend. You have to say that."

"No, I *have* to tell you you tried hard and great effort and amazing idea. I don't have to tell you I enjoyed it."

I press a kiss to his forehead, deciding right there that even if Benny was the only one, the whole night was worth it.

"Harrison?"

I glance up at the gorgeous Black woman with braids halfway down her back.

"Claribel," she says.

"Oh. Hey." I accept her hug.

"That was really amazing. Plus, all the plants you have for people to actually look at. Touch. Smell. You've done really well, especially considering you put it together in, what? A month?"

"A little longer but close enough."

"Good job. Mitch will be in touch."

"Mitch?"

"Our director."

"Umm ... okay. Cool." I already said I'd share my results with them, but something about her expression is smug.

"He's always on the lookout for new blood and big ideas."

"I guess I'll talk to him soon, then."

I'm still confused as she walks away.

"He's totally going to offer you a job," Benny says.

My heartbeat kicks up. "You think?"

"Definitely." He's frowning slightly. "It'll mess with our Colchester plans though."

"I won't take it."

"What?" His scowl deepens. "If he makes you a good offer, of course you will."

"Not if it means losing you."

"Why the fuck will you lose me?"

I'm thrown for a second. "Well, if you're on the other side of the country ..."

"It'd be one semester. If you can't handle being away from me for a couple of months while we both sort our shit out, we need to talk about you not being so obsessed with me."

I choke out a laugh. "You really are so romantic."

"I know." His hand slides into mine. "But there's no guarantee I'll even go. If there's a guarantee you could have a job you love, then for sure, go for it. The rest is up to us to work out."

"Thank you."

He shakes his head. "Don't start getting schmoopy with me."

"But you know how much I *love* being schmoopy with you."

Benny sighs as I plant kisses all over his face.

"Like you could spend a few months away from all of this," I joke. His response isn't what I'm expecting.

"Unfortunately, I'm afraid you might be right about that."

34

BENNY

December passes as fast as a snot rocket. Between my assessments and Harrison's job offer and then us fucking off back home and meeting each other's families over the holidays, I barely have time to scratch my ass, but I do squeeze in more bugging Emmett.

He still hasn't made any decisions about what's next and acts totally comfortable chilling out in my room doing nothing. And he flat out refused to tell our brothers over Christmas about him being thrown out.

I was so fucking paranoid I was going to slip out a "pass me the potatoes and also Em's a dropout, thanks," over Christmas lunch, but he just sat there smiling like an angel.

West did love our tattoos though. Saving him the embarrassment of having to ask to check our palms was the best Christmas gift we could have given him.

Harrison's family was more incredible than I would have

imagined. He came out to them on the phone when he asked if he could bring his boyfriend home over the holidays. I could tell it threw them and they weren't expecting it, but when I visited, they went out of their way to make me feel welcome.

It's almost been a relief to be back at school, where things are quiet.

It's not until late when Em climbs into our window that night. His cheeks are flushed, and he looks happy, but I have no idea why.

He's been sneaking out, and every time I ask where he's going or what he's doing, it's always "going for a walk" or "found a hookup" or "took up a new career as a stripper, and now my billionaire boyfriend is being chased by the mob, and I have to go into hiding."

It'd be too bad if Em ever did get into actual trouble one day because I wouldn't believe him.

Harrison keeps telling me that Em will fill me in when he's ready, but asking me not to worry about Em is about as useful as telling me not to get hard when I see Harrison naked.

The universe has indisputable laws, and those are two of them.

"Let me guess; a mermaid washed up at Shenanigans, and you had to help her return to her underwater palace."

Em blinks at me. "Well, that's just ridiculous."

"Great to know your stories have *some* limits."

He tosses his hoodie into the corner of the room. It's a cooler night, but he's dressed like we're still back in Vermont.

Needling him for more information is right on the end of my tongue.

"How's Harrison liking work?" he asks, like he can sense my curiosity. Probably can. Damn him for knowing me better than anyone.

Harrison had a meeting with Mitch at the conservation

group before we left and worked his first official shifts last week. It means less time together, but when we do see each other, we make the most of it.

"Loves it."

"I'm glad."

I watch Em kick out of his pants and pull some pajama bottoms on. I haven't told Em about my plans for finishing out my degree yet because I was waiting for the official diagnosis and a moment I could catch him alone. But it's just us now. I'm finished my schoolwork for the night, and I'm dying to talk it all through with him.

"I got my official diagnosis."

"Shit." His head pops up like a deer in the headlights. "How do you feel?"

"Not much different. I was expecting it."

"So, what's next?"

This is the hard part. "Doc thinks that with learning assistance, I'll be able to pass stats. It'll be hard but doable."

"That's awesome."

"But I'd have to tell people. Then they'll ask questions, and there's a good chance they'll find the right answers."

"They can't prove anything."

"I think my diagnosis does it for them, honestly."

He falls silent, and I know he's trying to think up a solution like I have been for months.

"I'm going to speak to West and Jas this summer," I say.

"Oh, fuck."

"Sorry, but I think it's the only way. They're going to be so fucking mad, but I need Jas to help me."

"Wait ..." Em walks over to sit next to me. "If you can't do it here, you'll—"

"Move home."

"Shit."

It hurts to even think about it. I might have told Harrison that one semester is no big deal, but it's going to kill me being away from him. There's no way in hell I could let him say no to this job, though, when it's exactly the kind of thing he'll love to do while he finishes his degree.

"Harrison already knows it's an option, and we'll work through it."

"There is no fucking way you'll survive being away from him," Em says. "You're sulky on the nights you don't get to see him. Constantly message him while he's at work. I never would have picked you as needy as fuck in a relationship, but apparently, he turns you into an idiot."

I hate that I can't even argue with him.

"It's my only option."

"Okay. We'll tell them together."

I'm not expecting that. "You sure?"

"Obviously, I'm sure. We do everything together. Including being murdered by our big brothers."

"I don't think Asher will be that pissed."

"No, but if murder's involved, you know he'll be on West's side."

I chuckle because he's right. I also know that as bad as it might be, as furious and disappointed in us as they're going to be, they're my brothers. They love me. They'll support me through it all and try to understand.

Even my by-the-book brother-in-law is a true Dalton. He might be head of the math department, but Jas will go to bat for me. For all of us. He'll probably even blame himself for not picking up on it, but I'd gotten good at hiding.

I lean forward and breathe into my hands, sure I've made a decision. Now I need to hope that Harrison and I can survive a semester apart.

"What about you?" I ask Em.

"Me?"

"Will you come with me?"

His face falls a little. "Back to Vermont?"

"I mean, it's still forever away, and you've got time to think about it, but ... what else would you do out here?" The familiar panic of being apart tries to creep in. "Not going to lie here, I don't think I could handle missing both you and Harrison at the same time."

He smiles and rolls his eyes at me. "Do you even need to ask? Of course I'll move back. And then here again and back again as many times as we need to."

"Really?"

"We've already worked out we can't be apart. I hope Harrison is prepared for that."

"I jokingly told him we'll all have to live together when we're older, and he just nodded and said, 'Make more money, got it,' and carried on with what he was doing."

"Good man."

"The best."

"Who's the best?" Harrison asks, throwing my door open.

Embarrassingly, I jump from the bed and throw myself at him. "I didn't think I'd see you for two more days."

"Yeah, but then on the way home, I was like *fuck that* and decided to come over."

Emmett snorts. "A whole semester, my ass."

"I'm going to do it just to prove you wrong," I tell him.

"Uh-huh. I'm going to ... do literally anything not in this room."

He leaves, and Harrison lifts his eyebrows. "You know, someone is going to start questioning why you're always out there when I visit."

"Em has been living here for five months, and not a single one of my brothers has noticed. I think we're safe."

That relaxes him, and he ducks his head to kiss me. "A semester is going to suck."

"Agreed."

"We'll talk every day though. And now I have a job with regular hours, I'll be able to save for flights to Vermont."

I quickly shake my head. "You'll be done with your master's and either studying more or starting as an ecologist somewhere. You can't risk that by flying out to see me."

"I might even be working in Vermont with you."

"We can only hope."

"Well, I'm not giving you up. No matter where we are or how long it takes."

How long. Yeah, that's what worries me. My doctor is confident I'll get there, but will a semester be enough time? What if I fail and need to take the class again? A semester is one thing, but *two*? One of the things about having time blindness is that sometimes a long amount of time will fly, but there's the flip side to that. A semester could feel like years. Not being able to process the time distance to seeing him again is going to be one of the hardest parts.

"Hey." He smooths a thumb over my forehead. "No more worrying. We've got over a year before we even need to think about it."

"Right."

"Which is a lot of time to spend together first."

That makes me smile. "I'll take all of the time. And all of the late-night visits. And just ... everything."

"Even my plant facts?"

"Even the boring ones."

He squeezes the life out of me. "I'll make sure to think up some extra-boring ones, then."

"Suddenly, that semester away is looking better and better."

His gorgeous brown eyes turn soft as he looks down on me. "You're such an asshole." It doesn't sound like an insult.

"And you're such a sweetheart." That does.

But it works for us. Total opposites. All cinnamon and snark.

We might have some rocky shit coming our way, but if I always love him like I do now, that won't mean anything.

We'll make it. Easily.

Because I might not have had to fight for much in my life, but he's worth fighting for.

EPILOGUE

HARRISON

TEN YEARS LATER

There's the slap of skin on skin, and I turn to glance at Benny. His whole face is scrunched in disgust as he lifts his hand from his arm and reveals the mosquito he got.

"Cute date," he deadpans.

I just want to tell him to bear with me. I've been saving for this trip for years now, and little does Benny know it's for a very specific reason. Our dream Australian vacation was less about beaches and fancy bridges and more about fungus.

One specific fungus.

Because Benny is worth it.

"Forests smell."

"This is the bush, babe."

"Bush. A bush is what's between your legs right now."

I laugh, if only to dispel some of the nerves. "You said you like the retro look."

"I'm going to say anything to get in your pants."

Trim the pubes. Got it.

We've been walking for an hour now, and I'm starting to get as frustrated as he is. We set out at sunset, and even though I was careful about making sure we stuck to the paths and have the exact mapping and coordinates set out, I didn't expect us to be walking for this long.

I'm starting to lose hope.

I've been researching, and getting firsthand recounts, and narrowed the dates to be the most common for these stupid things, but I'm still coming up empty. What the hell am I supposed to tell Benny if I suddenly decide we're done and head back frustrated and disappointed? This is less of a romantic night to remember and more the opening to a horror film.

"Are we lost?" he asks.

"No."

"You look lost."

"I know exactly where we are." The problem is, I don't know where *they* are. Years of planning have gone into tonight, and if, after spending my whole life being good to plants, they choose not to return the favor, I might just stomp on one.

Okay, I won't.

But I'll probably want to.

Might even kick a tree trunk if I'm annoyed enough.

"My legs hurt," Benny complains, and I finally stop.

This is useless. My hair is damp under my hat, and if we go any further, we probably *will* end up lost. That's definitely not the kind of trip I'd been planning.

So, with my heart lodged in my throat and disappointment churning in my gut, I force a smile. "You're right. Let's go back."

"Fina—" His eyes shoot wide. "What the fuck is that?"

My head shoots around, expecting to find a ghost or a man with an axe, but there's nothing there. I narrow my eyes, searching until—holy fuck. We found them.

I grab Benny's hand and drag him off the path, making note with my phone compass on which way we're heading as I pray no spiders jump out to ambush us.

"No, don't go toward the thing!" he protests, but I don't let him go, and when we step through a thick patch of shrubs, my mood soars.

This is better than I imagined.

A whole cluster of ghost mushrooms. There are four thick trees here, and growing all up the sides of their massive trunks are brightly glowing fungi.

"Wow," Benny breathes.

Wow, indeed. I've never seen so many together like this. It's like I'm on an otherworldly planet.

Benny wraps his arm around me, head resting against my shoulder. "This is what you were looking for?"

"Yep."

"It's ... fucking unreal."

"Yep." I take a deep breath, heart that was in my throat back in my chest and hammering out a fucking drum solo. "So are you."

I click off my flashlight, and the mushrooms glow brighter. They're not bright enough to see him clearly, but there are gaps in the canopy above, letting enough moonlight through for me to catch his smile.

"There you go being sweet again," he murmurs. Like he can feel it too. The something magical in the air that makes us whisper so we don't disturb it.

"You know I love plants, and you know I love you—"

"Probably in that order," he teases.

"Which is *why* when I did this, I knew it had to be this way."

Benny's eyebrows pull together, and when he slowly lifts his head, I know he's figuring it out.

"When ... when you do what?"

"Ask you to marry me."

"Oh my god." Both hands fly to his mouth as I pull out the ring.

"I know we said it didn't matter either way if we took this step or didn't take this step, but the truth is, I lied. Call me a romantic, but I *want* to marry you. More than I've ever wanted anything, and I'm pretty sure I've been planning this since I met you. Maybe not consciously, and maybe not actively, but there was never any other choice. I was always going to end up here. In Australia, surrounded by nature, asking you to be mine."

"Goddamn it, Harrison." He swipes at his nose, and I know that look. The one where he's close to tears. "You flew me to the other side of the world and hunted down some stupid glowy mushrooms, all so I'd know you were serious?" His voice hitches. "I know sometimes I joke around asking why I love you when you're being all dorky, but this is why. This is the dorkiest, sweetest, youest thing in the entire world, and when we tell everyone about this, we're going to leave out the part where I'm a dumb, crying mess, but I'm glad I am. Because I want you to know I'm serious too."

Shit, now my eyes are starting to sting. "Is that a yes?"

"You shouldn't even need to ask, baby. I'm yours. In every single way. And I can't wait to be your husband."

The tears come, and I don't try to hold them back as I slip the ring onto his finger and kiss him. Benny is everything I never knew I needed, and after ten years together, I still fall for him more every day.

THANK YOU FOR READING A STEALTHY SITUATION. I HOPE YOU ADORED BENNY AND HIS HARRISON.

If you want to know more about cutie Jordan from stats class, and those sudden muscles he's sporting, make sure you jump into Batting Style by Louisa Masters, book three in the Franklin U 2 series.

To see Harrison head home for Christmas with Benny and meet the rest of the Daltons, you can get their bonus scene by joining my newsletter or Patreon.

MEET ALL THE COUPLES OF FRANKLIN U2!

Perry and Theo
<u>The Hookup Mix-up</u>

Harrison and Benny
<u>A Stealthy Situation</u>

Blaise and Jordan
<u>Batting Style</u>

Jay and Ryan
<u>Level Up</u>

Silas and Everly
<u>Full Service</u>

Dex and Austin
<u>Tongue-Tied</u>

Chase and Amos
<u>Method Acting</u>

Emmett and Jonah
<u>Twincerely Yours</u>

AUTHOR'S NOTE

Thanks so much for reading these gorgeous guys!
The fact you keep showing up for me, release after release,
means the absolute world! My dream has always been to have a
career as an author and it's mind-blowing to me that I get to
live it.
If you're a lover of signed paperbacks, special editions,
audiobooks or merch, don't forget to check out my store.
You can find it through the link or QR code: www.saxonjame-
sauthor.com

ACCIDENTAL LOVE SERIES:
The Husband Hoax
Not Dating Material
The Revenge Agenda
FRAT WARS SERIES:
Frat Wars: King of Thieves
Frat Wars: Master of Mayhem
Frat Wars: Presidential Chaos
DIVORCED MEN'S CLUB SERIES:
Roommate Arrangement
Platonic Rulebook
Budding Attraction
Employing Patience
System Overload
Forgotten Romance
NEVER JUST FRIENDS SERIES:
Just Friends
Fake Friends
Getting Friendly
Friendly Fire

<u>Bonus Short: Friends with Benefits</u>
RECKLESS LOVE SERIES:
<u>Denial</u>
<u>Risky</u>
<u>Tempting</u>
CU HOCKEY SERIES WITH EDEN FINLEY:
<u>Power Plays & Straight A's</u>
<u>Face Offs & Cheap Shots</u>
<u>Goal Lines & First Times</u>
<u>Line Mates & Study Dates</u>
<u>Puck Drills & Quick Thrills</u>
PUCKBOYS SERIES WITH EDEN FINLEY:
<u>Egotistical Puckboy</u>
<u>Irresponsible Puckboy</u>
<u>Shameless Puckboy</u>
<u>Foolish Puckboy</u>
<u>Clueless Puckboy</u>
<u>Bromantic Puckboy</u>
STAND ALONES WITH EDEN FINLEY:
<u>Up in Flames</u>
<u>The Bastard and The Heir</u>
FRANKLIN U SERIES (VARIOUS AUTHORS):
<u>The Dating Disaster</u>

**And if you're after something a little sweeter, don't forget my YA pen name
S. M. James.
These books are chock full of adorable, flawed characters with big hearts.
https://geni.us/smjames**

ACKNOWLEDGMENTS

As with any book, this one took a hell of a lot of people to make happen.

The cover was created by the talented Natasha at Natasha Snow Designs with a gorgeous image by Wander Aguiar, and edits were done by Sandra Dee at One Love Editing, with Lori Parks proofreading the bejeebus out of it.

Thanks to Tal Lewin @caravaggia13 for the cover of my illustrated alternate edition.

Charity VanHuss you're the most amazing PA I could have ever dreamed up. Without you I'd be even more of a chaotic disaster and there isn't enough space to list the many hats you wear for me. Paige Treff and Lara Janz, you round out my team in the most incredible way and I'm always excited to see what fun ideas you both have next.

Eden Finley, thank you for being there for all the doubt spirals and hand-holding. Whether you wanted to be or not.

AM Johnson, Becca Jackson, Louisa Masters and Riley Hart thank you so much for taking the time to read. Your support is incredible and I really appreciate it!

A huge, huge thank you to Ariella Zoelle, Ashley Jeanette and

Mikaela Sweeney. Your insight was invaluable, and you helped make Benny who he is.

And of course, thanks to my fam bam. To my husband who constantly frees up time for me to write, and to my kids whose neediness reminds me the real word exists.